About

Pamela, who has enjoyed writing stories ever since she can remember has had two books and numerous short stories and poetry published to date.

Blood in the Snow, her third novel draws on her experiences of living for a number of years in many different countries and travelling widely all over the world. Now settled in Sussex she devotes her afternoons to writing unless gardening in her beautiful cottage style garden or socialising with family and friends!

Pamela also enjoys entertainment style cooking and loves having friends for dinner.

For Richard, Debbie and Simon with my love always.

Pamela D. Holloway

BLOOD IN THE SNOW

Pamela Holloway

AUSTIN MACAULEY PUBLISHERS™

LONDON · CAMBRIDGE · NEW YORK · SHARJAH

A CIP catalogue record for this title is available from the British Library.

ISBN 9781528904964 (Paperback)
ISBN 9781528904971 (Hardback)
ISBN 9781528904988 (E-Book)

www.austinmacauley.com

First Published (2018)
Austin Macauley Publishers Ltd
25 Canada Square
Canary Wharf
London
E14 5LQ

Acknowledgements

Many thanks to friends for encouragement and to Alfred Douglas for his eagle eyes and patience.

Prologue

1993 Bosnia

The woman stood in the street with the sleeping child in her arms. "Please take her," she implored. The engine of the lorry revved. The tears poured unchecked. "Please," the anguish sounded in her voice. As the lorry moved slowly forward, arms reached down, they were almost too late…but they had the child in their grasp. She was passed further down the lorry where it was slightly warmer.

A shot rang out, the woman sank to her knees then fell forward, her blood staining the white snow where she fell. Her last thought was for the child…at least Yana was safe.

In Brize Norton all was as ready as it could be. It was not the first mercy flight they had dealt with, and Michael surmised it would not be the last. A voice sounded over the speaker announcing that the plane was landing. Michael along with fellow doctors, nurses and social workers steeled themselves. There would be wounded and tortured bodies and certainly some tortured minds. They were organised and ready for thirty, but they thought it could be more. As the plane touched down, ambulances lined up in anticipation of those unable to walk, for the rest it was just a short walk to the prepared reception centre.

The next half hour was organised chaos. In a brief pause between assessing patients, Michael heard a child crying, following the sound Michael had his first sight of Yana. She was sitting on the floor, her face blotched and tear stained, she looked thin, too thin, Michael thought for a little one. Finishing with the patient he was with, he strode over to her and very gently picked her up. He spoke softly, knowing she wouldn't understand a word. She cuddled into him as if recognising a temporary refuge. Betty, a no-nonsense social worker came over. "Were you expecting a child?" Betty shook her head. "We'll have to put her into care if she is not travelling with anyone."

To Michael's astonishment, he heard himself saying. "We'll foster her for a little while until you get something sorted."

"What about your wife?" Betty said taking the child.

"I'll phone her; she can be here in half an hour."

"That's not quite what I meant," Betty began, but Michael chose not to quite understand her meaning.

He went to the desk phone and quickly explained the situation. He knew his Sue! Smiling broadly, he went back to Betty. "Sue will be here in no time," he said.

"Until she arrives I'll hold on to her, she seems to accept me."

With a sense of relief, Betty handed the crying child over and within moments she was smiling as Michael pulled funny faces at her. He had a few more patients and the paper work to complete and once Sue had collected the child, he would follow her home as quickly as possible.

The child fell asleep on the way home, she hadn't liked being strapped into the car seat and was quite hysterical for a moment or two, but then, as children can she quite suddenly fell fast asleep. During the short journey, Sue kept checking on her in her rear view mirror. Poor little child looked so vulnerable. Her twins would love having a little girl to look after for a few days. Thank goodness, their au pair was from that region, she might hopefully be of some use with language.

As she pulled up in the drive, the twins ran eagerly down the steps. Carol followed more slowly wondering why Sue had gone off in such a hurry. Sue lifted the little girl from the car and carried her, still half asleep, into the house. "Some warm milk Carol please and also some bread and butter." As she eased of the child's coat, she noticed a piece of paper sticking out of a pocket. It had been fastened there with a safety pin. 'Yana Brzekoupil 18.10.92.', followed by the figure 25 and a street name Sue presumed. "Yana," she said gently. Yana looked up from her milk. It was the first time she had smiled since her mother had handed her over.

Chapter 1

Lily and Lucy were as different as chalk and cheese. Yana loved them both, they were her big sisters. She loved Rupert too and it was good that she was no longer the youngest. She had been five when he was born.

Fourteen years she mused as she sat on her bed listening to her favourite music.

She didn't want to spring it on them. Sue and Michael had been the best parents anyone could have and she certainly felt like their daughter even though they had never adopted her. "She was," as they so often said when she was little, "their only foster daughter."

She hadn't understood at first, but they made it seem so special.

Now her exams were over and she was making plans that she somehow felt they might not approve of, and she really did want their blessing but she also knew she must 'go home'. Or rather to where home once had been.

Yana knew her story as far as Sue and Michael knew it, but she wanted to know why she had been sent away and what had happened to her family. She had a scrap of paper with her name, date of birth and a bit of an address obviously written in haste.

There was a knock at the door and Lucy came in. She was the youngest twin by ten minutes and Lily had constantly reminded her of the fact over the years. Lucy was home for the summer and as she came in, Yana looked up with a warm smile at what she secretly acknowledged to be her favourite 'sister'. They were so different, Lily and Lucy. All Lily wanted was her horses and eventing of one sort or another, she even reckoned she had a small chance of making the Olympic team at some point. It had been the same since she was nine and had been given her first pony; her life was spent mostly in the paddock making miniature jumps which over years became higher and ultimately professionally built. She currently had two horses. Days of Pony Club were things of the past. Jimbo was her favourite mount and Tess much younger, was still on a major learning curve but Lily felt she was beginning to show real potential. "She needs a rich husband," her father was heard to remark on an occasion.

Lucy on the other hand took after her father and was reading medicine at University College London. Now in her second year and enjoying every moment. Looking at Yana's expression she instinctively knew her adopted sister was 'up to something'. Cryptic remarks had not gone unnoticed by the astute Lucy and she was planning to ask outright what was afoot.

There was something so vulnerable about Yana, Lucy mused; she loved her dearly. Sometimes she felt she loved her more than her somewhat self-centred twin!

"Come and sit on the bed Lu," Yana patted the bed beside her.

"You're up to something little sister, aren't you?" Yana smiled. She loved Lucy to call her that, it made her feel so special.

"I am actually," she replied hugging Lucy as she sat down beside her. "I am planning a journey." There was something in her tone that gave Lucy a sensation of almost fear in the pit of her stomach. She knew, she knew already what Yana was about to say.

"I've got to do it Lu, it's not that I don't feel I belong here, because I do, but I have to try and find out what happened. Why I was sent away in such a pre-emptory fashion, I don't want to upset Sue and Michael though," Yana sucked her bottom lip, an old childish habit that she adopted when feeling stressed or uncertain. Lucy noticed and was concerned about her little 'sister'.

Yana had only ever called her parents by their first names, they had felt it important for the child to know that perhaps she had parents or extended family somewhere.

They had given her all the love they had given to their own children, in fact Lily had commented, somewhat crossly at times that they gave her more than their own children. But that was Lily being Lily thinking as always of numero uno!

"Well," Lucy prompted.

"I need to go to Bosnia – to see what really happened – if I can," she added a slight sound of desperation in her voice.

"Then I will go with you." *There is no choice*, thought Lucy. There was no way Mum and Dad would want her to go on her own. Things were normal, whatever that meant but Yana could or might be exposed to anything.

She is so lovely, Lucy thought fondly looking at the auburn haired beauty that Yana had become. Tall too, like a model but with proper curves, none of the emaciated, anorexic that seemed to be the vogue on the catwalk.

Yana smiled, her white teeth gleaming against her ivory, if slightly, freckled face. Rupert always called her freckles whilst she had nicknamed him Bear which he was now called by the whole family and friends.

"You'll come with me?" Yana had hoped, a faint hope, that Lucy might consider coming, but the spontaneous response was more than she had ever dared to consider seriously.

"Now we have to break it to the olds," she murmured. Seeing Yana's anxious expression, she hugged her 'sister' again. "Don't worry," she said with more confidence than she felt. "Leave it to me."

Yana was alone again, smiling happily. Lucy was coming with her. It had to be a good omen.

Chapter 2

Dinner was a noisy affair, no different from usual when all the family were together.

Lily held forth about the Badminton cross country she was determined to finish in the first three.

Sue had walked the course with her and once again was dismayed at the difficulties with some of the jumps. A moderate rider herself, she had never attempted anything so hazardous.

Lily shrugged off her mother's concern with a nonchalant toss of her head, her long brown hair waving like a horse's mane.

"I think she's part horse," Sue had confided to Michael on more than one occasion.

Lucy let Lily have her say. Bear wanted to talk about cricket with his father. They were both due to play in the village team on Sunday. Sue made a mental note to check Bear's whites.

Finally, there was a pause. "Coffee anyone?" Sue made to stand.

"Just a minute, Mum," Lucy began, shooting Yana a conspiratorial glance. "There is something we need to talk about." Something in her tone stopped them all in their tracks.

"Sounds serious," Michael said. Sue looked worried. Lucy decided not to beat about the bush.

"I'm going away for a few weeks."

"Where?" Lily and Bear said in unison.

"Bosnia." The silence was deafening. After what seemed like ages to Yana. Lucy added, "Yana is coming too, of course."

"There is no of course about it." Sue looked and sounded taken aback. About to say something else, Michael kicked her lightly under the table.

"What prompted this?" he asked, trying to sound as equable as possible. He knew things had settled there now but there were still sporadic problems. His parallel thought was that this really was no surprise. Naturally, Yana wanted to know her story. His mind shot back nearly fifteen years and he pictured the thin, tear-stained child he had first seen. "So, what is the plan and who is going to pay for it?" He immediately wished he had not said the last few words. Yana looked taken aback as if it hadn't even occurred to her. Lucy smiled winningly at both her parents. "You are, of course, Mum and Dad, we just knew you would, didn't we Yana?"

Yana looked down feeling embarrassed with her 'family'. "I will pay you back, every penny, really," she spoke breathlessly, feeling ashamed that she had presumed somehow that they would.

"Of course, we will pay for the trip. It is very important to you Yana darling, isn't it." Sue smiled at the girl as she spoke. Yana could only nod, her eyes had filled with tears and her voice seemed to have disappeared.

"Oh Yana," Bear laughed. "For God's sake don't cry, it makes your nose go red!" As ever, Bear managed to lighten the mood and they all laughed.

"Let's talk some detail tomorrow," Michael said, thinking it would give him an opportunity to find out more about routes and costs. But Lucy pre-emptied him. "Dad, I've been online, we can take a train to Zagreb and another to Belgrade and from there we will probably have to go by local bus to Yana's town." It suddenly seemed real, unlike the fantasy story they had all grown used to, of a little girl appearing as if from nowhere.

Chapter 3

It didn't take long before it was time for the girls to leave. Sue and Michael decided they would like the girls to fly to Belgrade, so the airline tickets were purchased with the return three weeks later.

Neither girl slept the night before. Lucy thinking about how much she must support Yana, for who knows what they might discover. Yana couldn't sleep either. Somewhere deep inside, she had an image. She wasn't sure if it was imagined or real, she had never let herself really think about it – but now as she lay in the security and peace of her bedroom she remembered being cold, really really cold. She had a picture of a small room in the dark and being held so tightly she could hardly breathe. She tried hard to block the sound that filled her head – the sound of screaming, such screaming, and she knew the person who screamed was the person who held her so tightly.

Never before had her memories been like this, it was as if knowing she was going back unblocked memories from the deep recesses of her mind.

As if on cue, Lucy slipped into the bed beside her, she felt Yana's shaking body and tears fell on her as she held her sister in her arms.

This is how it had been when Yana first came to live with them. Lucy would hear the little girl crying and slip into bed and hold her until she slept. Their closeness had begun fourteen years ago.

The girls slept and Sue found them in the morning arms entwined around each other. Without a word, she fetched Michael and putting her finger to her lips she pushed the door gently open and Michael saw for himself how this girl, his daughter Yana, had touched all their hearts.

The flight was uneventful apart from both girls being chatted up by the passenger in the third seat of the three. He was surprised to learn they were sisters – the only information they gave him. The journalist in him was intrigued. Two girls, so different, flying to Belgrade. They wouldn't even give him their names. The one girl with brown shoulder-length hair and the deepest of deep blue eyes that shone out of a delicately featured face. The other, an auburn-haired beauty. Her eyes were dark, but he couldn't tell if they were brown or very dark green. She had a sprinkling of freckles over the bridge of her nose, but otherwise her skin had a creamy beauty he had never seen before. "So who is like Mother and who Father?" he asked conversationally with a winning smile. They laughed, then looked at each other and giggled. He hadn't heard giggles like that since his sister and her best friend got together. It brought back memories of a happy childhood and he was now intrigued by theirs, but apart from saying they were staying for three weeks they gave nothing away. Finally, as the plane touched down and in despair at his lack of progress, he handed Yana his card.

"If I can help, or you want company, I am in Bosnia for a month – do call."

Yana tucked the card in her pocket and proceeded to forget all about it. Her mind and Lucy's were racing ahead wondering what, if anything they would find.

They planned to spend the night in Belgrade, it was early evening and already getting dark. They went to the Customer Services desk and were given a list of hotels and family run establishments. All around her, Yana was hearing Bosnian and Croat and words she seemed to understand kept hitting her in the face like a wet cloth. She clutched at Lucy's arm suddenly afraid of what she might find.

As if sensing this, Lucy put her arm around the younger girl. It's all right Yana, it will be all right.

They took a taxi asking for the nearest small hotel to the railway station. The place was small and modest, but scrupulously clean. The beds had big goose down duvets despite the warm weather and soon the girls slept, duvets pushed away their cotton pyjamas the only cover they needed.

Lucy woke first and glanced fondly at her sleeping sister. Yana looked so beautiful, it almost made her gasp. She knew her so well, yet she was constantly surprised how she had grown so beautiful.

She smiled to herself remembering as a five-year-old her first glimpse of the little girl who would touch all their lives.

As if on cue, Yana stretched, yawned and opened her eyes wide as she realised she was HERE. She was nearer to her home. Nearer to where she had been born, nearer to the place she had left so suddenly all that time ago. "Hi, sleepy head," Yana stretched again.

"I can't believe I'm really here. Can you?"

"It's different for me – but I can't begin to imagine how you feel."

"Hungry?" Yana laughed, leaping out of bed, "Race you to the shower…"

The owner of the hotel was very helpful, he liked the look of the girls. He told them which train they needed, but said in rather a strange tone he had never heard of the village they were heading for. Then as if suddenly remembering something, his attitude seemed to change and he seemed less friendly.

They talked about him as they travelled. "He'd heard of it I'm sure," Yana said. Lucy nodded.

"He certainly became a bit shifty. However, let's forget him. We're on our way – the way to your home, Yana dear." Yana's expression changed, she looked worried for the first time since the whole project had been mooted.

"I'm scared suddenly. I almost wish we could turn around and go home, home to England I mean."

Lucy squeezed her arm. "Don't worry Yana dear, we will go home to England soon. But you would never forgive yourself if you didn't make this journey."

Sometime later, they heard an announcement and as the train drew into the station the name flashed past. Lucy remembering some of the things Michael had told her before they left felt a momentary fear, but, she rationalised there was nothing to be afraid of, two sisters on holiday – no one would think anything else.

It was harder now to make themselves understood. Yana's few words seemed to have left her. Lucy tried German and that was more successful. She held out a map with the village very clearly ringed in red. The man they had asked looked from one girl to the other, *Strange place for foreigners to go,* he thought.

He pointed down the road to where a number of buses were gathered. "You will find the name on the bus."

Lucy nodded her thanks and almost dragging the younger girl, she led the way.

Finally, after looking at name after name it was Yana who spotted it. "Look. Bijeljina!" The girls clambered aboard and after a few minutes, they were pulling out from the bus station.

Yana's eyes looked, strained, and looked again. This was her country. These were her people, she had a longing to stand on her seat and shout. "I'm Yana, I've come back!" Instead she sat very still – seeing and not seeing. Her eyes were moist with unshed tears.

She put out her hand like she had as a little girl and as she had on so many occasions. Lucy took the proffered hand, with its long, slender fingers in her own and squeezed gently in response to the need.

A village, another village and finally the town of Bijeljina. Without speaking, the girls stood up and collected their back packs and scrambled awkwardly off the bus which pulled swiftly away. They stood alone in the silent street both wondering what to do next. They had arrived, now what?

Yana broke the spell. "Look," she pointed across the road. "A hotel." They crossed over and walked the few yards. Pushing open the door, they stepped into a dark and gloomy space which after the sunlight outside made it momentarily difficult to see anything.

Lucy hit the bell on the front desk and a moment later a man in his late forties wearing a large white apron came out from a door behind the counter.

He greeted them without even looking at them and getting no response to his usual ebullient greeting, he looked up from the registration book that he was turning 'round to face them.

Lucy spoke first. "We are English. Do you speak English?"

"A little," he replied looking up for the first time. His gasp surprised them both. He made a quick recovery. "You are both English?" He asked, with, Lucy noticed an emphasis on the word 'both'.

"We are sisters," replied Yana annoyed with the way he was staring at her.

"Of course, of course," he handed them a room key. "Up the stairs, second door on the left, overlooking the road." Taking the key, they made their way up the short flight of stairs.

"Why did he stare like that?" Yana thought aloud as they closed the door behind them.

"He recognised you."

"Lucy, how could he, he has never seen me before. Well not grown up anyway!"

"Perhaps, you remind him of someone," Lucy said as gently as she could. Poor darling Yana had definitely had a shock.

They had no sooner left the front desk before Janus, the proprietor of the hotel, picked up his mobile and disappeared into the office behind the desk. He quickly pressed the keys and rang his cousin. Kurt, Mikail's son answered on the second ring. Janus spoke with urgency in his voice explaining he needed to his speak to Mikail urgently. "Sorry, Uncle Janus, I don't know where he is. Can I give him a message?"

"Tell him the child has returned – he will know what I mean."

"Are you sure?" Kurt laughed. "It's a very cryptic message."

"It's enough nephew, quite enough."

The girls were tired both emotionally and physically. It was dark outside and they decided they didn't really want more than the fruit they had purchased earlier. Lunch had been particularly filling with a substantial meaty soup and lots of delicious crusty Balkan bread. There was a tray with tea and coffee in their room so they each had coffee, ate the fruit and fell into bed, both wondering what the morning would bring.

To her surprise Yana slept soundly, it was Lucy who tossed and turned wondering what mountains Yana would have to climb – what horrors she might have to cope with. For the first time, Lucy found herself doubting they had done the right thing. Perhaps Yana should have left well alone and continued with her life in England perhaps joining Lucy at University College to read medicine. She was, thought Lucy so diligent and bright, none of them had any doubts that her exam results would be anything other than good. She watched the younger girl still sleeping, her breathing so quiet and peaceful. Her creamy, almost translucent, skin against her auburn hair which spread over the pillow in soft waves. She was so beautiful, perhaps so like her mother that the owner of the hotel really thought he had seen a ghost. Certainly, once seen no one could forget Yana or anyone like her.

That's it, she decided, he knew Yana's mother. It had to be a starting point, then she remembered they also had an address. What would they find!

When they had arrived the previous evening, it had already been dusk and although Yana was longing to explore and get more than a glimpse of her hometown, Lucy had managed to persuade her it would be better in daylight when they would be feeling fresher.

Yana stretched and was instantly awake. She smiled happily at her sister. "I'm home, aren't I?" It was a rhetorical question that needed no reply.

Lucy nodded and smiled. "It's the first step of the journey," she answered, trying to rein in a bit of the excitement and tension in case disappointment or worse lay ahead.

They were starving. "Hardly surprising, really," Yana said between mouthfuls of cheese, meats and yoghurt and the strongest coffee they had ever had. It was an unusual breakfast for them, but substantial enough to fill their empty stomachs.

"How long are you to stay with us?" the proprietor asked in carefully prepared English as he poured out the strongest coffee they had ever had.

"We'll be flying with all that caffeine," Lucy replied, laughingly. She winked at Yana when they both realised he hadn't understood.

There was something about the man Yana didn't quite like. He kept looking at her quite strangely, and although she had planned to ask him for directions, she decided against it thinking instead it might be more special to find it for themselves.

It was already warm outside and the sun was warmer than either girl had anticipated. The hotel had been cool with its thick walls and wooden shuttered windows. They both tied their cardigans around their shoulders and without a spoken word started to wend their way slowly along the street.

There were few shops, it was, after all quite a small town. As they strolled past a bakery, the aroma of freshly baked bread filled their nostrils. There was a butcher with strange cuts of meat on chilled slabs. There was a gloomy-looking shop with buckets and brooms stacked up outside that they decided must be the hardware store.

Houses were interspersed with the shops. Small white numbers on equally small blue plaques about two inches square. They found number three. It was on the shady side of the street. Then number five and seven. One by one they walked on until there it was at the far end of the narrowing street number twenty-three, they must be almost there. They could see the crops now, fields upon field of cultivation and woodlands in the distance. Number twenty-five stood on its own a small fenced front garden with a metal gate. Yana waited trying to remember, something, anything.

The house was well maintained although the green paint had a slightly faded look. *What was she thinking?* Lucy wondered, as they both stood in front of the gate in silent contemplation. "I don't remember it." Yana was nearly in tears. This was her home – and nothing seemed familiar.

"It was a long time ago Yana, you were so very little." Not appearing to hear her, Yana pushed open the gate and walked purposefully up the path.

Before she could knock, the door opened. "We were expecting you." Kurt was nearly bowled over by the girl who stood a few feet in front of him. She was the most beautiful girl he had ever seen, his heart almost seemed to stop beating. He'd always scoffed at the idea of love at first sight – but he was in love! Momentarily, Yana hardly seemed to notice him she was so caught up in her thoughts she wondered vaguely who he was.

Kurt opened the door wider, "Please come in you and your friend." For once, Yana didn't correct the statement as she usually did to 'my sister'. Lucy smiled to herself, Yana was totally caught up in her 'mission', and she wondered if this good-looking young man was perhaps a relative.

Yana walked through the open door straight into a large room with a log-burning stove. For the first time her stomach lurched as she looked at it. "Don't touch Yana darling it's very hot." The words, although foreign to her, were so comforting and she understood them. She had a sensation, nothing more, of being held lovingly. She could almost smell her mother, she knew it was her mother.

All the colour drained from her face, she almost seemed to faint. Kurt held out his arms to support her wondering what vision was going through her mind to cause this reaction.

He led her to a chair and almost pushed her into it. Yana was aware of nothing – just desperately struggling to hold on to the feeling and sensations that were at the same time terrible and wonderful.

Lucy perched on the arm of the chair and asked Kurt the question she was sure Yana wanted the answer to. "Who are you and why are you living here?" If the young man was startled by the obvious feeling that lay behind the question, he was unable to reply because at that moment Mikail, his father returned from the bank.

Finally, Janus had managed to speak to him, and by God Janus was right. The girl, no doubt of it was the image of the girl they had both loved and lost to their old school companion. The one who had died so horribly in front of their very eyes.

Now, the daughter was back to haunt them. To make them relive the terrible past when neighbours had become enemies and innocent victims like Yana's mother had been shot dead in a terrible mistake they still could not talk about.

Kurt was looking very unlike the schoolmaster son he was so proud of. He looked besotted already with the vision from the past.

"I can't introduce you to my father," Kurt said smiling. "I don't know your name."

"My name is Yana, and this is my home; why are you living here?" Fortunately, Kurt who taught English, understood what Yana had said unlike his father who had understood a little but not enough. In a way it was her tone of voice he understood more.

"This is my home," Kurt said firmly but with a smile that softened the statement. "I came to live here, when I was eight, with my father, mother and grandmother. Sadly, my mother and grandmother are dead so it is just the two of us."

"This is my home," Yana repeated firmly as she produced the scrap of paper Michael and Sue had found pinned to her clothing.

The paper was now carefully pressed between two sheets of laminated plastic. She passed it to Kurt. He read her name, date of birth, the name of their town and the address. Kurt passed the laminate to his father. Mikail only glanced at it, he knew only too well what would be on it.

His mind went back to that afternoon, that cold snowy afternoon fourteen years ago.

Chapter 4

They had been hiding for two days. They were cold, tired and very hungry. It had snowed heavily in the night; they were hiding in the old bakery. The oven had long since gone out.

The British lorry had been driving up and down snow packed roads collecting the dead and wounded from both sides of the recent battle. It had been hell for months now, spring seemed determined not to arrive and the weather seemed colder than ever.

It had been a near massacre and now survivors huddled in cellars, many of the houses above them destroyed by fire or the blasting of guns. His own mother, wife and son Kurt had been driven from their home. "Please God, they are safe," they said to one another, "let it be over soon."

Their commander was a professional soldier, not like them forcibly conscripted. He was a ruthless man and they had seen things that made even the strongest stomach turn. It was Christian Serbs versus Muslims and old friends, people they had played with as children were suddenly sworn enemies.

Now, as they looked out, the last of the lorries seemed to be leaving. A woman, it was Maria! Hardly recognisable so wrapped up against the cold. Strands of hair had escaped from her scarf and Mikail was shocked to see it had turned white. The shock, no doubt of seeing her husband garrotted in front of her. She had been raped too on the orders of the Commander. Thank God, not by him at that point, but by Janus who had wept as the Commander held a gun to his head.

Maria had her child – the child with red auburn hair just like hers. *She was holding the child up like an offering,* Mikail thought. Even from their hiding place in the bakery they could sense her desperation, and imagine her pleas. The lorry started to move, arms reached down at what seemed the last possible moment and the lorry was gone. As it pulled away, "fire" yelled the Commander. As if automatons, they raised their rifles. Only one shot was fired and no one said then, or ever who fired the shot.

Maria fell, first to her knees then forward her face hitting the compacted snow which was quickly stained with her blood. They watched helplessly, unable to go to her as they had been told, whether in in pain, or close to death they were not to give away their hiding place.

Yana pulled the paper from his fingers. He looked strained as he looked at her slightly oddly. "I knew your mother," he said slowly. Yana didn't understand, she thought he had said he knew her mother. Had he said that? She looked at Kurt.

"He knew your mother," he repeated in English what his father had said.

Lucy stood up. "But that's wonderful. Isn't it Yana?" Yana stood too. She repeated her earlier question. "What are you doing in my home?"

Kurt looked at his father, it was obvious Mikail couldn't or wouldn't speak, so he spoke instead. "The people who lived here – they went away. A lot of houses were badly damaged. We had to rebuild part of the upper floor. We were 'assigned' the house."

"I know it is my home."

"It was your house, but…"

"How can you have been assigned this house? I know it is my home."

"It was your home," Kurt responded in a considerate voice and with a gentle smile to take away the cruelty of his words. It was cruel, he knew that, but then war was cruel. So much had happened, so many people had died, sent to camps and never seen again or tortured to death in their hometown.

He had never asked about the house. As a nine-year-old, he accepted what his father had said about being assigned a new and better home as the original owners had 'gone away'. Later, he realised it was a euphemism for something entirely different."

On the rare occasions he had asked his father about the previous occupants, he had been met with a curt reply. "It's in the past Kurt – the bad past – the time is now."

Now, Kurt felt guilty. It wasn't his fault, all that had happened had happened, but now faced with this beautiful girl who claimed the house as hers he felt ill at ease.

The authorities would be on his side, his and his father's, but it didn't make it any less terrible for her. He tried to explain, but Yana was having none of it. "Lucy, come on, we're going to the police."

Kurt sighed. "It won't do any good," he said. But Yana and the other girl had already left leaving a silence between father and son like no other before.

"Tell me what happened to her family. You know, don't you?" His father nodded briefly and sank into the recently vacated chair.

"I know," he said wearily. "I knew this might happen one day – but I hoped it never would."

They sat, the two of them for several hours. Mikail explained how he was conscripted. How good neighbours became, in some cases, hated enemies. He didn't tell all. He couldn't talk of the rape of Yana's mother, but he told of her death in the snowy street right outside of where they now lived.

Of the shot ringing out and seeing her fall, her blood gushing out staining the white snow.

His father sat head in hands, it all came back so vividly. Kurt felt a mixture of revulsion and anger.

By rights, this was her home. By rights, they should move out and let her take back what was hers.

He knew though that this could not be. Things had moved on and life in the village was not what it had been. Now, once again people lived in relative harmony. Justice had been seen to be done with trials of the then leadership and the long prison sentences had placated people to a major degree.

But the murder of a young woman trying to save her child was unforgiveable and it could have been his own father who fired the shot.

The girls sat at a pavement cafe. The colour had returned to Yana's face. She was angry now and Lucy was relieved, anger seemed better than that awful stricken face she had witnessed a short while ago.

They ordered coffee. Once again it was very strong and accompanied by a small glass of water. They were silent, each wrapped in thought. "What am I going to do?" Lucy became brisk and purposeful. "The first thing is to have some lunch and then we can formulate some sort of plan."

27

Yana put her hand in her pocket searching for a tissue. Her eyes kept filling with tears and she didn't even know what, specifically, she was weeping about. Though inside her she knew she was weeping for everything she had lost. Flashes, images, kept popping into her head. A card that had been in her pocket fluttered to the ground. Lucy glanced at it. It was the card given them on the plane by the young journalist.

Without saying a word, she put it in her own pocket wondering if he might be able to help in any way. There might be something he could do. It was certainly worth a telephone call.

They spoke at the same moment. "How about contacting…" Lucy began.

"I keep remembering things," began Yana. Lucy didn't speak. Yana looked so traumatised. "Oh no," she moaned, clutching at Lucy.

"What darling, what is it?"

"It was the stove. This morning when I saw it I remembered something. I remembered a voice. It must have been my mother. She was telling me not to touch it. Now I remember something else, so horrible," She began to weep copiously.

The Restaurateur came out with more coffee. He spoke no English but asked if the girl was all right. "Was she ill?" Lucy didn't understand but recognised concern. She smiled at him in gratitude.

He was the first person to treat them naturally. "It's okay," she said. Okay is understood everywhere.

"Okay," he smiled. "Okay," and he returned indoors.

It was not okay, far from it. Yana had once again turned as white as a sheet. She had stopped crying and now stared blankly into space.

"Do you want to tell me?" Lucy asked softly.

For a moment there was silence. "It must have been my mother," she began. "On the floor near the stove. I was near the stove too but it was not hot, it was so cold. I remember being so cold." Lucy remained silent, holding Yana's hand as she relived and remembered.

"She was on the floor – there were men – not my father. They were laughing and one lay on top of my mother. She said something to me," Yana closed her eyes. "She said, 'don't worry little one, this is a game'. It wasn't Lucy. It wasn't."

"No darling, Yana, it wasn't. How brave she was, your mother."

"I remember being in a lorry. Someone wrapped me up," her voice broke. "But it wasn't my mother, what happened to her. I have to know Lucy. I have to know!"

Lucy spoke soothingly. "I have an idea Yana. Let's go to the police, and if we don't get the information. The facts we need, then we'll ring that journalist." She glanced quickly at the card. "Peter Jordan. He said he'd been coming here for years, he probably speaks the language and he might have useful contacts."

Yana smiled. "You are brilliant Lu – whatever would I have done if you hadn't come too?"

"There is no way we, the family and me, in particular, would have let you out of the country on your own. You mightn't have wanted to come home!"

"Never," Yana smiled. "Never," she repeated firmly.

Chapter 5

They had some lunch still sitting at the same table. A lovely salad and a beef stew of some sort with dumplings. It seemed slightly incongruous eating dumplings associated in their minds with winter sitting as they were in the lovely spring sunshine but they ate everything on their plates and washed it down with quite a rough red wine. "That's better," Yana said. "I always think better on a full stomach."

The restaurateur brought them a selection of cheeses. "No, thank you," she waved them away speaking in hesitant Bosnian as she did. If the restaurateur was surprised, he didn't show it. In fact, he thought how nice the one girl had taken the trouble to learn a little of his language.

After a final coffee, to which they agreed they were becoming far too acclimatised, they set off in the direction of the police station. They had noticed the building in the small square off the High Street.

The police station stood next to another, quite imposing building which they assumed was the Town Hall.

"Come on then," Yana said taking a deep breath. "Let's see what they have to say."

A young man sitting at a desk behind the counter stood up as they walked in. He smiled pleasantly and asked what he could do for two such beautiful girls. Neither girl understood what he had said though Yana was understanding more and his encouraging tone and friendliness was just what they needed. "Do you speak English?" Lucy enquired feeling her sister was having to deal with so much.

"No English," he replied with a flashing smile. "Wait." He disappeared through an archway and they heard him knocking on a door.

The Chief of Police for the district had been expecting them. The town was too small a place for their disturbing arrival to

30

have gone unnoticed, and anyway he had received a telephone earlier from an angry Mikail. "Who does she think she is?" he had demanded of his friend, trying to claim our home after all this time.

It was guilt speaking. The Chief of Police knew his friend all too well, they had grown up together and with Janus they had called themselves the three musketeers after the Dumas book they had studied at school.

Of course Milo was upset but he had a responsibility too.

He remembered that night so vividly, and casting his mind back the child had been there. The Commander had laughed, he remembered, and beautiful Maria had called out to her child. He couldn't remember what she had said but remembered thinking how brave she was.

No one ever admitted to the shooting when as ordered they had raised their rifles as she stood in the snow. Only one shot was fired. They never mentioned it again.

He pulled himself together, these were bad thoughts. He took his hat off the peg and went through to the front desk, his emotions now under control.

His intake of breath when he saw her was heard only by himself. It could have been Maria herself. That hair – the purity of her skin. It was as if Maria had returned to wreck vengeance on them all.

"You are English," he began. "What can I do for you?" Though heavily accented, his English was good, thanks to that schoolmaster from England all those years ago. Yana smiled with relief, and Lucy's spirits lifted. This was going to be easier without a language barrier.

Yana began to explain about the house. She passed him the laminated sheet. There he saw a scrawled hand, Maria's no doubt – who else. Her husband had gone to the camp and they had heard he had died under torture. The boy who must have been about five had been found in the street stabbed to death. He looked carefully at the handwriting he was sure it was Maria's.

He handed it back. "It is not proof of ownership."

Lucy started to speak. He held up his hand to silence her. "No one was living there. It was quite badly damaged. People arrived from other towns, or locals moved into unoccupied houses if theirs were uninhabitable. It was legal then and it remains legal now and that is the end of it. I'm sorry," he seemed to add as an afterthought.

There was no point in continuing. The younger policeman gave them another flashing smile and shot 'round the counter to open the door for them. When he turned around to ask what they had wanted his Chief had already returned to his office and firmly closed the door behind him.

"That's it," said Lucy. "We are going to ring Peter Jordan." They walked slowly hand in hand for comfort, and seeing fields they walked through a gate and sat in what seemed to be a wild flower meadow and Lucy took out her mobile. "We'll phone Peter Jordan first, then I think we should phone Mum and Dad and bring them up to date, don't you?" Yana nodded, she seemed, perhaps unsurprisingly, distracted. She had a feeling that the people of her home town were ganging up against her. Somebody knew something of that she was convinced.

The phone call home provided a touch of reality. Michael and Sue were full of questions most of which they couldn't answer. Yes, they had found Yana's home. Yes, she had been inside and met the people who lived there. No, they were not related. Yes, they had been to the Police Station. They didn't add that it had been a fruitless experience.

Sue and Michael were so happy to hear from them. Bear was playing in his first junior county cricket match and Lily and her horse had done extremely well at Badminton. She had come second in her class. Apparently, she had fallen once, but got straight back on barely losing time and her second circuit proved to be a perfect performance; she finished only two points behind first place. Everyone, including Lily and the family seemed to be getting terribly excited about her prospects.

It all seemed so normal, and both Lucy and Yana were inwardly wishing they were there. But, it was a momentary weakness only, and their resolve hardened having spoken to Peter Jordan.

If he was surprised to receive Lucy's call he tried to sound calm and serious, though in fact he raised a fist in the air and mouthed 'yes!' to himself.

He listened carefully to what they had to say. First Lucy then Yana. "Come back to Belgrade," he said finally. "You are probably making people in Bijeljina feel uncomfortable and they won't open up. I have good contacts here, would you like me to book you in to my hotel?"

The girls had a quick consultation. "Is it horribly expensive?" Lucy sounded a bit worried.

"No, not at all," he assured her deciding to make some arrangement with the hotel or his editor. There was a story here and he could perhaps not only help them but help himself too.

Several people saw the girls leave and later that evening Janus, Mikail and Milo met for a brief meeting.

"That is that." The Chief spoke firmly

"Let's hope so," Mikail and Janus spoke together.

Only Kurt was sorry to see them leave. He would, he decided never forget Yana and he determined to ask his father why they were living where they were and if they had the right to do so.

He had no idea but he determined to find out and who knows perhaps he could persuade her to come back to the town of her birth.

Chapter 6

The journey back to Belgrade though tedious was uneventful. The excitement and speculation of the outward journey had been replaced by a mixture of frustration and anger.

As arranged, Peter Jordan met them. He was once again bowled over by the two girls; in particular, he felt very drawn to Lucy.

The hotel was in a quiet street and Lucy had a quick glance at the tariff. Yana had seen it too. "Don't worry girls. Special journalistic rates for you both." They believed him! He thought he might have an argument on his hands but he was obviously more convincing than he thought he was.

The three of them had supper together that evening in a small Bistro that Peter knew well. The owner greeted Peter warmly and chatted away in Bosnian, which Peter not only understood but seemed to speak fluently as well.

As they ate, both Yana and Lucy complimented him on his language skills. He shrugged nonchalantly. "I have a Serbian grandfather, my sister and I used to spend summers with him in the old Yugoslavia. My mother is half Serbian and half English. Now tell me all about your visit to Bijeljina, and I mean ALL."

It was good to eat French food, and as they ate and the wine flowed, Yana told him all that had happened. Every now and again she was too overcome with emotion and Lucy would fill in the gaps until Yana regained her composure and could continue.

The more Peter heard the more interested he became. The story had all the ingredients that would make a great article – at the very least. Dating from Yana's precarious start and her journey to England. Her life with an English family and the seeming recognition of her by a small number of the town community.

Finally, the story was told. "I think I am right," Peter began. "In saying that town was under a particularly vicious commander. He hated anyone connected to the Muslim community, perhaps you are connected Yana. He was brought to trial, quite rightly. In fact I am here on some follow up stories connected with the trial."

Yana couldn't help herself. "With your connections are you sympathetic towards him?"

"You must appreciate my interest, but I can assure you – passionately," he added to emphasise his views. "That although some of my roots are here my feelings about what took place during that time are filled with revulsion. There are good and bad in every nation as I am sure you are aware."

"Of course we know that." Lucy was annoyed at what she thought was a somewhat patronising comment.

Yana sensing an atmosphere smiled at Peter. "Please Peter. I think you may be my only hope. You may be able to find out how I go about claiming what is my home." The more she thought about it the more upsetting it became. That man and his son living there in her home as if she had never existed."

"What proof do you have?" Once again Yana produced the laminate. "You have nothing else?"

"Isn't that enough?"

"We will need to trace your birth certificate and some record of your parent's ownership of the house." The girls fired questions at Peter, wanting to know how easy or difficult it would be to do all the necessary traces. "Harder in some ways and easier than it was in others!"

"Peter, that's nonsense," was Lucy's response. *The whole scenario is nonsense*, he thought to himself. Why wasn't Yana content to stay in England where she had a good home and family. Ah, his mind ran on then he would not have met the delightful Lucy!

The three of them walked slowly back to the Hotel mostly wrapped in their own thoughts. Having felt a certain impatience Peter was now thinking more positively again about what a great story it would make.

They said their goodnights in the foyer. It was only ten thirty but Peter had a couple of 'phone calls' to make before he could really turn his energies to the 'new story'.

Peter's telephone calls paid dividends. He had a Serbian friend who was also a journalist. Without giving too much away Peter asked one or two leading questions. He then 'phoned' his editor and told him the story as he knew it. He explained that he wanted to stay on and research the story and leave his current assignment for the meantime. There followed a bit of healthy argument/discussion and finally his editor agreed to his request providing they had exclusive rights to the story.

Crossing his fingers and touching available wood, Peter assured him this would be the case. He had never lied to his editor before, but felt so compelled to both help the girls and dig out the facts that he put his scruples to one side even though he knew in his heart of hearts there was a possibility that Yana would not want her story published and he would be bound to accept that, but he had allowed his editor to gain the opposite impression.

It had also been agreed that the hotel expenses and other basic costs would be covered. Peter assured his boss he would keep him up to date with developments. Switching off his phone Peter knew he had made commitments he might not be able to keep and he realised for the first time that he was putting his job in jeopardy.

Next morning, he was away early for the final day of the trial of the 'butcher' as he was known by large numbers of people. It had taken so many years to track him down, he had been 'protected' by an array of fellows Serbs. Eventually though, even the most hardened had come to accept that the man himself, and those under his command had committed unforgivable atrocities.

For Yana and Lucy, it was a day of window shopping and the purchasing of a dictionary and phrase book. Yana was picking up her language quickly. The first three years of her life when she had heard nothing else were coming back to her though she had to dig deep into the recesses of her mind. She kept delving into the dictionary and phrase book, and constantly amazed Lucy with her grasp, or re grasp of her mother tongue.

They bought little gifts for the family. A beautifully carved horse for Lily. A white polo shirt for Bear and a lovely crystal bowl for Sue and Michael.

They hardly saw Peter over the next few days but when they did, he told them he was making progress. They saw a ballet and went to the opera. Then Lucy had the idea of going to the hospital and explaining she was studying to be a doctor.

To their surprise, the girls were made very welcome and they spent two days being shown everything from Pathology to Maternity. There were differences with the way some things were run but they were both impressed with the well-run and disciplined atmosphere. There seemed to be no shortage of nurses, and Lucy confided to Yana that she wouldn't mind working in a hospital that was so well run. "That's it," said Yana who was hoping to follow Lucy to University College and read medicine too. "That's what?" Lucy laughed.

"I'll come back here when I'm qualified – perhaps even to my town."

Lucy was horrified – the thought of Yana leaving them for what seemed, for the most part an unfriendly community. But she wisely said nothing, there would be a number of years before she was even qualified.

Yana had spoken without thinking. She sensed Lucy was hurt at her keenness to leave them. It was probably a stupid idea anyway, she pushed all thoughts of her future out of her mind.

That evening Peter was obviously impatient to see them. There were several messages waiting for them at reception asking them to phone his room and several messages left on Lucy's mobile which she had switched off.

They decided to shower and change first, both feeling hot and sticky after the day's sightseeing and shopping. In their (hotel provided) white towelling robes, they sat on their beds and Lucy, at Yana's request telephoned Peter's room. She held on for ages, thinking, like them he might be taking a shower but finally she put the phone down. "No reply," she said ruefully, "and his mobile is off too."

"Well, that's rather a let-down. Now what?"

"Let's order some food and watch T.V," Lucy suggested sensing as she did, Yana felt rather let down too.

They were like a couple of kids pouring over the menu finally both deciding on club sandwiches and salad with a side order of pomme frites followed by crème brulee and a bottle of white wine to wash it down with.

They turned on the television and found B.B.C. World Service. There were the usual dramas of politics. A resignation of someone they had never heard of in high dungeon about something and a front bench spokesman who had been hauled in by the police for down loading child pornography. "Sick," Yana muttered.

"We need something more cheerful." Lucy agreed changing channels until she found an episode of *Friends* they had enjoyed in the past. Supper arrived halfway through the episode and they put the tray on Lucy's bed and sat either side of it. *Friends* made them laugh. Chandler trying yet again to remember how things should be put back in the cupboard according to Monica's decree, and getting himself all worked up because he knew she would be furious with him. This was followed by the trite but amusing *Will and Grace* and by now the girls' eyelids were beginning to grow heavy.

"I'm going to clean my teeth and go to the loo."

"I'm for bed too," Lucy replied. "I'll follow you in."

The telephone rang while Yana was still in the bathroom. "Peter?" she said as she picked up the phone. "No Miss. I'm sorry. Front Desk here. Another message from Mr Jordan. He sends his apologies and he will see you in the morning." Lucy thanked him and put the phone down with some impatience. What was he doing messing them about like this?

"Did I hear the phone," Yana enquired her head wrapped in a towel. She had decided to have a quick shower and hair wash before going to bed.

"Mmm, you did," Lucy nodded. "That wretch has sent us another message – he'll see us in the morning apparently."

"I hope he really is going to help," Yana sounded upset and not a little worried.

"He better," said Lucy with a grimace. *Or he will have to answer to me*, she said inwardly.

The girls went down to breakfast at eight o' clock. Peter was already there at a table for four.

"Are you expecting anyone?" Lucy asked.

"You two I hope." Peter replied smiling at Lucy in such a way she felt her heart miss a beat. Pity he was so good looking, because he wasn't her type at all.

Their order taken, Yana wanted to know what he had found out. Peter grinned. "Do you want the good news or the bad news?"

"Oh, for God's sake stop messing us around Peter," snapped Lucy. Peter looked instantly contrite.

"I am sorry about yesterday evening. There was a big story breaking and I had no choice. Forgive me?"

He was so disarming that they chorused 'we forgive you'. Though Lucy added darkly. "This once."

Breakfast arrived and as they started to eat, Peter told them what he had ascertained so far. Unless Yana could absolutely substantiate her claim to the house, the status quo would remain as it was.

"But how can I do more. I have my full name and date of birth, and my address. What else do I need? I don't have a birth certificate though," she added thoughtfully.

"There is a central bureau but many records were deliberately destroyed. This has caused tremendous anger of course, but that doesn't help unless we can find out your baptism date. The name you have is Christian so we might find a baptismal record in the church in the village."

"So, it's back to the village again," Yana said slowly.

"That is only the first step. Armed with a copy of baptismal records, we can then seek a copy of your birth records and from that trace your parentage and records of the house purchase."

"So, it's not all gloom and doom." Lucy surmised rather dreading thoughts of returning to the rather unwelcoming, unfriendly community.

Peter expressed regret that he was unable to accompany them as he was rather tied up in something but assured them he would keep in close touch and up to date with anything he found out from this end.

Part of Yana wanted to go back, but she also had an awful sense of foreboding. "I wish you could come with us," Lucy said. "It is so strange there isn't it Yana."

"It is rather – something seems wrong – it is as if they are all aware of who I am, but no one will tell me anything."

Chapter 7

Their return was unwelcome, with one exception. Kurt was delighted to see the beautiful Yana again with her sister. His father was in a foul mood! He had just received a phone call from Janus. He had slammed down the phone and cursed as Kurt had never heard him before.

Kurt cast his mind back.

He vaguely remembered arriving at the house, his father still dressed in military uniform. It was cold and his father had soon got the stove going. It was good to be warm again, thought the boy, after their own home was destroyed and he and his mother had shivered alongside some nuns for a few days.

His mother had seemed happy enough, though from the whispers the boy overheard they had moved into a house where they had known the previous occupants; hardly surprising in a small community. The upstairs was damaged but downstairs in the warmth life seemed good. He heard his mother talking about the people who had lived there before. "How sad," she had murmured to her husband. "How stupid too, marrying a Muslim."

"It was okay then," his father had replied.

The boy was so glad to be warm he didn't wonder who had lived there before or what had happened to them.

Now, thinking back he remembered a family living there, he realised it must have been Yana and her mother and father. He found himself wondering what had happened. Yana must have been so little. How did she finish up living in England and what had happened to her parents? He found himself puzzling over the circumstances and was determined to find out more.

His father had poured himself a drink and was sitting in his favourite chair by the big stove. The stove that had been so cold when they arrived all those years before.

He sat down opposite the older man. "I think you owe me an explanation," he began. "I owe you nothing, nothing. I gave you life didn't I – what more! You were educated well at the school. You went to college. You are a teacher, a respected man in this place."

Kurt listened to the older man 'sounding off'. "Father who lived here before? Was it that girl Yana who came here with her sister?"

"She has no sister."

"Who?"

"The girl who left. Forget it, it is not good to know too many things." Kurt sighed.

"Father, they are back you know. You know it, the truth. You have got to tell me the truth now."

"What is the truth?" the older man replied cryptically.

"It's no use Father, we shall sit here until you tell me."

"Are you threatening me?" Mikail blustered.

"If that is what it takes. Yes."

There was a long silence Kurt began to think he would not get to hear anything. Finally Mikail began to speak, it was almost as if he was speaking to himself he seemed to be in a sort of reverie.

"He was a bully, that commandant. Things happened then to people, we had all got on well with, in the past. She shouldn't have married him. What a waste – she was so beautiful and she married that Muslim." He almost spat the word out.

Kurt was shocked he had never heard his father speak in such a vehement tone. "We live together alright now."

"Stupid boy, stupid. We did before, but underneath we hated them and for Mohammed to marry her. For her to accept…what a waste, what a waste."

"Who is the 'she'? Was she Yana's mother?" The older man nodded.

"We killed her. Her blood ran, was in the snow." He buried his face in his hands and wept.

"Tell me about it, please father." There was a deep raw silence. Mikail sat staring now, straight ahead of him as though conjuring up the dreadful scene.

Finally, speaking slowly, as though dragging the words from somewhere deep inside him, he started to speak.

"We turned one against another in this village, like most of the towns and villages in our region. We turned against the Muslims. You know the history. You must respect that circumstances change behaviour."

"So, what happened to the people who lived in this house?" Again, a long pause, Mikail seemed to be in another place, his face full of pain. Finally, as if the words were being dragged out of his very soul, he spoke.

"I don't know what happened to Mohammed, I saw him being dragged away and..." his voice broke. "And the boy too..."

Kurt sat very still, waiting for the dreadful story to continue wanting to know all, and at the same time almost wishing he had not asked the question.

"The boy was crying. He was about five I think. They shot him then and there. Then Mohammed was dragged away screaming for his son. Later, I saw. I didn't want to see. But I saw his body. He had been tortured horribly. I can't talk about it anymore," he finished brokenly.

Kurt reached out and held his father's hand. "It was not your fault." His father looked up.

"No, not that, not that," he repeated. "The other."

"What other?" Kurt was appalled. He knew, of course he knew atrocities had happened on both sides, but his father. The man he had loved and respected had been caught up in something so dreadful and seemingly had no choice over. By all accounts it was kill or be killed.

"So, what happened to Yana's mother?" Kurt prodded gently.

There was a shuddering sound from his father. "She was raped, here. Where we are sitting now. Right here in front of this stove. We had no choice," he continued. "The commandant said he would kill us else."

"Oh, my God." Kurt moaned. "Who raped her – did you?" He was shocked with his own question.

"Did you?" he repeated.

As if dragged out of him by force Mikail nodded a weak yes. Kurt was silenced.

"And then," he prompted finally.

"Then we left. We went to the bakery. The British were coming so we hid there. Me and my friends and the commandant. The lorries came. Everywhere was searched but we had hidden behind the ovens six of us, and they didn't look there. They loaded up some wounded and I think some prisoners Then as one of the last lorries was pulling away 'she' came out of the house carrying the child."

"Maria?" His father nodded.

"She handed the child up. As the lorry pulled away he told us to fire. We all put our guns up but only one shot was fired. She fell and I saw her blood spilling, spreading on the snow."

"Was she dead?" It was a question Kurt knew the answer to. "Who fired the shot?"

His father looked at him anguish in his face. "I did," he whispered. "I did."

All sympathy was gone. Kurt could not believe his anger. First rape. Then killing. Killing Yana's mother and finally moving into the house with his wife and son and living there in a home that had seen rape and murder by his own father.

Kurt's emotions were beyond anything he had ever felt. He paced around the room wondering if the rug he was walking on was the rug on which Yana's mother had been raped.

In fury he slammed out of the house and bumped into Yana and Lucy as they walked slowly down the road.

They had been looking for the priest's house but as there was no answer to their knocking they had been drawn once again to pass number twenty-five.

Kurt's ashen face and frenzied demeanour was impossible to miss. He took one look at the girls, and without even a word of greeting walked sharply in the opposite direction.

"How strange," Yana murmured.

"Very," her sister replied. "This place is so odd."

"Hey, you are talking about my home." But as she spoke she realised nothing was further from the truth. Home was England with Michael and Sue, the twins even Lily, and certainly Bear.

They walked back to the hotel in silence. Janus greeted them with a strained smile. He had just had a telephone call from a very stressed Mikail. "I've told Kurt the truth" was all he had said.

Janus was worried – the truth might cause them all problems.

43

Kurt walked through the fields to the woods and up the hill to his favourite vantage point over the village.

It was peaceful here and normally provided the peace and tranquillity he sought. Today, though, his mind was spinning. His all too vivid imagination could visualise the horrors his father had described. How could he ever touch his father again? How could he respect or even love him?

He shuddered thinking of the dark days of his early childhood and wondered how he would have behaved had he been old enough to be involved.

Gradually, he calmed. He thought about his mother who had died shortly after they moved into the house. For the first time he was glad she wasn't alive now. She would have found it impossible to forgive the rape let alone the murder of a young woman like herself, possible even a friend.

He stayed there until it was dark. Marshalling his thoughts – planning his future. Finally, he stood up from the log which he had been sitting on and carefully walked back down the familiar path. He didn't need daylight to find his way, it had been a route he had taken hundreds of times before.

He welcomed the dark and looked upwards at the stars. It was a clear night and there they were; all in their places, untouched by the world below. The world that he felt would never be the same for him.

Chapter 8

"I wonder what was the matter with Kurt." Yana speculated as they ate their supper, once more in the little restaurant where the patron was one of the few people who treated them normally. He hadn't given Yana a second glance that was what she had almost become accustomed to in this place.

"Perhaps he moved here after the war." Lucy surmised.

"Um. Who knows? So what next, back to the priest's house?" Lucy nodded, her mouth full of the delicious plum dumpling.

An hour or so later they were, once again, knocking at the priest's door. He answered the door himself. He was a man about forty, very thin and pale, though friendly enough and seemingly delighted when Yana tried out her ever-increasing vocabulary.

Both girls were working at the language, but Yana's very early years seemed to give her a distinct advantage and Lucy thought she sounded quite fluent at times.

"I'm Father Gregory. How can I help you?" he asked widening the door as he spoke and indicating they should enter. He led the way to an untidy book-lined room which they assumed was his study.

They sat as he waved an arm in the general direction of some chairs. Before they could sit both girls had to remove books and papers. "I am rather untidy," he smiled. With relief both girls realised he was going to be friendly as he looked from one to another questioningly.

Taking a deep breath Yana began. "My name is Yana Brzekoupil. I was born in this village 15 years ago. I left when I was three so I remember very little." The priest sat forward in his chair, obviously interested.

"Where did you go?"

"England."

"Ah. How fortunate for you." Yana nodded.

"I need a copy of my baptismal records. I feel sure I would have been baptised."

"If your parents were good Catholics there is no doubt. But…" he continued, "It will mean going through a great many records," and with a self-deprecating smile, he added. "I'm not the most organised fellow as you can see," he waved his arm indicating the general chaos. "However, I will look. It may take a day or two."

If Yana and Lucy were disappointed they were too polite to show it. Out of deference to Lucy's lack of the language the priest had reverted to English, albeit heavily accented.

They all stood up and about to show them out the priest suddenly struck his head with his hand.

"Of course. Father Ignatius."

"Who?" they chorused.

"He was here during the fighting. He is an old man now and a lot of the time quite confused. But he might remember your parents, and who knows even your baptism.

"That would be wonderful," Yana said, giving such a joyous smile, the priest was determined he would do all he could to help her in her quest.

"I still need proof though," Yana added.

"Of course, my dear. I shall start searching as you leave!"

"And Father Ignatius. Where can we find him?" Lucy queried.

"In the garden."

"Here?" Yana was excited.

"Of course. Just go around the side of the house and you will find him sitting underneath the trees or just pottering around. Good luck with him," he added as an apparent afterthought.

"Isn't this good news. The first good news. He may actually have known my parents," Yana could hardly contain her excitement. She walked so quickly Lucy could hardly keep pace with her.

It took a moment or two. The garden, like the house was untidy. Tall multi-coloured hollyhocks and bright yellow sunflowers seem to have taken over. The grass had been left untended, so that a variety of wild flowers provided succour to a multitude of bees and other insects.

They found a path of sorts, and in single file walked cautiously along it. From time to time prickly bushes catching their skirts as they walked.

Just when they thought he couldn't be there, they ducked under a heavily laden archway. The climbing plants almost blocked their way completely and there in the stillness was a rustic looking bench where an old man sat his stick firmly in his hand.

His hair and beard were white and unkempt and he appeared to be asleep.

Lucy cleared her throat not wanting to startle the old man. Yana spoke in her mother tongue.

"Good morning Father Ignatius." He opened his eyes moving his head slightly at the sound of her voice. "Why Maria," he said. "I thought you were dead." Yana gasped and sank to the ground, almost as if her legs could no longer sustain her weight. "I am Yana," she whispered.

"Maria speak up. You know I am deaf. Where have you been? I haven't seen you at confession since…" he broke off. "Maria?" he repeated, this time his voice was questioning.

"Perhaps I look like my mother." Yana whispered.

"Ask him about Maria," Lucy whispered back not having understood a word the priest had said but hearing the name Maria several times realised it must be significant. "Ask him," she repeated.

"Why did you think I was Maria, Father?" she asked gently.

"Maria is dead. Who is this then? Maria came to haunt me. I did my best child. I tried to bury you but the ground was too hard and all the men were fighting and killing.

He closed his eyes and seemed to disappear into himself. "Father," Yana repeated once or twice. But the moment was gone. He was away living in some dream world of his own.

Lucy helped Yana to her feet. The younger girl was crying, almost soundlessly. Lucy glanced again in the direction of Father Ignatius. "He must have dementia or something similar. Triggers like you will open up something in his mind, but he will probably have forgotten already. You must look so like your mother, Yana. No wonder people have been looking at you as they have, they must have thought they were seeing a ghost."

47

"He tried to bury her," Yana said brokenly, "but the ground was too hard. How awful. My mother lying cold and neglected because there was no one to help dig a proper grave."

"He will have given her last rites." Lucy said wisely knowing at least that much about Catholicism.

"I hoped she might be alive."

"I know you did darling – but she must have known she was in danger or she wouldn't have made what was such an enormous effort to save you."

They walked arm in arm back to the street. Father Gregory had said he would come to the hotel when he found any evidence.

Chapter 9

True to his word, Father Gregory arrived the following morning as they were eating their breakfast. He accepted their offer of coffee before producing a piece of A-five paper from his pocket.

"This is only a photo copy. The original remains in the records of course."

At the top of the headed paper he had typed: 'This is a true copy of records held at the Church of the Basilica in the town of Bijeljina'.

The middle section was taken up with the detail and Father Gregory had signed and dated the paper at the bottom of the sheet.

Yana took it eagerly. "There is no mention of my father." Father Gregory looked grave.

"There are two explanations for that, both of which will be difficult for you I fear." He was speaking in English again for Lucy's benefit.

"Well," Lucy said, a shade impatiently longing for Yana to be put out of her misery.

"The first is that you may have been born out of wedlock; but that in a way would surprise me because this is a small community and had your mother been pregnant under those circumstances I believe pressure would have been put on her and the baby's father to marry."

"And the second possibility?" Lucy enquired glancing her Yana's stunned expression as she spoke.

"I fear this is the most likely. Your father may have been a Muslim and many atrocities were committed at that time."

"That does not explain why his name was not on the registration certificate, or whatever it is."

Yana interrupted her sister. "Please explain," she said. Her voice full of unshed tears. Father Gregory sighed. "To be married in the Church both parents must be accepted into the Church.

Maybe she, your mother, may not have been able to marry in our Church, but as a good Catholic she would have certainly wanted you to have been baptised." He didn't add that he had found a record of an older brother, for now he felt that was better left alone.

"Undoubtedly, Father Ignatius was prevailed upon by the family, your family, to perform the baptisms. Baptism," his quick correction did not pass unnoticed by Lucy who decided this was not the moment to comment on it.

"So, my surname – that is not a Muslim name?"

"True," Father Gregory answered. "It was undoubtedly your mother's family name. I'm sorry," he continued. "I don't seem to be the bearer of cheering news."

Yana's conscience smote her. Poor man had probably spent several hours finding this information amid the chaos of his records. Good manners came to the front as she thanked him for all his trouble and felt sure it would be helpful in proving her identity.

The priest rose from the table feeling troubled about not mentioning the other baptismal record, but shook hands before he left them, deep in thought about the sickening history of the place he now called home.

Yana felt the need to be alone. They were close enough to understand each other's needs. "Why don't you go for a walk?" Lucy suggested. "You could walk to that beautiful field we found."

Yana nodded. "Just what I was thinking. You don't mind?"

"Silly," Lucy patted her on her backside. "Go on. Off you go and leave me in peace."

As soon as the younger girl was out of earshot, Lucy retrieved her mobile from her bag and rang Peter Jordan. He sounded pleased to hear from her and whilst Lucy brought him up to date, his mind was rushing ahead looking forward to their next meeting.

If Yana's father was a Muslim, the story was just getting better and better; but he made no mention of this to Lucy. *Timing is of the essence, my boy*, he thought to himself.

"We'll leave after breakfast tomorrow." Lucy confirmed thinking that would leave the balance of the day for anything that might crop up. "It's so obvious that Yana's presence is making some people uncomfortable."

"I'll bet," Peter replied cryptically. After they said their goodbyes, Lucy found herself smiling as she thought about him. He always seemed so positive and enthusiastic. She thought about her father and Bear, the latter getting more and more like the former. Her father she thought was always kind and generous-spirited if perhaps a trifle boring. She brought herself up with a jolt.

Just because Peter seemed to lead quite an exciting life did not make her father boring and she loved him dearly.

The other men in her life were all fellow medical students. All slightly mad at times managing to party through exhaustion caused by their long hours and the tensions of their study. She had determined never to marry doctor if she could help it. One per household she reckoned more than enough!

Chapter 10

Yana squeezed through the gap in the fence and skirted around the edge of the field. She had her sights set on the hill, a well wooded area that looked intriguing.

She soon found a path that seemed to have been used quite recently. Grasses had been flattened by someone or some forest creature. For a moment, she felt slightly fearful hoping a wild boar wouldn't cross her path or some slithery snake. Yana soon forgot her momentary fears as the gentle slope led her slowly upwards and she delighted in the peace interspersed with bird song and the sound of crickets chirping vociferously. A frog hopped out of her way and she wondered where he found water in the woods.

She eventually found herself nearing the top. The trees provided shade but shafts of sunlight through the trees provided warmth which she welcomed. She continued upwards and finally came across a large boulder. She immediately noticed the 'M' carved on it and saw a carved line at the end of which was another M obviously done by the same hand. For a moment it occurred to her that the first M could be for Maria, her mother, and the second for her father. She realised this was wildly speculative but as she ran her fingers over first one and then the other she felt a warmth flooding her and a calmness that made her smile with happiness that was completely unexplainable.

There was a sudden sound. A cracking twig, she turned – immediately a bit fearful. She was a long way from Lucy. She was alone. She needn't have worried, it was Kurt! But a Kurt she barely recognised. He was pale and unshaven. His face went even more ashen when he saw her. She started to say something, but he turned on his heel and left as abruptly as he had arrived.

The silence was still golden though for Yana it was now tinged with something else.

What had happened to make Kurt behave so strangely, he had almost looked as though he hated her. Why had she ever come back, the whole venture was a terrible mistake.

She turned around and set off down the route she had enjoyed only a short while before. Now, she wanted to leave this place. To be with Lucy. To never, ever, under any circumstances to come back. It was the past, it was best left well alone. At least she had seen where she was born. She had learned that her mother was Maria and that she, Yana, looked like her. Now she could look in the mirror and visualise her. That was the only good thing that had come out of this mess.

She walked slowly down the road and couldn't help but give number twenty-five a quick glance.

It was like all the houses shuttered against the sun. From behind the shutters, Kurt saw her glance before she continued along the road.

She was so beautiful. It almost made his heart stop when he looked at her. He could no longer see her and with an impatient sound he went into the garden where he knew his father would be having his after lunch beer before dozing off in the sun.

"I'm leaving," he announced startling the older man out of his reverie.

"Where to?" his rather gruff voice sounding as fierce as ever.

"I can't stay in this house a moment longer. Too much happened here – and anyway it belongs to the girl."

His father gave a derisive snort. "It was all agreed, legally. The house is ours and will become yours."

"Never," Kurt replied. "I shall find an apartment near the school in Sarajevo." For once his father was nonplussed. "If you leave, you go forever." As a response Kurt turned away, staying in the house only long enough to pack a few things.

Lucy had just made her second telephone call. After a long conversation with Peter Jordan she had a longing to talk to her Mother. "Oh, Mum," she began. "It is all so complicated, but it is beginning to come together." She filled her mother in, telling her the facts as they appeared at the moment, and answering Sue's questions as far as she could.

Then she wanted to know what was happening at home. Sue went into a bubbly description of the house she had just found for a rather difficult client. She ran a company called 'Home

53

from Home' and worked hard to find the perfect home for each client. Today was her greatest success ever.

"We shall really be able to splurge out with the lovely percentage," she continued happily.

"Well done Mum – must go now," she added hastily, as Yana came into the room. "Mum sends her love," she said looking at Yana and noticing she looked distracted and a little upset.

Taking a deep breath, Yana looked out of the window and noticed Kurt walking along the road suitcase in hand. She felt curious as to where he was going, there was something about him that appealed to her and she wondered if she would ever see him again.

Lucy sat on her bed and patted the space beside her. Rather than ask questions, she chatted about the phone calls.

Peter's earlier conversation was repeated verbatim along with the promise he had made to have dinner with them. "Yana giggled. "I'll believe that when it happens!" Lucy grabbed a pillow and threw it in her direction. Then as Peter had suggested they started to pack so they could check out first thing the next morning.

"Tell me about your walk." Lucy asked as they ate another fattening and delicious dinner that evening.

Yana explained the linked M's on the large boulder. "It's silly I know, but I felt somehow it was them – my parents – but of course I have no idea what the second M stands for."

"Why not ask Janus." Lucy suggested. Yana shook her head, then smiled.

"Why not. He is rather odd with me so I don't hold out much hope that he might be helpful. But you never know," she finished with a wry laugh.

The next morning, they paid their bill and Janus hoped this would be the final time he would see them. He and Mikail had talked long into the night and for the first time Mikail told his friend what Janus had always suspected, that he had fired the fatal shot.

In a way it was better now that it was out in the open between them. "Are you going to tell our third musketeer?" Mikail shook his head.

"He is police now, that makes a difference. What he doesn't know he doesn't know." Janus nodded understandingly. The men parted with hugs and Mikail slept better than he had for a while. He was sorry Kurt had gone, but the boy would return.

They paid their euros over and taking a deep breath Yana asked the question she had carefully worked out. "You knew my mother Maria, didn't you?" Lucy watched Janus pale under his tan.

With difficulty he nodded. "You look like her."

"And my father?" Janus's colour changed again. This time he went bright red. He shook his head. "I know nothing," he said, turning away from them.

They both knew he was lying but what could they do, he was giving nothing away.

He sighed with relief as he stood by the door and watched them board the bus. Now perhaps life would go back to normal.

Chapter 11

As pre-arranged, they met Peter in the bar. His eyes lit up when he saw them and once again he realised how drawn he was to Lucy. They ordered drinks, both girls ordered wine and Peter ordered another gin and tonic.

"Let's sit over there," he indicated a small table tucked discretely in a corner. Lucy went near the wall with Yana on her right and Peter on her left. He really was very charming, she decided happy to see him again.

"So, have you got it Yana?" Pleasantries had been exchanged, it was now down to business. Yana produced the copy of the baptismal certificate Father Gregory had given them. Peter took it eagerly, then after a quick perusal he looked up in surprise. "No father listed!" Yana explained what Father Gregory had said that perhaps Yana's father was a Muslim and of course a marriage would not have been acceptable in the Roman Catholic Church.

"The baptism was a Christian one. It might have even taken place secretly," she added, a thought that had occurred to her recently.

"So as not to upset your father perhaps," Lucy suggested.

"Exactly."

"Well," Peter said slowly. "It will of course now be harder to trace any sort of marriage certification. Though a state marriage at the equivalent of our registry offices will be recorded under both their names. Using your dreadful surname! How do you pronounce it by the way?"

"Checkopeal," Yana responded gravely.

"Ah," Peter grinned. "I would never have got that! Anyway, with that name we can search through the records for your grandparents' marriage. It might give us a clue."

Both girls smiled. It was, after all a sort of progress.

"Now," said Peter. I have some very good news. My editor is keen to follow your story Yana, and how you settled in with Lucy's family and…"

"Stop it, Peter, stop it," Yana spoke fiercely. Lucy too looked shocked almost as if she had received a body blow. Was all his kindness solely to do with getting a story and publicity, and what else?

"How could you Peter," she said in a pained voice. Peter looked stunned, he hadn't anticipated this reaction at all. It was a good story, maybe even a great story and he was a journalist. Surely they realised.

"Was our stay here subsided by your newspaper?" Lucy demanded. Peter looked a bit shamefaced.

"We…ll, yes," he admitted with reluctance.

"Then we shall pay it back," said Yana standing as she spoke and wondering how they could have been so naïve.

Lucy stood too. "Goodnight, Peter," she said coldly, as both girls swept out of the bar. Reading each other's thoughts, not for the first time, they then walked through the lobby and out into the street.

"What a nerve," Yana began.

"Absolutely," agreed Lucy. "I am very disappointed in him," acknowledging as she spoke that she had been attracted to him and now that was spoilt. She never wanted to see him again.

"Let's fly home in the morning," Yana suggested. "We should be able to transfer our tickets."

With that in mind, they found a small restaurant for dinner, and before they returned to their 'subsidised' hotel they phoned the airline company who were fortunately able to arrange for them to transfer their tickets to an early morning flight the following morning.

Once back in their room, Lucy telephoned the front desk to ask for their bill and explain they were checking out early; only to find their account had been settled.

She put down the phone in fury. "Who does he think he is," she muttered more to herself than Yana.

"What now?" Yana wanted to know, and when Lucy told her she felt equally mad. They both felt they had been duped.

******

57

Once at the airport Lucy phoned home again. Sue was delighted they were returning home early.

"You will be here for Michael's 60th birthday party. He will be so thrilled." She agreed to meet them at Guildford Station having been assured they did not need to be met at the airport.

"We've only hand baggage Mum, really." Lucy had protested when Sue was all set to meet them off their flight.

It was good to be home again. Yana went straight upstairs and closed the door of her bedroom leaving Lucy to fill her mother in with all the happenings.

She had a sudden desire to be alone. She looked in the mirror and spoke softly to the image she saw. "So I look like you mother Maria, at least I know your name now." She sat on the comfortable bed and kicked off her shoes as she lay back and closed her eyes. Images from their time in the village floated in front of her…

The old priest thinking she was Maria. "Oh, God," she said out loud remembering what he had said about not being able to bury her. "Poor Mama," she whispered. She so longed to know more but she doubted that she ever would. She had at least found her roots and she would have to try and be content with that.

******

Kurt had found a one-bedroom flat. It was furnished in a rather more fussy style than his personal taste but at least he was away from number twenty-five. He could not think of that as home anymore.

As he unpacked his things, he thought about the girl Yana wondering if he could write to her to explain why he had walked away from her the last time he saw her.

On a sudden impulse he phoned Janus and found his assumption was correct, Janus did indeed have an address in the guest book they had signed when they originally checked in.

Janus was curious. "Why do you want it Kurt my boy?" Kurt was not to be drawn.

"There is something I forgot to mention," he answered not prepared to be drawn.

It was, thought Kurt, the most difficult letter he had ever written or ever hoped to write. He began by reminding Yana who he was and saying how very much he had enjoyed meeting her.

The first two sentences were written and re written and, he thought to himself, he hadn't even arrived at the difficult part yet. Finally, he decided to write exactly what his father had told him explaining as he did that he had to drag the words from his father who had carried the burden of his crime these past fourteen years.

He wrote with no thought for himself, though he knew, given the choice he would have enjoyed writing a very different letter telling her of his feelings for her.

He sighed deeply as he signed his name, thinking as he did so that she would hate him now if for nothing else, being his father's son.

His last sentence read: 'This has been the most difficult letter I have ever written. I felt it my duty to tell you the truth, awful though it is. I hope over time you may come to forgive me for who I am and for having lived in your home for all these years. Kurt'.

He didn't have the full address but he printed her name clearly on the envelope, followed by The Old Rectory, Guildford. England. He hoped the postal system would manage to find her.

Chapter 12

It was an exciting day. Yana's exam results arrived. She had thought she couldn't bear to go to school to pick them up. She had not wanted them emailed as she wanted to share the moment with her friends. They had agreed good, bad or indifferent, they would support each other.

She had done better than she dared hope. Three As and a B. It was better than the offer she had received from Cambridge so she felt ecstatic.

When she arrived home, it wasn't long before she and Sue were dancing 'round the kitchen and when Michael arrived home for lunch, a huge grin spread over his face as he looked at the paper Yana handed him. "I never doubted it," he said. "Now I shall have two daughters at med school. He hugged her tightly and once again Yana acknowledged to herself how fortunate she was to have the loving home and family she had.

"There's a letter for you Yana dear." Sue suddenly remembered the intriguing missive with the foreign stamp. She laughed. "It looks as if it has been to several Old Rectories before it found you."

Yana took the letter and turned it over. There, clearly written was Kurt's name, but with a different address. "I wonder why he's written. He behaved so strangely last time we met."

"Open it darling girl before we all die of curiously!" Michael hugged her as he spoke.

Yana tore it open eagerly. She had enjoyed meeting him and acknowledged to herself that she had been a little hurt, as well as taken aback by their last encounter.

His written English was a little stilted but as she read she sank weakly on to one of the kitchen chairs. Sue and Michael heard her sharp intake of breath and watched as her face turned paler than pale. The tears were now pouring furiously down her cheeks and a sob wrenched at their hearts.

Finally, she finished reading and wordlessly handed the letter to Michael. He and Sue stood close and read it together, reading the words that Kurt had so laboured to put together.

As they read the last words Lucy burst excitedly into the kitchen. "How have you done little sister?" Then seeing Yana's tears and the expressions on her parent's faces was shocked to think she has not done as expected.

"She has done brilliantly of course." Sue spoke quickly her mind still caught up in what she had just finished reading. Lucy laughed happily. "Then why are you all looking so miserable?"

Sue took the letter from Michael and handed it to Lucy. "May I?" she asked Yana who just gave a brief nod. Like her parents, Lucy read the letter with mounting horror. "No wonder he behaved oddly at the end."

"In all fairness," Michael spoke quietly. "The boy knew nothing of this until recently. Imagine how he must feel." Yana gave a cry and grabbed the letter before running back to the solitude of her bedroom to read the dreadful letter once again.

After a while she got off the bed and walked to the mirror. "Oh, Mama," she whispered looking at her own reflection. "How brave you were." A sudden picture came unbidden into her mind. She stood once again shivering by the cold stove. Her mother lay on the floor. *It's only a game darling*, the disembodied voice in her head said. A racking sob tore through her. She vowed never ever to go back to her country of her birth, never to go back to the house where she had hoped she might find a happy truth. Instead, she had found rape and murder and Kurt's own father had committed these crimes against her mother.

There was a quiet knock at the door. "May I come in Yana?" It was Sue, who not hearing a reply came in anyway. Yana was still standing in front of the mirror, her eyes wild with shock and her body trembling. Sue put her arms around the girl and led her gently to the bed. Yana sat as her racking sobs cut through to Sue's heart and she held her foster daughter close to her, wanting only to ease her pain.

Time passed and gradually the girl quietened. Sue released her hold and took Yana's hand in hers. *If the eyes are the mirror of the soul*, she thought, *Yana is in a living hell.*

Days went past. Yana barely ate or spoke. Michael and Sue became increasingly concerned. Strangely enough in the end, it was Lily coming home that helped Yana.

Chapter 13

Lily arrived as she always did, or so Michael said! She roared up the drive in her Suzuki Jeep – scattering the stones and churning up a dust. She had as always dropped the horses at the paddock, unhitched the horse trailer and put it just inside the gate. She was a capable girl of that, there was no doubt. She was also continuing to get noticed in circles that mattered to her.

She burst into the house brown Labrador as always at her side. "Hi everyone," she said coming into the kitchen. It was a Sunday morning and apart from Yana the family were altogether.

"Hi Luce, good trip?" Before Lucy could answer Lily moved on. "Mum, Dad," she continued blowing kisses as she sat down in her usual place.

"Hi kiddo."

"Don't call me that." Bear almost growled. She always managed to rub him up the wrong way.

"Where is Yana then," she demanded next, helping herself to a piece of toast which she spread liberally with Sue's home-made marmalade.

The silence around the table made her pause mid-bite. This was never a silent household. "You didn't leave her in Yugoslavia or whatever it's called these days, did you Luce?"

"No," Lucy's answer was brief even by twin standards.

"Yana had a horrible letter from a man who lives in her house," said Bear sounding cross with his older sister. "She's upset."

"She is more than that," Lucy added.

"Oh well, I better go and cheer her up. Perhaps I'll cheer her up by telling her all my news first."

"What news." Michael and Sue spoke together. Lily was so unpredictable, heaven knows what she would come out with now.

Lily bounded up the stairs two at a time, Beth, her ever faithful hound following close at her heels as always.

She knocked on Yana's bedroom door and without waiting for a 'come in' went straight in.

Yana, still in her pyjamas was sitting on the stool at her dressing table staring bleakly into the mirror. Her hair brush was in her hand but her hair looked tousled and untouched from her night's sleep. *But*, thought Lily, *she always looks gorgeous*. Not today though. Her face was blotched with tears and she had dark circles under her eyes which made her skin look whiter than ever.

For once Lily was taken aback. *Must have been some letter,* she thought. "Here Beth." The dog obediently came to her mistress who pointed to the door where the dog lay down patiently waiting for whatever came next.

Lily sat down on the bed. Talking about herself (as usual) she said to herself with a slight grimace, but it might also distract Yana and anyway she was longing to tell somebody.

Yana swung 'round and gazed fondly at Lily. Dear Lily, always so dramatic. "You've what?" she said in response to what she was hearing.

"You heard. Come and sit here and I'll tell you all about my gorgeous beau!" She had made Yana smile with her extravagant language. "Go on, ask me some questions." Yana laughed in spite of herself.

"Right," she said. "You've asked for it. Who is he? Where does he live? Is he English? Does he have horses? Oh and how old?"

"Yes, yes, et cetera et cetera. I've forgotten the others," Lily laughed delightedly. "His name is Adrian MacDonald. He is twenty-six. He is on the Olympic Team. Oh, and his father is Lord somebody or other."

"Oh Lily, it all sounds too wonderful for words. What have Sue and Michael said."

"They don't know yet. You are the first member of the family to know."

"I'm honoured," she said, happily wondering just why Lily had told her first. She kissed her sister. "Well, when are we going to meet this knight of yours?"

"Tomorrow, would you believe? Tomorrow. And in this day and age, he is coming down to ask for my hand!"

"I think he sounds perfect."

"He is." Lucy answered dreamily. "He really is."

They sat for a while and finally Yana showed Lily the letter. Lily read it through once, and then again and to Yana's surprise tears ran down her sister's face. "The bastard," Lily muttered. "How brave of, what's his name, Kurt," she said, looking at the signature again. "How brave of him to be so honest, pretty hard for him to do, wouldn't you think."

Yana didn't reply. Kurt and sympathy were the last thing on her mind – but of course Lily was right. It had been brave – even courageous, but she couldn't forgive him for being his father's son.

Down stairs Sue and Michael were clearing away the breakfast dishes. "I do hope Lily isn't saying the wrong thing."

"Have a little faith darling," Michael said. "She isn't heartless you know."

"Just self-centred!" They laughed quietly together exchanging a brief kiss.

Sue picked up the envelope and without even thinking put in her kitchen filing system, the back of her diary.

The girls came down the stairs chattering as they came. A glance passed between the parents.

Their eldest daughter had worked some magic. "Now parents prepare yourself for my news."

"Do we need to sit down?" Sue questioned with a somewhat anxious smile.

"You certainly do. Right Yana," she said with a grin at her younger sister, who appeared so much happier than she had been since her return home.

Yana had not forgotten the letter or its contents but she had, thanks to Lily's effervescent joy, managed to file it away in her special, don't-think-about-it-department that served her well at times of stress.

They were all seated and gazing expectantly at the still standing and excited Lily. "I'm going to get married," she announced solemnly. Then burst into peals of laughter. "What do you think of that?" she demanded.

After a silence in which you could hear a pin drop, Michael stood up and walked around the table to where Lily stood. "If you are happy – we're happy. Right Sue?" he added as he hugged the bride-to-be.

"Oh darling, yes of course," she said jumping up and joining the hug.

"Come on, Yana, you too." It was Lily, who she had always found a little difficult who was managing to ease her pain away with her joyousness and also the feelings they had shared in the bedroom had brought them closer in a new and an unexpected way.

"This calls for champagne. I have always said it was good to keep a bottle on the ready in the fridge." Michael sounded happy and as Sue fetched some champagne glasses from the dining room, she hoped it really was good news. She wanted to know so much more.

Soon they were toasting Lily and her future happiness, toasting each other and generally being 'the happy family' they were. Glancing at Yana she noticed the shadows gradually lifting from the girl's face and realised that Lily had been the cause of the change. Whatever they had talked about upstairs, including the exciting news, she had obviously been able to reach Yana in a way none of the rest of them had. She said an inward 'thank you God'.

Lily went on to repeat all she had told Yana, including his father's title. "Oh dear," Sue said in a worried voice. "I do hope they are not terrible snobs."

"They are lovely, easy going relaxed people." Sue looked doubtful.

"Darling Sue we are a match for anyone, title or not. I'm certainly not going to touch my forelock to a mere lord." Michael made them all laugh.

"Tell them when he is arriving," Yana said mischievously.

"Tomorrow."

"Tomorrow," Sue and Michael said in unison.

"For lunch. Tell them why Lily."

"He is going to ask for my hand. Actually, he wants more than that but he is going to do the right thing!" she and Yana collapsed in giggles.

"He sounds better by the minute." Michael muttered sotto voce to Sue.

******

His visit had been a great success. Lily knew her parents would like Paul. He had been charmingly deferential towards them. He had a sense of humour which Sue gave him points for and he fitted in as easily as if he had known them forever.

"I do love your daughter," he told them as they sat drinking coffee after a delicious lunch. Sue was grateful she had a filet of beef in the freezer and had made boeuf en croute. Whilst Yana at the special request of Lily had made her speciality, apple crumble.

"I love Lily," he repeated. "That is why I wanted to visit you and make sure you had no objection to my marrying your wonderful daughter."

"Glad to be rid of her," Bear said cheerfully. "I have far too many sisters!" They all laughed.

"So, may I take it Sir that you will allow me to get engaged to Lily?"

"We would be delighted to welcome you into our family," Michael said, smiling at Sue and speaking for them both.

Out came a new bottle of champagne and Adrian with a wink that did not go unnoticed by the family, produced a beautiful diamond and ruby ring. "Lily, as you know this ring belonged to my great grandmother and I would love you to accept it as a sign of my love and also a welcome into my family."

Lily who was well primed smiled and looked at him lovingly. "Why it fits perfectly," he said.

"Just like Cinderella's glass slipper, and you are my prince."

"Oh yuck." Bear could contain himself no longer. "I can't stand this soppy stuff." They all laughed and talked and the family felt additionally happy because Yana was smiling again.

-0-0-0-0-0-0-0-0-0-

Yana's troubles were put to one side. She had other things to think about. In October she would join Lucy at University College, having decided that the opportunity to share a flat and do the same course as Lucy was more compelling than her offer of Cambridge.

Michael had decided that it would be good sense to buy a small flat rather than shabby rooms somewhere, as Lucy had

67

previously. The girls had fun flat-hunting only really made possible by both of them being in the same city.

Finally, they found what they considered to be the perfect flat. Euphemistically called a garden flat, it was actually a basement flat with a small garden of which they would have sole use.

With two bedrooms, a tiny bathroom and equally tiny kitchen and one living, dining room which would make an excellent party space!

Lucy called home straight away saying that at last they had found the perfect flat. Michael agreed to make an offer that would at least hold it for twenty-four hours while Sue dropped everything and took the train straight up to London.

Fortunately, Sue also thought it was perfect. It was located in a cul-de-sac, so no through traffic, and off Kensington High Street. Surveys organised and completed, price agreed, contracts signed and the flat was theirs.

Chapter 14

Sue and Michael drove home feeling very happy. They had just spent a pleasant afternoon with Lily's prospective in-laws. Sue had been a little apprehensive and Michael was totally laid back and relaxed as usual.

They had agreed they would make an effort for Lily's sake whether they liked them or not. In the event however they found the couple totally charming, like their son and felt Lily was fortunate to have such delightful people as future in-laws.

Sue had adored their mansion, for that's what it was. Quite Downton Abbey ish, Sue had commented as they had driven up the sweeping drive with its beautifully maintained lawns. And large clumps of azaleas and rhododendrons. "They must look magnificent in the spring," she had murmured. Michael had agreed.

"I really liked Meg and Paul."

"It would be difficult not to," Michael said.

Wedding plans were in the air. Lily for once interested in clothes. The wedding dress she said emphatically, had to be a simple column of cream silk, more she didn't know. Her bridesmaids would be Lucy and Yana of course and Paul's sister Christina. As Christina was a tall blonde – the bridesmaids would be a beautiful trio of colour with Lucy's dark hair, Yana's auburn and Christina's blonde. They were all much of a height too – all tall and slim.

After much talk and discussion and with a dressmaker recommended by Meg MacDonald, they settled on pale primrose silk which would work with their diverse colouring.

Bear would be an usher, Lily told him firmly. He was just relieved that until THE DAY, which was to be December 1st, he could keep a low profile.

People were always at the house these days, thought Yana, glad that in a week she would be joining Lucy in London.

Marquee companies, caterers, florists were forever having meetings at the house. Yana was amazed they were even considering a marquee in the middle of winter but Sue assured her heaters would keep it warm and cosy, although she admitted to inwardly she was a little concerned but kept her worries to herself.

There would be a greeting point in the lovely square hall of the Old Rectory then guests would walk down a tented corridor to the main marquee on the lower lawn.

Sue began to think of her own outfit. It could be very cold, or wet or even a lovely crisp winter's day. Her mind was in a whirl and the wedding seemed to have taken control of her life!

Yana was in heaven. The course was all she had hoped for and more. As always, she absorbed everything like blotting paper to the chagrin of her fellow students who would have hated her had she not been so lovely in every other way.

She was teased of course, but that had happened at school when she regularly achieved ninety nine percent. Yana saw very little of Lucy. The older girl was working very long hours and sometimes almost a week would go past without them having so much as a coffee together.

Lucy sometimes slept for a few hours during the day when Yana was studying and at other times she was up before dawn and back after midnight. She looked tired and pale, but she told Yana she had no regrets and had decided she wanted to specialise in dermatology which she found was becoming increasingly interesting with some of the exciting developments to aid some of the more dire conditions such as psoriasis.

Yana smiled at Lucy's enthusiasm. She knew exactly what she wanted to do. She wanted to be a doctor in the community. To get to really know patients rather than see them just passing through as in hospital. She had always known this is what she wanted but had hugged it to herself. Now Lucy was shocked. "But Yana you are so clever. You could be anything, a brain surgeon or cardiac surgeon."

"I want to be a general practitioner, I want to help the people in the community where I live, wherever that might be. So that is that," she added with a finality that brooked no argument.

Chapter 15

Home in Guildford, Sue was totally caught up in lists of all descriptions. The telephone seemed to ring ceaselessly. At night with her mind buzzing, she paced around downstairs unable to sleep trying to cope with her business as well as the multitudinous wedding details.

Finally, Michael had had enough. "My darling," he said looking at her pale face across the breakfast table. "You won't be fit to go to your own daughter's wedding if you don't calm down."

"I am calm," she answered in a tone that belied her comment. He reached over and put his square capable hand over hers.

"My Sue," he said in a tone of endearment. "For once, you are going to listen to the doctor." She glanced away.

"Goodness, look at the time," she said about to spring up.

"Sit down Sue." His tone was uncompromising unlike the Michael who let things happen around him only interfering when he felt it necessary to intervene.

They talked for an hour. Finally, Sue admitted to feeling tired and run down. Michael went to his bag and got out some tablets. "Just one now and one at bedtime."

"Yes, doctor," Sue said meekly, but belying her meek voice with a flashing smile. "I love you Michael. Thank you for being so caring."

Life progressed at a more even keel from then on, though Lily's frequent visits and at times temperamental behaviour were an unwelcome strain. She was living mostly at Paul's cottage now, but having to be discreet as his parents she knew would not approve.

The cottage – in the grounds was fortunately sufficiently far away from the main house for discretion to be observed. However, Lily's gold four by four was known to all the staff on the estate who smiled indulgently. 'Why not', was the consensus of opinion. Times have changed.

Of course Lord and Lady MacDonald eventually heard, but after a short outburst by Meg to her son on how to behave; her own good humour prevailed, and she acknowledged things were certainly not as they had been in her young days.

Meg thought back to her early married life. Her mother-in-law had been a dragon, making her first few years of married life pretty terrible. Constantly putting her down in front of both her husband and small son. Meg determined that Lily – who seemed delightful, would never be treated in such a manner.

The wedding day dawned. The first of December had arrived. Sue woke early and pulled the curtains back from the windows. It was still dark, but she could see the ghostly silhouette of the tunnel and the marquee. At least, it wasn't raining. She shivered slightly in her silk nightgown. "Come back to bed and give me a cuddle," came a sleepy voice from the bed.

"It's rather cold." Sue giggled as she slipped off her nightgown at Michael's behest.

"You will always be my beautiful bride," he whispered. He ran his hands gently over her body, squeezing her nipples then kissing the soft mound of her stomach before parting her legs and slipping his fingers into the warmth and wetness that told him she wanted him too.

After a shower, Michael went down and made them a cup of tea whilst Sue had a leisurely shower herself. *Probably the only quiet moment of the day,* she thought as she towelled herself dry.

The heating had come on while they were still in bed and now she sat in one of the two comfy chairs in front of the window waiting for Michael and the cup of tea he would bring with him.

Dawn was breaking showing there had been an overnight frost. With any luck, the bride's mother thought, it will be a lovely winter's day.

Soon the couple were enjoying the hot lemon tea they enjoyed every morning. Michael had started making it when the twins were born, and it had become a well-established part of their morning routine.

He would go downstairs and let the dogs out for a run. The two elderly spaniels and the young dalmatian they had, in his opinion, foolishly acquired six months ago. He was proving quite a handful and Michael was quite glad that all three dogs would be collected at nine am and spend a couple of days in the local kennels.

"Woman cover yourself," he growled as Sue's robe fell open displaying her soft full bosom and her long, shapely legs. "Or I shall not be responsible for my actions!" Sue pretended to be horrified but she was inwardly delighted that Michael still fancied her. He had always been an attentive lover and her best friend in the world.

"We haven't time," she said as sternly as she could, but with a slight regret in her voice.

There was a knock at the door and before they could say 'come in', Lily was in the room with them. "Oh Mum, Dad, I've been such a pig, haven't I."

"Well," drawled Michael.

"Yes, you have darling," Sue responded. "But as the bride you are almost entitled!"

"Is there any tea left?" Michael nodded and without a word took his cup to rinse out for her in the bathroom. "Here you are bride-to-be, I have dogs to track down and feed." He walked into the dressing room and left mother and daughter together.

Lily poured herself a cup of the Earl Grey tea they all loved and sat in the chair vacated by her father. "Is the dress okay. Really Mum – really."

"It's beautiful," Sue said and meant it. It was just as Lily had wanted it to be. A tube of cream silk with narrow sleeves to her elbows. The bottom of each sleeve had five silk-covered tiny buttons which corresponded with identical buttons that started at the bottom of the deep v on the back of the dress, and continued to where some tiny pleats then softened the dress and continued on downwards to form a tiny train at the bottom. She was going to wear her hair up and Meg had loaned her prospective daughter-in-law a narrow diamond tiara which she had worn at her own wedding.

Soon, the whole family were around the kitchen table. Sue was in her element Michael thought watching her produce eggs of all descriptions and crispy bacon. Bear was tucking in as usual and teasing the bride-to-be, calling her bride-to-bed. Lucy and Yana were deep in conversation about something that had happened at the hospital. Michael overheard the word pornography. "Goodness they are not teaching that in med school these days, are they?"

"No such luck." Lucy laughed. "No, we were just talking about the SHO who was found to have been downloading porn during his shifts."

"How on earth." Sue sounded aghast.

"All too easily. The computers are everywhere and it's not exactly difficult to get into the web sites."

"Talking porn on my wedding day is not appropriate."

"I agree not quite the topic for discussion, please girls." Lucy winked conspiratorially at Yana, her twin playing up again, the wink seemed to say.

Yana smiled back. She was looking forward to the wedding, she and Sue had spent all of the previous morning helping the florists decorate the church. Everywhere was now a bower of cream and yellow roses even the archway around the door. The ushers and main guests would be wearing yellow roses. The groom wearing a cream rose to pick up the colour of the brides dress. The bridesmaids would be carrying Victorian style posies with the theme continued of yellow and cream.

Bear had been trying on the morning suit Michael had bought him for the occasion. He had told Bear he hoped his would last as long as his own had! Sue had checked it over for him to make sure it was still worthy and they both found it strange, that he would be walking his daughter down the aisle in the same suit he had worn to marry Sue twenty five years before.

They were both aware it was a little tighter but Sue told him it looked as good as ever. In fact, she had said as handsome as ever which pleased him inordinately.

It was such a happy day, albeit a long one thought Sue, finally kicking off her shoes. The invitation was for twelve thirty with 'carriages' at midnight. It had been twelve solid hours on the go and it felt like it – at least she thought, drinking a glass of water – her feet felt like it.

Michael joined her by the sink. "A great day…"

"Such a happy one. Didn't she look utterly beautiful."

"Nearly as beautiful as her mother."

"Flatterer," she laughed happily. He walked to the fridge.

"A last glass of champagne then bed." Sue nodded walking across the hall to the family room where she sank gratefully into one of the chairs. "I may never move again," she said taking the proffered glass. "The church looked lovely," she murmured. "The choir sang their solo so much better than expected. Everyone seemed to enjoy the service, wouldn't you say Michael? Charles can always be counted on for that and his homily was perfect." Michael grunted his agreement beginning to think longingly of bed.

Sue continued to rave about the food, the weather, the sun actually shining for the photos.

"It was all wonderfully organised. You did a great job my darling. I agree the food was delicious as was the cake, and the disco was a great success for the 'youngs'. They certainly threw themselves into it. Now come on woman," he added affectionately.

Sue put her glass down and held her hand out. Michael pulled her up and hugged her lightly before starting to turn the lights out. Sue shook her head. "The children are around somewhere, probably still in the marquee. Let's just leave the lights on for them and go to bed."

Chapter 16

There were lots of students Yana liked, particularly among her year group. However, their attitudes were all quite similar, slightly madcap, particularly the heavy drinkers – off duty of course, and sex seemed to be forever on their minds.

"Too much testosterone." Lucy laughed when Yana talked to her about it on one of their rare suppers together.

Lucy, Yana felt was being a bit mysterious these days. There was something she was not telling. Usually the two girls shared their secrets knowing nothing would go further.

Lucy was dying to confide but for once she needed thinking time. She was, she admitted to herself feeling a bit confused. The reason was the wretched Peter Jordan. He had texted her at intervals and she had ignored every one of them. Then she received one that said 'am going to the U.S.A, goodbye'.

Damn him, she thought. I couldn't care less whether he is going to the moon, but inwardly she felt a brief flicker of disappointment.

Finally, she rang his mobile. It was of course on answer phone. 'Peter Jordan here please leave a message. I promise to call you back'.

Without thinking she spoke. "Lucy here. How long are you going to the States for? Good Luck."

When she rang off, she realised she had asked him a question. *Damn him*, she thought not for the first time. That was an invitation to reply.

Her phone rang just after she had fallen into one of her deep exhausted sleeps. Looking at her clock she saw it was two a. m. What did he think he was doing ringing her at this time. She knew it was him, but his voice made her heart race a little faster and despite herself she acknowledged the sound of it excited her.

"I leave the day after tomorrow, Lucy. Please meet me for lunch or dinner before I go."

"I can't make dinner, working," she muttered sleepily.

"Lunch then? The Ritz Bar."

Pretentious, she thought.

"Noon," he added.

"I'll be there." She turned her mobile off and was asleep again before her head even touched the pillow.

Lucy dressed with care. She was due at the hospital at three p. m. and she could hardly turn up over-dressed. She chose a simple but elegant skirt with a pretty blouse which she partly covered with one of the gorgeous cashmere sweaters that Sue bought for her daughters when she was feeling flush! Apart from a simple gold chain around her neck, she wore no other jewellery.

She brushed her hair. It was below her shoulders now she had, at the request of her twin let it grow, now she couldn't wait to go back to her just below the chin length which is what she preferred.

Her pale face, due mostly to long hours and lack of sleep made her dark hair appear almost black. By comparison, and the only good thing about it she felt, was that now, freshly washed it gleamed.

Glancing at her watch she realised she was running late. Grabbing her faithful camel coat and bag and forgetting her gloves she ran all the way to the tube.

She was only ten minutes late but Peter waiting anxiously by the bar wondered if she was coming.

When she walked through the door he was almost bowled over. God, she was beautiful. About to kiss her on the cheek he took the proffered hand instead. "I've got to be away by two thirty," Lucy said by way of greeting.

"Right I'll pay for my drink. I thought we'd go to a little Italian place around the corner, I wasn't sure you would find it which is why I suggested we meet here instead."

Lucy felt a sense of relief she didn't see herself as a Ritz person!

The restaurant was charming and Peter was clearly well known. He explained that Lucy was a doctor in a hurry and their steaming antipasti arrived amazingly quickly.

"Now tell me what is taking you to the States?"

"It's a colleague really," he began. "His wife is very ill and he has taken leave of absence to nurse her. I gather it may be terminal."

"How sad," Yana murmured.

"You don't know the half of it. They were only married a year ago." Lucy was silent thinking of the recent family wedding that had been such a joyous occasion. To lose someone so soon, after only a year.

She was miles away, Peter thought. "Hey Lucy, come back."

"Sorry Peter, thinking of weddings made me think about my twin."

"There are two of you!" His tone made Lucy laugh. "We are not identical twins."

"I think I'm relieved." Peter grinned. "Two such beauties would be difficult to be around." They chatted easily – and Lucy warmed to him again. After two years of refusing to answer his text messages and phone calls, she began to wonder if she had over reacted just a little.

"Will you come and visit me in New York, Lucy? All above board and all that."

"With no subsidised accommodation," she couldn't resist the jibe.

"Touché," he retorted. They laughed companionably and Lucy realised she found his company more enjoyable than the medics she seemed to date. There were nice enough chaps but with rare exceptions BED still seemed a high priority.

When they parted, Lucy agreed to consider a visit to New York. "You have my number," he said kissing her lightly on both cheeks. "I'll wait for your call." She was smiling as he hailed her a taxi and she felt an inward warmth that was rather delicious. She was still smiling as the taxi dropped her off outside the hospital.

******

As Lucy and Yana chatted over an early coffee one morning, Lucy's mind kept returning to her meeting with Peter and all the texts and telephone calls that had transpired since.

"Come on Luce, you are keeping something from me –tell."

"I'm not sure you are going to be very happy about it." Lucy began diffidently.

"If you are happy, then so am I. You know that Luce."

"It's Peter Jordan."

"What!" Yana couldn't help herself. "That creep," she said involuntarily.

"Yana, you promised." Yana looked shamefaced.

"I did, didn't I. Tell me from the beginning."

So, Lucy told her about all the 'phone calls she had ignored. For almost two years she had done nothing. Finally, she had sent him the text 'leave me alone'.

"And," Yana asked. "Did he?" Lucy smiled.

"It seemed to work for a while, then it began again. The messages were sometimes very funny and made me smile. Sometimes it was a joke he had heard or a bit of gossip he assumed I might enjoy.

"Then finally he sent a text saying he was going to live in the States and would I at least meet him for a farewell drink." Yana raised her eyebrows questioningly.

"Yes, I did," Lucy replied, a shade defensively to the unasked question. "We had a drink," she continued, "over lunch actually, at a little Italian restaurant. I found to my surprise, I rather liked him. Though I hadn't forgiven him at that stage. Then he went to New York. He phoned once or twice a week and I found I was rather looking forward to his calls. I even phoned him once just to let him know I was doing a double shift and wouldn't be able to answer his calls. Now he has repeated his invitation to me to go to New York for a weekend and I think I might go, Yana. I really think I will go," she ended firmly. She looked fondly at her foster sister wanting something, not exactly approval but at least acquiescence.

For a moment Yana was silent. Then she leaned across the table and kissed Lucy on the cheek. "I think you must go Luce, it seems to me like destiny."

It sounded a bit profound to Lucy, yet, she rationalised they had been drawn together from that very first meeting on the plane. Whatever his motives, he had been helpful in Belgrade. He made her laugh. Her mother always said humour was a good thing to look for in a man. He was also thoughtful and seemed to be caring. *I'll go*, she decided. *I will go*.

Peter read the text message from Lucy with a broad grin spread over his face. She was coming, she was actually coming. It was a huge step. He immediately booked a room in her name. There must be no confusion, this time she could pay her own way completely! The next three weeks would seem a long time but it was her first free weekend. He decided he must do some research on young doctors' hours. She seemed to work most of the time… There had been a fuss years ago and the hours were supposedly modified; but he had been shocked at the shadows under her eyes and her pale complexion. It was as if she seldom saw daylight!

Peter was enjoying New York. The pace was if anything more frenetic. The deadlines were as tight as back home but he enjoyed the more laid back and friendly atmosphere wherever he went. For the first time he rather envied the colleague he was standing in for; then felt bad as James' circumstances were not at all enviable. They had spoken once or twice and James had implied it was more likely to be weeks rather than months for his adored American wife.

Peter wanted to make the weekend special for Lucy. Not too hectic as her life was that anyway. He bought tickets for a Broadway Show he thought she would enjoy and made reservations for an early dinner before the show at a highly recommended Italian restaurant. She had commented that Italian food was her favourite 'eat out'. Apart from that, he wanted her to relax. Perhaps a ride in a horse-drawn carriage through Central Park and a visit to ground zero. The area where the twin towers had so proudly stood before nine eleven.

He couldn't stop smiling and attracted a number of glances as he travelled on the metro. A smiling, attractive young man was a pleasant sight on a grey New York morning.

Three weeks had both dragged and sped by. The days had gone in a flash he was so busy. But his free time had dragged. He was invited out a great deal a young bachelor Englishman was quite a coup in certain areas. Several of the women surprised him with their very upfront attitudes.

Had Lucy not been so very much on his mind, he would have taken at least one of the women out.

They were beautiful, very well groomed and very well dressed. Certainly, they were ahead of the English women he generally came across in his field, but he loved Lucy just as she was. He stopped in the middle of the pavement causing people behind him to curse as they walked around the mutt standing stock still whilst everyone else was rushing somewhere or another.

He loved Lucy! His mind said it again. He knew he fancied her. He had fancied her from the first moment he saw her in the plane. She was beautiful with her glossy swinging hair. Her greeny-grey eyes, her skin. He started to walk slowly forward. He loved her, not only that he wanted to spend the rest of his life with her. He even wanted to marry her. He had a mental picture of he and Lucy – and he and Lucy – with children. My God, he didn't even really like children. What the hell had happened to him. His elation fled as quickly as it had arrived, he wished she wasn't coming to New York. He wished he could never see her again, and in the same moment he longed for her.

The plane touched down. It had been a long three weeks for Lucy. Because she had been so busy she had only been able to think about Peter at infrequent moments. Sometimes she giggled to herself at some of the inappropriate moments like sitting on the loo, or studying a patient with bad psoriasis she would find herself wondering about Peter's epidermis. Skin was such an interesting field.

His epidermis, she decided would be smooth and firm with perhaps a hairy chest which she personally found manly and sexy. She wondered how his skin smelt. Smell was so important, he must use deodorants, she had never smelt a hint of sweat though. She smiled to herself, that could be sexy too…

Her eyes scanned the faces. With only hand luggage, she was ahead of the main crowd. Customs had a look in her pull along and studied her correctly completed white form which was duly stamped. Her passport was perused and checked on the computer and with a wave of a hand she had permission to continue.

She somehow had expected Peter to hug her, but they both seemed rather restrained and shook hands! Despite the long journey, Peter thought she looked as lovely as ever and she seemed more relaxed. She had, in fact, slept for the entire journey and suddenly realised she was starving. He suggested they dropped off her bag so she could freshen up, rest or whatever.

"I'd like to drop off my bag, a quick wash and then Peter I'm starving. Can we eat?"

It broke the ice and arm in arm they went out to find a cab. "It's my first time in New York." Lucy confessed. "I've always wanted to go in one of these yellow cabs."

They were soon in down town Manhattan and the cab drew up at a smart looking hotel.

Peter hovered whilst Lucy checked in and then as she finished at the desk he told her he would wait in the lobby for her. He waved in the direction of some comfortable looking chairs and sofas as she headed for the lift.

The bedroom, true American style had two queen-sized beds – a fabulous bathroom and more, soft white towels than she could use in the entire visit. She washed, brushed her hair, replaced her lip gloss and touched up her mascara. Then with a quick look in the long mirror she let herself out of the room and went to find her friend.

Peter was surprised at her speed remembering time consuming tidying up by other women. He thought she looked great with her slim fitting black trousers worn with her camel jacket. She looked smart enough for anywhere yet casual enough for sightseeing. "Lunch?"

"Yes," she replied firmly but accompanied with a warm smile.

This time they walked hand in hand. "Two blocks. Alright?" Lucy nodded feeling surprisingly light hearted.

Chapter 17

Back home in London Lucy explained that the weekend had gone well. "One of the best." Lucy confided. Yana looked at the happy face in front of her and hesitated to ask 'what next'.

As if reading her thoughts, Lucy told her that Peter was coming back for some special meeting, so she would see him in around six weeks. The girls fell silent, each wrapped in thought.

Lucy was remembering Peter's lingering kiss at the airport. He had been quite restrained during the weekend and Lucy could have no idea what strength of character that had taken. Once or twice she almost willed him to kiss her, there were so many opportunities. The carriage ride, at the bedroom door, when all he had done was place a chaste kiss on each cheek.

Then at the airport it was as though he could let his emotions out! Lucy's heart had raced and she felt her lips melt into his. Afterwards they looked deeply into each other's eyes – their expressions serious at first as they both recognised a major change had taken place in their relationship. Then they smiled and reached for each other's hands.

"This is the beginning Lucy." Lucy nodded, almost fearful to speak lest she damage a fragile moment. "I must go, the flight."

"I know, it's been called. I'll ring you." She leaned forward and kissed him lightly on the lips.

"Thank you for a wonderful weekend." She turned away, and was gone. He saw a glimpse of her as her boarding pass was re-checked, she turned to look but didn't see him. He saw her look of disappointment and felt happy in the knowledge that she was disappointed!

It was a marvellous weekend, Lucy continued dreamily and Yana felt a sudden tug at her heart; she was going to lose her dearest sister and best friend. She felt happy for Lucy and sad for herself.

******

Sue was transferring various facts from the current year's diary to the new one. For several years every time she came to the end of the year she came across the folded envelope along with other odd semi important items. It was the envelope that had contained Kurt's letter to Yana. The letter that had caused her such distress. For the past three years Sue had unfolded the envelope, looked at it, and placed it at the back of her new diary held in place with an elastic band. This year she was about to repeat the process, when on sudden impulse she pulled out a piece of headed notepaper from her desk drawer and started to write.

It was not an easy letter, but she felt Kurt had shown courage and although late, he deserved a response. She wrote of Yana's distress at receiving the letter, and how it had made the girl unhappy for quite a long time. Sue tempered this by writing how courageous she thought he had been to write such a letter in the first place and that she was sure Yana was glad she knew the truth, awful though it was. She continued by telling him that Yana was now in her fourth year of medical studies and that they had enjoyed two family weddings as both her twins were now married and she was looking forward to being a grandmother soon. She wrote about Michael, and how he had first seen Yana as a terrified barely three year old and that she was of course like one of their own daughters and had been almost from day one; when she had at Michael's bidding collected the tiny child from the military hospital and strapped her in Bear's car seat. She wrote about Bear explaining that his real name was Rupert and that if he, Kurt, liked cricket he might even have heard of him as he had recently been invited into the English team. She wrote about their home, their dogs and how they used to have horses too; but now Lily had the horses at her home with her husband who was a trainer of horses for Trials and Events and that Lily had been first reserve on the Olympic Team; but she hoped she might one day actually ride for the Team.

Finally, she wrote of her own sad news. That only six months earlier, a few months after Lucy's happy marriage to Peter Jordan, her own beloved Michael had been killed in a crash

84

involving a non-insured driver who did not even possess a driving licence. She didn't mean to, but Sue found herself telling of her aloneness now and how she missed her darling Michael who had so filled her life with love.

Sue pulled herself together. She was after all writing to a complete stranger. The final paragraph became surprisingly formal. Your letter did find us eventually, but the full address and postal code is at the top of this letter. If you write again, it will make it easier for the post office. She underlined the postal code and unusually couldn't bring herself to read the letter before putting it in an envelope. It had covered two pages. She carefully copied the address he had put at the back of his envelope and then copied it into the address part of her diary. She propped the letter against one of the 'photos on her desk so that she would remember to post it when she went out.

"Well, Michael," she said to the air. "I've finally written to Kurt. What do you think?" There was no reply of course and with feeling of sadness threatening to overwhelm her she called the dogs. It was just Abby the black Cocker Spaniel and Dally the Dalmatian, her closest companions these days. Abby was sweet but at twelve she slept a great deal of the time. Dally on the other hand seemed sensitive to her moods and even licked the tears from her face when she had one of her quiet weeping sessions.

She, who had not cried for years, wept frequently behind closed doors. The family, friends and everyone thought how wonderfully she coped; but Dally knew the truth and listened patiently to her mistress's sorrows, seeming to understand every word and putting a comforting paw on Sue's knee as she sat. Or leaping on the sofa, which was not officially allowed, and resting her head on Sue's lap.

Chapter 18

It was Janus who telephoned Kurt to let him know his father was ill. Kurt thanked him for letting him know and was about to end the call when Janus asked if he was coming. Kurt's answer was a brief "No".

"This feud has gone on long enough. Your father is dying, he needs you."

"My father knows I am not returning to the village and that is final." Janus was silent for a moment. He had known Kurt since he was a small boy. He could be stubborn, true – but he was also loyal. Janus tried again. He explained clearly what the matter was, how much care and attention he needed. How bad the pain was, Janus was no fool, the boy would return home.

"I won't come," Kurt replied abruptly turning off his mobile, but Janus was right. Kurt was loyal. He started thinking about his childhood. Mikail hadn't been a bad father, what had happened had happened in war. He so wished it had not been HIS father and of all people, Yana's mother – but it was done. Over. It couldn't be put right.

He rang the school principal giving a brief explanation and saying he needed compassionate leave. He was a good teacher and made learning languages interesting – he made things come alive.

He would be missed, but a dying father takes precedence. Kurt packed a small bag and drove back to the village. There was a light burning in an upstairs window, but apart from that the house appeared to be in total darkness.

Kurt took his bag off the passenger seat and locked the car. Using his key, he let himself in to the house. A pale light shone from the kitchen and he put his bag at the foot of the stairs before calling out to his father so that his sudden appearance would not be too much of a shock.

The room smelt of death. The curtains were drawn and only a small bedside light illuminated the gaunt face of the man who lay there.

Mikail appeared to be asleep but he had heard the footsteps on the wooden stairs. Despite his pain, he felt a surge of pleasure. Kurt had finally come home. He tried to speak, but his mouth felt dry, he reached out for the glass of water on his side table; but Kurt was there first, and helped raise his father's head as he held the glass to the man's lips.

"What can I do for you?" Kurt asked, feeling helpless in the company of such suffering.

His father shook his head. "You are home," he finally managed to say.

After a while Kurt left the room leaving the door slightly ajar so as to hear if his father called in the night. His own room just along the landing, was neat if slightly musty. He opened the window and the chill of the night air seemed wonderfully fresh and clean.

He returned downstairs put some logs on the fire, made himself some coffee and returned upstairs carrying the coffee and his bag.

A routine developed quite quickly. Every morning and evening the nurse would arrive with pain-killing medication. Father Gregory would call in before lunch and various neighbours would leave casseroles and prepared salads.

Kurt's father seemed such a pathetic figure now, and Kurt found it hard to continue to hate him. In fact he found it hard to reconcile this dying cadaver with the big strong man he had so looked up to as a child.

He washed his father twice a day as tenderly as he would have washed a sick child. If his father was grateful, the only indication was the occasional grasp of his hand. His bony fingers clutching feverishly at Kurt's steady hands as he prepared to do the necessary ablutions.

Every day he lifted his father into a chair he had brought up from downstairs. He had padded it with cushions and Mikail sat there watching every movement as Kurt put clean sheets on and shook the duvet out of the window. The kindly next-door neighbour did the laundry, as Mikail had never bothered to update the kitchen and an old boiler was the only laundry facility.

Kurt thought back to conversations about washing machines. "No modern trivia in my house." Mikail would state emphatically.

"Silly fool," Kurt muttered thinking back to those conversations.

"What, what, what," his father demanded querulously before sleeping back into a morphine-induced sleep.

It was three weeks that Kurt would never forget, and finally, when it was over and when he saw the sods of grass being laid over the grave he knew a great sense of relief.

The house belonged to Yana, and with that in mind Kurt set about making arrangements to make it right for her. First he threw out every piece of furniture, every cup, saucer, plate, and cutlery. He kept a picture that hung in his room which he liked, and also he had a memory that his mother had given it to him. He had a builder rip out the old kitchen and replace it with an upmarket, and he thought rather special one. There was now a new oven, dishwasher and fridge and upstairs an elegant bathroom with a shower.

In the attic he found an old cot and some toys, some were moth-eaten but a Russian looking bear had escaped the ravages of time. He found a round table and four chairs that he had never seen before and instinctively knew they had belonged to Yana's parents. Certainly he had no knowledge of them,

He looked carefully at the attic. It was really quite big, with one window overlooking the street and another, the garden. It would make a wonderful bedroom and to that end he asked the builder to put a small bathroom in one corner. After much head scratching and measuring the builder suggested a shower, rather than bath plus of course toilet and hand basin. He also suggested cutting a hole in the roof and putting a window to add additional light to the room.

With a new boiler and extra radiators, Kurt knew the house would be warmer and cosier than it had ever been for when Yana 'came home'. For one day, he convinced himself, she surely would. Leaving everything in hand, and promising to return once a week until the work was completed he left the builder and his mates to get on with it.

He arrived back at his flat to a pile of post, most of which was junk mail. His heart missed a beat though, when he saw the letter with the English Stamp. Dropping the other mail on the table he hastily tore the envelope and reached for the letter inside.

Dear Kurt. It began. *We have never met...* He turned to the last page his disappointment palpable. It was signed, *Sue James*. With a deep sigh of disappointment and almost inclined not to continue reading it, he turned back to the first page. He read it slowly savouring every mention of Yana.

At the end of the letter he almost wept. This Sue had written from the heart. Her sadness came through every word along with her joy and pride in her family which so clearly included Yana.

Yana, a doctor – how wonderful. He wanted to write back straight away. He had given up all hope of seeing her ever again. It seemed almost a miracle that his letter had ever found her. How glad he was that he had started the work on her home. Tomorrow he must see a lawyer and make sure the deeds were officially transferred to her.

Much later that night he started what was to be the first of many letters to Sue.

Chapter 19

She was a grandmother – she had been with Lucy and Peter as their little girl was born. A beautiful baby weighing six pounds and thirteen ounces; not big, but big enough Lucy had said wryly! It had not been a particularly easy birth – but that was already forgotten. Lucy and the baby were back at The Rectory. The old crib had been recovered and a small room that had been called the nursery for many years, was once again the nursery.

Peter had left for Russia, a big political conference with many heads of states. Sue was hazy about the details, something to do with pipelines she thought. But much more important than that, as far as Sue was concerned, was that there was a baby in the house again and of course Lucy as well.

She didn't think ahead, she knew it was for a matter of weeks, but she was going to make the most of it every single day. The baby was to be called Leila Susan, and Sue not madly loving the first name was flattered by the second. Peter had become like a second son to her and seeing he and Lucy together reminded her so much of she and Michael.

"Well Dally, what do you think Michael would think about being a grandfather." She had stopped talking to Michael and found instead that talking to Dally about him was quite helpful. His responses varied from utterly bored to extremely interested, particularly if she was preparing food at the time!

Peter was away for almost three months as one assignment had led to others. Sue, Lucy and Leila had organised themselves into a routine acceptable to all three of them and the dogs obliged by fitting in too.

Sue was always up first and they arranged that Lucy would express a feed for the early morning which meant if she had a disturbed night she could relax knowing grandmother was in charge. It was a part of the day Sue grew to love. The delicious smell of a newly bathed baby nuzzling up in her arms whilst she gave her the first feed of the day, as her mother slept blissfully on.

The day continued with Leila in the baby sling taking the fresh air as together they walked the dogs. Leila, enjoying the warmth of her grandmother's body would coo contentedly like the sound of doves Sue thought happily. They walked in the rain too with Leila zipped inside Michael's old Barbour jacket which provided the baby the space needed and kept her dry.

Lucy would make a sleepy appearance about ten o' clock and mother and daughter would sit together while Lucy tucked into warmed croissants from the Aga and freshly brewed coffee.

It was a time Sue would always hold cherished memories of, and she and Lucy, always close, seemed to each provide each other with what was needed.

"I couldn't have coped on my own, Mum." Lucy confided one day. "I've missed Peter terribly, but it is wonderful to have been so spoilt, and you are so fantastic with Leila."

"It's something to do with being a grandmother I think." Sue answered with a smile. "None of the responsibility and all of the pleasure."

Then as suddenly as Sue had them with her they were gone. Peter had flown in to Gatwick and driven straight to Guildford. He stayed for two days and then Sue having watched them load everything into the car waved cheerfully as they drove off down the drive back to their home in Putney.

Sue went indoors. The breakfast table with its detritus of used cups and saucers, half eaten croissants, jars of her home-made jam and marmalade still open, a slab of butter with the butter knife resting on it. The dogs went to their beds as if aware it was all change again.

Very purposefully Sue put the kettle on and getting the small cafetière out of the cupboard she added some freshly ground coffee, before pouring the now boiling water in. Leaving it to stand for a few moments she started clearing away and then noticed one of Leila's tiny rattles under the table.

She picked it up and started to sob. These were not quiet tears like her grief at Michael's death, but deep racking sobs that came from nowhere and that she didn't seem able to control. Even old Abby came and sat at her feet and Dally stood nuzzling her until she finally took notice. "Oh, Dally what a fool I am – but I shall really miss Lucy and Leila so much. The smell of freshly brewed coffee permeated the air and she felt calmer now. The telephone rang and it was Lucy.

"Hi Mum, just to say thank you from your granddaughter and me." For a moment Sue could hardly speak. "Hey Mum, are you okay."

"Of course, darling." Sue's voice sounded brighter. "Just made some coffee and clearing up after you lot!" She even managed a light laugh. She sensed relief in Lucy's tone.

"Right Mum, speak to you tomorrow."

Once again, she was alone, she felt even more alone having loved her life being filled with family so recently.

o-o-o-o-o-o-o-o-o-o-o

Several weeks had gone by since Lucy had returned to London. It had been hard at first and Sue had been doing some serious thinking about the house. They had made so many plans for when Michael retired. They would, they had decided stay there and it would always be a base for the children, their partners and any subsequent children – but that was then. *This is now*, she thought.

The house seemed too big and empty for one person and two dogs. Lily and Adrian were completely tied up in their new venture, a horse rescue and rehabilitation centre. They only seemed to leave the estate for riding events and work was progressing on new barns and stable blocks. What had started as an undemanding vision was now a major investment, both in time and money.

Lily had always had a way with horses. She didn't claim to be a horse whisperer, but in her own way she was developing techniques that enabled her to calm unhappy, difficult, injured or even just bad tempered horses. The past three years the business had taken off and now she was approached both privately and by trainers who sought her help.

The horses would arrive for a week's assessment and depending on the circumstances she could then have them with her for as long as three months.

At Paul's suggestion they had put in a hydrotherapy pool which helped with both the well-being of rescue horses as well as some 'high profile' horses belonging to high profile riders. "It was," Lily told Paul over lunch one day. "A dream come true."

Meg and her husband continued to be delighted with their charming and competent daughter-in-law. They loved the way she called them Mil and Fil, short, she told them for mother and father-in-law. They only had one grumble – where were their longed for grandchildren. They had dropped hints several times and Lily was aware of their frustration, but she had Paul, her horses and dogs and felt not the slightest desire to have children. It was a nuisance really because Paul was beginning to nag her, albeit gently about the duty of producing an heir to the title.

With many misgivings she finally agreed to try for a baby. To her consternation she conceived almost immediately and a few months later was horrified to discover she was expecting twins. *At least*, she thought morosely. *I will get it over all in one.*

Lily didn't tell anyone, apart from Paul until it was difficult to conceal it any longer. His parents were thrilled with the news and opened Champagne immediately. Paul was on pain of death not to tell anyone it was twins. "Everyone will fuss, fuss, fuss if you do," she said. "I'll drop them easily."

"You are not a horse or a dog Lil." Paul gave her a light-hearted warning. Lily though, was determined to keep fit by working as hard as everything would, in her words 'be a doddle'.

Sue who had finally been told it was twins invited herself down as the birth date drew nearer. She brought Dally and Abby with her and as always they settled happily in to a dog's paradise.

Like all good labours, Lily started hers in the early hours of the morning. Paul drove dangerously fast to the hospital with Sue following at a more sedate pace.

Things seldom go to plan in childbirth and Lily's assurances that she would have the babies like clicking her fingers turned out to be wrong.

After forty-eight hours when mother and babies were exhausted Lily had an emergency caesarean.

Paul was beside himself with worry and promised himself there would be no more children. A little girl was lifted out followed by her brother. They were small, but perfect and Sue when she saw them was taken back to the time she first held Lucy and Lily in her arms. It had been one of the happiest moments in her life, until Bear had rounded off the family so perfectly.

Lily was exhausted, as far as she was concerned it had been the worst forty-eight hours in her life. She barely looked at the twins wanting only to sleep and wake up as if nothing had happened. Before closing her eyes, she glanced at the twins and declined to hold them.

The doctors and nurses explained how tired she was and Paul who had an instant love affair with his children put her lack of interest due to the experience she had been through. Sue was more concerned but kept her council and five days later when Lily was allowed home a nanny had already been installed.

Lily claimed she was not strong enough to breast feed Amy and Andrew and Sue felt saddened that they were bottle fed from the start. She tried to influence her daughter to change her mind, but Lily, always the stubborn one was adamant and her decision brooked no further discussion

Sue stayed for a month, primarily at Paul insistence. He spent as much time as possible with his son and daughter and he gradually accepted that Lily had no maternal instinct. That side of her nature was given to the care of the horses.

Sue talked to Paul's parents who felt things would improve, though inwardly she thought 'might' would be a better word, although she hoped when the babies become little people the situation might improve.

Meanwhile, they had two doting grandmothers, one equally doting grandfather and a besotted daddy!

Nanny Liz proved a great success and was persuaded to stay on permanently, or for as long as the twins needed her. With an easier heart, Sue headed back home to Guildford.

******

There was the usual amount of junk mail. Recognisable writing that indicated letters from friends. A couple of 'stiffies', invitations that would be quite smart events – and to her delight a letter from Kurt.

She opened his letter first wondering how he would have responded to her letter, feeling rather bad about the way she had let her hair down to a stranger. The letter started. *Dear Mrs James – or may I address you as Susan?* It made her smile straight away and lots of what he wrote made her smile.

He responded to a number of things she had written and then continued by telling her of his father's death. The clearing of the house. The putting in of a new kitchen and bathrooms, adding. *Please don't tell Yana. I want her to be surprised* – he wrote. He then went on to say he had been in touch with the lawyers and had arranged for the house to be transferred back to her, Yana's ownership, as the natural heir to her family home. He said in due course the deeds would be sent to England addressed to Yana.

Sue wrote back immediately and that was the beginning of the regular interchange of letters. She learned about the school where he was now the deputy principal, and how much his work meant to him. He described his walks in the meadows and woods. The tumbling streams and the bird song.

His descriptions were so vivid that she could visualise his walks.

Kurt finished his first and subsequent letters by requesting, quite formally, that his good wishes be passed on to Yana.

Sue looked forward to his letters. She liked what she read about him, his humour when he talked about some of the children he taught. His sensitivity when he talked of Yana. His gentleness when he referred to Michael. He had read all about the horse rescue centre and Lucy's baby. About Bear and his cricket. Always making appropriate comments.

Back to the present. An invitation to a ruby wedding dinner and dancing. She wondered if Bear would escort her. Another invitation, this time to a husband's sixtieth birthday bash. Thoughts of Michael and how she missed him were inevitable. A year ago she would have refused the invitations but time is a great healer and now she could think of him with love and warmth rather than the deep sorrow she had lived through. *That was progress,* she thought happily.

As she gave the dogs their dinner, her mind was thinking about Kurt's letter. The mention of the deeds of the house prodded her into action. For months now, she had been contemplating getting a valuation on the house. More and more she felt it was not sensible or practical to live alone.

On impulse she looked up the number of a local estate agent, who she was aware also had branches elsewhere including London. They were keen to view and she arranged for them to come round the following morning.

Paul phoned to make sure she had arrived home safely. She felt guilty for not having rung as promised... "How are Lily and the twins," she enquired longing to hear Lily was beginning to bond with her babies.

"As when you left." Paul replied a little sadly.

"Don't despair Paul. This is quite a common problem," she repeated what she had already said on several occasions, not quite believing her own words. She had begun to wonder whether Lily who hadn't wanted children in the first place would ever be able to change her attitude towards her babies.

Bear phoned. He had just returned from a tour of the West Indies which England had won so the whole team were cock-a-hoop. He wanted to bring a few friends down for the weekend if that was okay. Sue agreed happily, and then gave him the date of the dinner dance and asked him to be her plus one. There was an imperceptible hesitation. Sue instantly wished she hadn't asked him, but he came back strongly then saying he would be delighted to escort his lovely Mother. "Black tie?"

"Of course, darling."

The house agent arrived at exactly the time they had arranged and Sue rather wondered if he had been sitting at the bottom of the drive so that he could arrival time could be precise.

"He was one of those exclaimers." Sue explained later to her friend Jose. "He exclaimed about the lovely spacious hall. He exclaimed about the magnificent staircase. He exclaimed over the drawing room, dining room and study. He thought the kitchen was remarkably friendly and was glad to see an Aga." Sue had begun to lose interest as each of the bedrooms and three bathrooms received lavish adjectives and, when he walked through the gardens with its eight acres, swimming pool and tennis court he was ecstatic!"

"We can sell this easily," he concluded. "What figure had you in mind?" Sue pulled an exorbitant figure out of her head bearing in mind what Lucy and Peter had paid for their Putney house.

"Oh, I think we can improve on that quite considerably," Sue said nothing actually feeling rather gob-smacked.

When he asked if she wanted a quick sale, Sue felt her first moment of panic. How could she sell? Where would she go, and she hadn't even mentioned it to the children! "Definitely not," she replied firmly.

That evening she wrote to Kurt. She hadn't meant to write so soon but she needed to tell someone of her dilemma, someone who wouldn't try and influence her. Once again she found herself writing about things that troubled her. Lily and the twins, and the confusion and uncertainty about selling The Old Rectory.

******

Lily was fed up. She had to get outside as quickly as possible, but her stomach pulled and her back ached from, she supposed, the epidural she had received during the long hours of labour that was supposed to make the whole thing painless. *Joke,* she thought cynically!

She supposed the twins were quite sweet but a new foal excited her more. Paul was being so bloody patient she could scream. The more understanding and patient he became the more irritating she found it.

She walked slowly out to the yard. Horses whinnied with pleasure to see her. She talked to each one of them for a minute or two, breathing gently close to their nostrils which calmed as well as communicating. "You are so beautiful," she whispered to each in turn even the latest 'rescue' who had been so terrified when he arrived. Now he neighed with pleasure at her approach rubbing his head against her outstretched arm. She put her right hand in her pocket and pulled out a piece of carrot. It had been the first food he had taken from her when he arrived. His head collar so tight that it had cut deeply into his flesh. Soon they would be able to introduce him to the herd, for a herd it was becoming with a clearly defined pecking order in which he would have to find his place.

Perhaps one day he might be able to be re homed, but perhaps not. He was quite small – almost a child's pony; perhaps some eight or nine-year-old. For the first time she felt a tremor of excitement imagining Amy and Andrew at eight years, a much better prospect than the helpless bundles they were at present.

To date Lily had managed to avoid even changing a nappy. When nanny was off duty either Paul or Mil took over. There was now an unspoken acceptance that Lily could or would not become involved. The more everyone said 'give it time', the more resentful she felt – and the harder to make the first move. She was constantly told how good they were, though as far as she was concerned they seemed to cry most of the time. She was thankful nanny was in total charge with Paul or his mother as back up.

Several weeks went by. Every day Lily felt stronger. Her mother telephoned regularly and Lily made polite conversation. She felt completely detached from everyone including Paul.

Lucy came for a short visit. One child in a car seat in the back and the new baby in the special back facing baby seat beside her. She sang and chatted to the two little girls, and played nursery rhyme songs on the cassette.

"We have too many girls in our family," looking at the new baby, who she thought looked like one of hers. "So, my eldest niece is called Leila," thinking as she spoke it was a dreadful name. It sounded to her like a kitchen cleaner or a room freshener. "What is the brat called?"

Lucy had ceased to be shocked by Lily years ago. "She may be a brat to you Lily but she is the sweetest baby in the world. Her name is Louisa."

"She'll be called Lou."

"Whatever," Lucy responded equably. "Now I want to meet the twins." They walked upstairs to the nursery. All was silence – bliss was the word that sprang unbidden into Lily's mind. Lucy carried Louisa, holding her toddler by the hand to help her up the stairs. She was hoping the children could meet their cousins for the first time while they were awake.

Lily seldom came to the nursery and when she opened the door she was surprised that the twins were not sleeping but lying on play mats on the floor, cooing happily.

"Oh, they are gorgeous," Lucy said, thrusting Louisa into her Aunts unwilling arms. Lily held the baby uncertainly. It was, she thought remarkably ugly – just like her two. "Nanny here take this," she gave the baby in to nanny's willing arms. "My they could be triplets." Lucy looked closely at the twins. There really was a tremendous family likeness. "What fun," she said. "It is great that they will have cousins so close in age." Leila was already down on the floor kissing one baby and then the other. "We only one baby."

"Yes darling. Aunt Lily had two babies at the same time. Isn't she clever?" She saw Lily scowl. Mum was right all was not going well with the twins and their mother.

Nanny insisted that the sisters went off on their own for a while. She was in her element, three babies and one little girl. "What a treasure." Lucy breathed. "You are so lucky to have found someone so good Lil." Lily merely grunted. They went into the kitchen where Lily made them some of their favourite freshly ground Brazilian coffee. Handing a mug to Lucy she suggested they went to visit the horses. Lucy who just wanted to spend time with, in her opinion, troubled sister agreed and they strolled outside in the pale autumn sunshine.

For a while they talked horses. "What about your career?" Lily demanded suddenly. "What is the point of all that study when all you do is produce babies," Lucy laughed.

"I have a great daily who doubles as a baby sitter so I can do two clinics at the hospital a week. That will keep my hand in until the children go to nursery school."

"My career comes first."

"Before your children?"

For a moment, a brief moment, Lily hesitated. "Yes. Before my children."

Lily had always been inclined to shock her younger twin but this shocked her to the core. How could she possibly put her children after her horses; but there was no doubt, she meant it.

For a few moments, there was an uncomfortable silence. Then Lucy realised there was nothing she could say which would do other than inflame her sister, so they talked of everything other than children.

After a noisy lunch that drove Lily to distraction and afterwards introducing Leila to the horses it was with relief that as evening fell Lucy piled her little family in the car. She had brought overnight things for that had been the original plan but it seemed obvious that Lily was only just coping and it would be better for her to take her little girls home. Glancing at the sleeping children she smiled contentedly, she was happy with her life but it was sickening obvious that Lily was not. Or at least she was not coping as she should. She needed help of that there was little doubt but whether she would be prepared to accept any was another matter.

Chapter 20

Once again Yana was waiting for exam results, her finals. This time she felt pretty confident. She had enjoyed every moment of her medical studies from the various disciplines she had covered to her contact with patients on the wards and on her general practitioner postings when it had confirmed for her, the desire to work in the community. She still had a year to complete at the hospital and she particularly looked forward to her Accident and Emergency assignment.

She was driving home for the weekend. None of the family was quite used to the cottage but after some heart-searching, Lily, Lucy, Bear and herself understood Sue's reasons for wanting a smaller place.

It had been hard for Sue at first – disposing of pieces of furniture that had been part of all their lives. But as Sue prosaically said, "Furniture is only furniture. It is the memories that count."

The cottage was sweet. Three bedrooms, one with a tiny en suite and a separate shower room with a toilet for guests. It meant that Sue could cope with the steady flow of family visits. Yana hadn't been home for more than six weeks and was longing to see her 'Mum' again.

She still missed old Abby who had been such a friend to her when she was little but at least Dally was still around.

Yana drove through the village thinking again how pretty it was and still convenient to Guildford and the shopping there. The cottage was on the fringe of the village which had attracted Sue in the first place, she wanted to be able to keep herself to herself if she choose to. Yana parked at the side of the cottage next to the open garage where she saw Sue's new Volkswagen convertible.

Sue came out of the kitchen door holding her arms wide open to give Yana a warm hug. They had always been close, these two, and they seemed to grow ever closer.

Lily and Lucy had such full lives. Lily with her horses and even the twins to an extent. Now they had their tiny Shetland ponies, they were becoming more like real people to their mother. It had taken Lily a long time to recover from their birth and she had vowed never to have more children. Paul didn't mind as the twins were his joy and delight. He and Lily had continued to build the centre which now had become internationally acclaimed.

Many a frustrated owner brought a difficult horse to them and Lily always rose to the challenge often feeling she had more empathy with horses than with humans, including her own family.

"Darling Yana, how lovely to see you. You look as if you need a wind down weekend."

"How right you are Mum. I have been so looking forward to coming down." Arm in arm they went into the charming cottagey kitchen. There on the round table was one of Sue's special afternoon teas. Dainty sandwiches, tiny scones with home-made strawberry jam and cream. Lemon drizzle cake and short bread biscuits.

"Oh Mum, just what the doctor ordered!" They both laughed happily.

A recent letter from Kurt was propped up on the dresser and behind it the brown envelope that had arrived several years ago. Would Yana finally open it this weekend?

Sue had tried everything, persuasion, cajoling, being cross and explaining patiently and not so patiently how rude it was to Kurt not to open it. Sue had, with some difficulty managed to restrain herself from telling Yana the contents which she knew from all the correspondence she continued to have with Kurt. *He was so patient*, she thought, writing only that Yana would open it when she was ready. Meanwhile, her home was ready and waiting for her when she was ready. *No matter how long it takes*, he had added philosophically.

They sat down at the table. Dally as ever, pleased to see her, though she too was getting older and a little calmer. "Do Dalmatians ever really grow up?" Yana smiled as she spoke,

Dally nuzzling her as always. "I don't think they do! She is such good company, I would be lost without her."

"Perhaps you should consider getting another puppy. How old is Dally now?" Her mouth full of scone, jam and cream Sue held up both hands.

"Ten. Gosh where have the years gone."

"I may never have another dog." There was something so sad and wistful in her tone that Yana wanted to find a way of cheering her up. Her eyes alighted on the brown envelope. As always in a prominent position.

Perhaps finally she should open it. She had no idea what it contained only that Sue and Kurt exchanged letters from time to time and he had sent that for her. Sue had, on several occasions offered her one of Kurt's letters to read but she felt such hostility when she thought of him, she couldn't bring herself to take any interest in them whatsoever.

Getting up from the table she crossed to the dresser and collected the brown envelope carrying it back to the table. Sue said nothing trying hard to control her delight. At last, she was thinking, at last.

As she sat down, she gave a slight shiver. Sue noticed, and again said nothing, just watched Yana turn the letter over scrutinising the address as she did, which surprisingly was not the address she expected.

Yana picked up a knife and slit the envelope open pulling out a paper the contents. The papers, quite thick vellum were folded in three and looking at the address Yana thought it looked like a law company. Slowly and carefully she began to read the attached letter before looking at the document. It was surprisingly easy to read, just a carefully written letter explaining that the owner of number Twenty-five, Main Street, in the village of Bijeljina, Bosnia was to revert to the original owner as the only descendant of Maria Brzekoupil. She, Yana Brzekoupil was now the legal owner of said property. It was signed by someone whose signature was indecipherable followed in type by an unpronounceable surname.

Yana's heart was racing as she looked at the second vellum sheet. It listed all the owners of the property since it was first built. It included her own parents and the final name on the list next to theirs was her own; so Kurt's family had never officially been the rightful owners.

"I don't know why he has done this."

Sue laid her hand over the girls.

"Because he truly believes you are the rightful owner and it belongs to you – that's why darling."

They talked for hours that evening. Sue passing on some of the things Kurt had written about. They had developed a pleasant and easy friendship and each looked forward to the others letters. It wasn't totally altruistic. Kurt looked forward to news of Yana and Sue felt it important to keep it going so that Kurt would not lose all hope of Yana ever accepting his hand of friendship along with the house.

Kurt had agonised with Sue over her selling of The Old Rectory and delighted in the photographs she sent of the cottage. Meadow Way Cottage – it sounded delightful. He shared her joys and anxieties about her children and grandchildren and she supplied him with photos of the little ones as they grew. Birthday photos of Lily's twins on their first ponies. Lucy's little girls on their see-saw. He learned that it was difficult to be a mother and a doctor but Lucy now worked three full days a week at the local hospital, while her now, live in cleaner had become housekeeper and child-minder taking the children to and from school. He heard how Bear had finally found the perfect girl. She was French and surprisingly loved cricket! She was matron at an 'all boys', boarding school in England, and when Bear was not touring he enjoyed being with his wife at the school and helping out with cricket coaching, which made him very popular with boys and staff alike.

He loved Sue's letters with all their newsy tales, and he read with particular interest anything that concerned Yana.

Monday morning arrived all too quickly and Yana left at six am in order to get back to the hospital for her shift. She was due three weeks holiday and as she and Sue had walked Dally Yana had talked about her plans for the rest of the summer. She had decided in the wee small hours of the morning to drive over to Bosnia and visit her home. As she explained to Sue she wasn't even sure she wanted to go. Her first visit years ago had been quite a traumatic experience. "Come with me Sue," she had suggested. For a moment Sue was tempted. It would be good to meet Kurt after all this time and to see for herself where Yana had come from those years ago. Sense prevailed, she knew it would be better for Yana to face all she had to deal with on her own. She made some excuses that sounded lame to her own ears, but Yana didn't seem to notice, her own mind buzzing with questions that needed answering and the more she thought about it the stronger her resolve grew.

Sue stood with Dally watching the car until it disappeared from view. She felt lonely, they all had such full lives and she – well, she just pottered on with little or no purpose. She straightened her shoulders and made a sound that felt purposeful. She was going to do something positive about her life.

Chapter 21

The results of the finals were not due for several weeks, though it had been intimated that all had gone well. Her senior tutor kissed her on the cheek and told her to go off and enjoy herself.

Feeling happier, she decided to arrange her journey to Bosnia as soon as possible. After checking the route on her maps, she resolved that flying might be better and she would hire a car once there to give the freedom and flexibility she wanted. It would she decided, be a good opportunity to explore the country of her birth without the unhappiness and complications of her previous visit.

She decided to fly to Belgrade and explore that city first and then with a hired car head to the village stopping when she felt like it. She had kept up with her with her language skills as one of her colleagues was from that part of the world and they had made a point of meeting weekly over several years for an evening out and a chat in the language of their birth. Sophia and her parents had fled during the troubles at the same time Yana was arriving in England.

At the cottage Sue was in her element. Amy and Andrew, Leila and Mia had come for a visit. They all adored their grandmother and they liked being together too. Sue allowed them to cook their own scrambled eggs while she watched with a very careful eye! She also showed them how to make real hot chocolate by melting the chocolate first. Together they made and tossed pancakes and if the weather turned wet they would turn their hands to making home-made toffee from a recipe of their great grandmother's.

Amy and Andy as he preferred to be called these days particularly enjoyed the 'kitchen time' as Sue called it. "We never do this at home," they choroused, as so often seeming to think and speak together. They also seemed very close unlike Lily and Lucy who were chalk and cheese as children and still were. Leila and Mia had become the toffee experts and it was the favourite thing they made. Sometimes they had picnics in the rain, they played hide and seek in the adjacent copse and Sue taught them how to lay trails with twigs and stones.

At night they all sat on Sue's big bed whilst she told them stories about when she was a little girl and she found herself remembering things long forgotten. The magical two weeks sped by and although somewhat exhausted, she had loved every moment with her three granddaughters and one grandson.

To her delight on the evening they left and she was missing the noisy household, Bear phoned. Chantelle, who insisted on calling him Rupert but as she said it without the final 't' it still sounded slightly Bearish… Chantelle and he were expecting a baby. The scan showed it was a boy. Chantelle chatted to her mother-in-law saying that her mama and papa were excited too as this would be their first grandchild.

"Well Dally it's all quiet again." Dally sat beside her on the sofa and gave a contented grunt, she liked a bit of peace and quiet these days.

******

The flight was delayed by about half an hour but after that everything went smoothly. Yana flew Serbian airways and was pleased to be able to communicate in her mother tongue. At first, she felt rather shy about using it but the woman sitting next to her chatted virtually none stop, asking questions, not bothering to wait for an answer before launching into another saga.

Yana let her mind wander, wondering what lay ahead and what she would find. Would she meet Kurt again? She knew how much Sue enjoyed their correspondence and wondered how she herself would feel face to face with the son of the man who murdered her mother.

She hired a Ford Focus and once out of the airport, studied the satellite. After some thought she decided not to explore the city until her return, and instead decided she would drive for about an hour and look for a small hotel for overnight then she could arrive fresh in the Town on the following morning.

After about a forty-minute drive when she was very conscious that she was driving on the right not the left side of the road she arrived at a pretty village. It was already almost dark but the hotel she saw straight away was well lit with the outside tables well occupied. Timing seemed providential and she pulled into the small parking area with a sense of relief.

A young woman at reception assured they had a pleasant room available overlooking the garden, which would be quieter Yana thought gratefully, beginning to feel rather tired.

She ordered a light supper which was delivered to her room within ten minutes of her arrival.

After eating and a quick refreshing shower she climbed into bed, and was asleep before her head touched the pillow.

She awoke early the next morning with the sun streaming through the open window and by nine she was once more on her way. As she drove she felt a tug at her heart strings. This place, this country was her birth place. She revelled in the hills, the fields, the wild flowers growing by the road side.

Once she parked and walked to a small bridge looking down into the clear sparkling water below. So hard to imagine now, a war torn land that had killed her parents and sent her into the unknown.

She had few, very few memories to cling to – but at least she was returning to the house where she was born and spent her first nearly three years. Just to walk through the house, then put it all behind her and return to her life and family in England.

The hotel where she had stayed with Lucy looked completely different but she decided not to stay there anyway. She parked on the edge of town leaving her small pull a long in the car. The town seemed much bigger than she remembered the only part that seemed familiar was the Main Street, but even that had changed with a huge supermarket and numerous other big stores.

The law office had kindly sent directions and she tracked it down easily in one of the many side streets. The envelope addressed to her was awaiting collection at the reception area and a young man handed it to her with a smile. Just as she was about to leave a door opened near reception and a plump, balding man wearing a heavily pattered tie and a crisp white shirt appeared. Seeing her with the envelope he indicated she should follow him into his office. Yana felt he was not happy with her for some reason, and remained standing when he sat behind his desk. She felt that he did not approve of Kurt's decision and speaking rapidly he said just that. Yana was stunned. Things had been going smoothly, if emotionally. Now this, an attitude, she certainly didn't need. "It is legally binding though," he concluded. "The letter I sent, the legal one. I acted under duress, as far as a number of people in this town are concerned the house will never belong to a half Muslim." Yana gasped, she did not know such hostility still existed. Holding firmly onto her emotions, and speaking as politely as she could, she thanked him for his opinion and walked out of his office. A moment later, she was outside holding the envelope containing the key in her hand. She longed for Lucy to be with her as before, and had to remind herself she had been seventeen then. Now at twenty-four, going on twenty-five she could cope on her own!

The little restaurant a few yards along the road attracted her attention. Its bright awning and welcoming music drifted gently along the street. She glanced briefly at the handwritten menu on a blackboard propped up against a pillar, liked what she saw and found a table adjacent to the pavement enjoying the ambiance and atmosphere. People passed by. Couples holding hands. An old man walking slowly, leaning heavily on his stout stick. Some young women, girls really. The nearly twenty-five-year-old Yana smiled inwardly feeling much older than they. Their chat and laughter drifted back to where she sat absorbing and enjoying the scene before her.

The patron came out to serve the beautiful lady he had spotted sitting down a few moments earlier. She smiled up at him and he blinked. She really was a beauty, with her gleaming auburn hair tied loosely back at the nape of her neck. Her cream silk blouse fell against her skin outlining her full breasts; and he had noticed how tall and slim she was as she had paused to glance at his menu.

A model, he thought, sad that she was alone. No one like her should be alone. "I would like to order," Yana repeated, jerking the patron out of his reverie. He bought her a glass of iced water, and at her request a small carafe of red house wine.

"It is local," he said proudly placing the carafe in front of her. "My brother has his own vineyard."

Yana smiled which seemed all that was required, and her host hurried away to tell his cook to serve up the best possible lunch for this lovely lady.

It was odd he thought, she spoke the language – but she seemed to have the air of a foreigner. Just come from another part of the country he rationalised, as he busied himself with other customers.

It was, thought Yana one of the most delicious meals she had ever eaten, even allowing for the fact she had been extremely hungry. The wine was almost like a burgundy, she thought sipping appreciatively finishing the carafe with no trouble at all.

Feeling very mellow, she meandered slowly back to the hotel – glancing in shop windows and mentally translating the euros into pounds. It was one of the thing she loved about England, the stubbornness that made them want to retain their individuality as a country.

The hotel owner was in Reception and gave her a warm smile wondering at the same time what she was doing in their town. He wondered about her profession. An actress maybe. Or an upmarket sales person for cosmetics or even pharmaceuticals. He looked again at her entry in the guest book. Dr Yana Brzekoupil, with and address in England. He glanced up as she walked up the stairs, never, he noticed, taking the lift. A doctor he mulled and with a local name. Intriguing! He quite suddenly remembered a promise he had made what seemed years ago. He opened a drawer and looked in a small box in which he had put the details. It seemed very possible that she had finally arrived and he telephoned the number on the paper. "I think your lady has arrived," he said to the disembodied voice at the other end of the line. A quiet thank you was the only response.

It was the next morning that Yana decided she could not put off action on the house any longer. It was market day. Stalls piled high with vegetables, the smell of fresh garlic filling the air.

A cake and bread stall tempted her, freshly baked bread kept warm by the sunshine. She walked slowly along the street savouring the sights and smells.

"Yana?" a voice called somewhat hesitantly. Surprised, she turned. A woman of about sixty stood smiling at her. "You must be Yana. Am I right?" Yana nodded. "I would recognise you anywhere – so like my friend – my dear friend Maria."

"You knew my mother?" Yana's voice was barely a whisper. This was more, so much more than she had even dared to dream about.

"Come," the woman said, her voice full of understanding. "Come with me – to my home – we shall have coffee together."

Yana felt like an automaton. She walked silently. It was almost like being in a time warp, it felt neither like today or yesterday or any other day. "My name is Daniella." Yana followed her companion through the door of the brightly painted house with its colourful flower boxes on every window sill. Daniella indicated a chair and Yana sank gratefully into it. Her legs felt like cotton wool and her throat was dry. She tried to talk, but felt so emotional she could feel the tears forming in her eyes threatening to run down her cheeks.

Daniella seemed to sense Yana's turmoil as she went about making coffee which she brought on a tray and put on a small table near Yana. Then without a word she left the room. Yana hardly seemed to notice. A few moments later she was back; in her hand she carried a small wooden box which she put on the sofa beside her. "Take some coffee Yana. It will help. I have something to show you."

Yana took a sip of the scalding drink. It jerked her back to reality. Here she was sitting in a room in Bijeljina with someone who knew her mother!

Daniella opened the box and took out some photographs, after a moment she pulled one out and handed it over. "Maria, my friend, your mother," she said softly smiling a smile that conveyed so much sadness that Yana wanted to cry.

She took the proffered photograph. There, staring back at her was a young happy-looking girl that, apart from the clothes, could have been Yana. The hair the same colour, but much longer. The smile, the eyes. It was like looking at herself in a mirror. No wonder Daniella had recognised her.

Yana recollected the strange looks she had received when at seventeen she and Lucy had visited her hometown. Of course, they all knew who she was. "This, my dear, was your father." Yana took the photograph with trembling fingers. It was a man and a woman. He was looking down at Maria who was looking up at him smiling happily. His dark moustached good looks leapt out from the picture. Yana closed her eyes tightly, for the first time she had a memory of him carrying her high on his shoulders and singing at the top of his voice.

"Look," Daniella continued. This time a picture of her parents and a little boy of about five. Her mother held a baby in her arms and the tender look on her face as she looked at the sleeping child caused an ache in Yana's throat. "My brother," she whispered.

"Yousuf, your brother's name was Yousuf."

"I remember him. I remember..." She did remember. Shouting, crying, him being taken outside, her father too. She buried her face in her hands. "It is all too terrible. I don't want to remember," she sobbed; her body rocking as she clasped her arms around herself.

Daniella picked up the photographs and moved close to the girl. Putting her arms around Yana she held her to her amble bosom until gradually the girl grew calmer. Putting the photographs to one side she made fresh coffee and insisted on the grieving girl drink a full cup. The caffeine would revive and the photographs she was sure, would one day provide joy rather than sorrow.

Taking a large envelope, she put the precious pictures inside. She had treasured these for so many years, always looking at them on Maria's birthday. Now, they didn't belong to her any more. They belonged to Maria's daughter.

Yana stayed with Daniella for quite a long while, and when she left she went straight back to her room. There, once again she looked at the photos and this time she smiled. She smiled at the smiling faces. She smiled at the mischievous expression on her brother's face, and the love in each and every smile she looked at. These were her family, her very own flesh and blood. At last, she had found her roots. Sue would want to know, she owed it to Sue.

Picking up her mobile, she keyed in Sue and moments later she was speaking to her dearly-loved foster mother. She explained what had happened – how distressed she had been – but now she felt a kind of peace and homecoming. "I'm longing to show you the pictures." She sounded so happy that it lifted Sue's spirits too. She hated Yana being so far away, but it seemed that the girl finding her roots was the most wonderful thing. She had always belonged with them but now she knew where her life had begun and whose beloved child she had been.

They said their goodbyes. It had been good to speak with Sue who instinctively seemed to understand how she felt.

Leaving thoughts of visiting the house to one side she decided she needed to go for a walk to clear her head and think calmly and quietly about her birth family. She found the meadow where she had walked and the path that led up the hill.

Slowly, enjoying the bird song as she walked steadily upwards she remembered the last time she had come this way. It seemed so long ago and yet it also seemed like yesterday. She had been seventeen, so determined to find her roots yet she had left the town feeling angry and betrayed.

Tomorrow, she resolved she would go to the house. Her plans for today had gone awry meeting her mother's old friend and seeing the photographs. Now she carried the pictures of her family and after the initial distress she had a sense of peace.

There was the rock! The carved linked 'M's were still there. Once again, as she had before she ran her fingers over them wondering, yet knowing, they were connected to her parents, perhaps in their early, trouble free courtship days. She laughed aloud at the old fashioned word 'courtship', but she somehow imagined that's how it was.

The waterfall was a bit further on. Kurt and she had stood there together, as they both watched the tumbling waterfall with shafts of sunlight giving it an ethereal feel. She had been drawn to him at that moment but later anger and fury had taken over – holding him responsible for his father actions.

As she returned the way she had come she was thoughtful, she supposed she hadn't really been fair to him. At the time however, she felt her anger was justified.

The next morning, she was determined not to be distracted. She thought back briefly to the pompous and unfriendly lawyer. For a moment she wondered whether she was doing the right thing. Then she remembered the photographs. It was HER home. Her family home. Without another thought she collected the keys from her bedside drawer and set off, walking with purpose.

It took her about ten minutes looking at the numbers as she did. Things seemed the same, much as she remembered them. Taller trees maybe, thicker shrubbery and then, there she was at number twenty-five.

She wouldn't have recognised it! The shutters were painted white instead of the dull brown she remembered. Flowers hung festooned from window boxes on the upper window ledges. Two box type trees in matching tubs stood either side of the freshly painted front door.

Yana put the key in the lock for some reason expecting it would be stiff. It turned easily though and before she knew it she was inside, with the door closed behind her. For several minutes she leaned back against the door her eyes tightly closed. It was, the thought entered her mind, like one of those television shows were contestants hardly dare open their eyes for fear of what has been done to their homes.

It was not like that though. It was really a fear deep within her about facing reality. Slowly she opened her eyes. The stove…she walked towards it, touching it, resting her hands on it. Then turning she took in the rest of the room.

It was empty apart from a moderately sized round table in the centre. The floor had a rush mat covering the main area and around the edges she could see the patterned ceramic tiles.

The walls were painted just off white and from her vague memories, it all appeared very different; the stove was the only original thing that remained. Yana walked through the door into a small tiled hall, a door was open showing a modern kitchen with a large refrigerator and a range oven. From the window, she noticed a small but neatly well maintained, garden. Puzzled, she continued to explore. There were two further rooms downstairs neither of which she had seen before. Upstairs the doors were all closed. Wooden floors creaked slightly as she opened the first door feeling a little like Goldilocks looking for a perfect place to rest! This room overlooked the street and on a beam above where she presumed a bed had once stood she saw two Ms, this time intertwined. It made Yana smile thinking of the Ms carved on the rock, she had felt such a strong connection with her mother the first time she had seen it and now seeing these confirmed for her that her parents had probably had their secret trysts there.

Her expression changed. This room had been defiled by Kurt's father. He had slept here, she shivered slightly, all the warmth she had felt leaving her in an instant. She left the room closing the door firmly behind her.

The next room was considerably smaller and to her surprise a cot stood in the middle. She cried out seeing a small bear propped up in one corner. It was Mishkin, her own little bear! She leaned over the cot and reached for the bear. How she had loved this little bear. A series of picture memories flashed through her mind. Her mother handing her the little Mishkin and soft words, perhaps even lullabies.

Still holding the bear, she opened the third door to find a modern and well-fitted bathroom. Still puzzled she climbed the narrow staircase to the top floor. She had no memories of this floor and she was surprised to find a large light room with a window at the front and back and a lovely dome shaped window in the ceiling. This she decided with a smile is where she would sleep if she ever came back.

As the thought entered her head she pushed it rapidly away. Why should she ever want to come back. There was nothing, nobody here for her and England and the family were 'home'.

There was what looked like a big cupboard in the corner. Intrigued she opened it and to her astonishment found a small bathroom. An attractively glassed enclosed shower with a wash basin with storage and a toilet. It was gleaming white apart from the tiled floor which had tiny swirls of delicate colour.

Yana was puzzled wondering when and who had modernised the house so thoughtfully. From the top floor she looked down on the back garden again. It really did look well cared for, not just neat. The grass was clipped and edged. Tall hollyhocks and sunflowers towered over the walls and then in the distance she could see the hill she had climbed up with such pleasure.

Returning to the narrow wooden stairs she made her way down the two flights. Once again, she was in the hall with its gleaming tiles and white walls. She returned to the room with the stove and with her back to it she relived what Kurt had written in his letter about Maria's rape.

"It's a game darling, don't cry." Yana could hear her mother's voice in her head. She turned feeling the cold iron stove with her hands as she did so. She could almost hear the sizzling of a kettle and smell the logs that were stacked high in the corner, just as they were now.

Yana jerked into action. The logs were ready to be used. She opened the stove all laid ready to be lit. Someone had taken a lot of trouble with this house. It had been modernised and cleaned until it gleamed. The aroma of wax polish had greeted her as she had walked in to the house. There were flowers on the round table. Putting her finger in the vase, she found the water came almost to the top. These flowers had been placed there quite recently.

On impulse, thinking about all the things she had discovered, she walked to her new friend Daniella's house. Daniella, who had been her mother's closest friend. Daniella who had saved all the photographs and given them to her. Perhaps it was she who had a hand in the renovation and care of number twenty-five.

Daniella shrieked with delight when she found Yana on her doorstep. "Come on in dear child. How lovely to see you again," she hugged Yana warmly, and once again the girl delighted in the warmth of her welcome.

"Come out to my kitchen, I'll make coffee and we shall sit in the garden and you will tell me all about your life since you left us."

Yana watched as the coffee was freshly ground thinking as she frequently thought that the amazing smell of freshly ground beans was often better than the taste! In this case she was proved wrong, as when the daintily laid tray with its pretty china cups was carried into the garden and she was handed a cup of the steaming brew she knew it was going to be special.

They sat on a small wooden bench with a white painted coffee table in front of it. Yana marvelled at the neat rows of lettuce, beans, sweet corn, spinach and abundant tomatoes.

Daniella noticed her appreciative glance. "I grow all my own vegetables and sell quite a lot in the market."

"Only self-seeded ones that the birds provide me with." She laughed happily. Yana sipped the hot coffee appreciatively, she thought she had seldom tasted anything more delicious. "I love flowers, but I love my salads and veggies more." Daniella continued to chat about gardens, weather, the town market, whilst Yana continued to enjoy the relaxed atmosphere interspersing the coffee with sips of the, always provided water. It would she thought, be odd to go back to instant coffee the standard fare in most hospitals which bore no relationship to 'proper' coffee.

As if suddenly aware that she was talking too much and that Yana might have had a specific reason for her visit Daniella put her hand on Yana's. In a business like voice she stopped her chattering flow and said. "You didn't come here to listen to me rattling on, did you?" Yana smiled self conscientiously.

"Daniella, you are too astute by half. I have a mystery that I thought you might be able to solve." She described the gleaming woodwork and smell of polish. The flowers on the round table. The obviously new kitchen and two new bathrooms. Even the crib and Mishkin her childhood toy; and finally, the neat and extremely pretty garden. Did you arrange it all?"

Daniella put back her head and laughed, her ample bosom heaving. "Oh no my dear, not me, not me at all."

"Then who," Yana wondered aloud.

"I am surprised you need to ask. I really am. Isn't it obvious child?" Of course, it was. How could she have been so stupid, it was as Daniella said 'so obvious'. "You know now," Daniella laughed.

Yana nodded. "I know now," she repeated like a mantra.

Much later after far too much coffee and happy tales of Maria and Daniella's childhood. Their schooling, and church going with the strict Father Ignatius, who had apparently died, not long after Yana had met him on her first visit to the town seven years before. He had thought she was Maria and she had reluctantly realised his mind was in a somewhat confused state.

Finally, and choosing her words carefully, Daniella told of Maria's love for Mustafa and their secret marriage in the village of Popovi only eight kilometres away. "You must go there, it is so pretty by the river with a few buildings with their legs in the water." The way she described it made Yana smile and she was determined to go there and see it for herself.

Daniella continued. Her tone was now more serious. She explained how Maria, who was a favourite of Father Ignatius had persuaded him to secretly bless their marriage. The civil ceremony had seemed lacking, particularly to Maria.

"It was better in those days. Some boys scrapped while still at school, but for the most part Christians and Muslims rubbed along."

"So, my father was Muslim? I don't understand the name though, it is Serbian, isn't it?"

"Your father's father was Serbian, hence the name. It was your grandmother who was a Muslim. You inherited yours looks from your Serbian ancestry, through your mother, my dearest friend in the world." Yana was silent, absorbing all she had heard. There was more…

"They didn't live together properly for some years. It was so sad. Your grandparents found it totally unacceptable that their only daughter had married a half Muslim. They used to meet up on the hill by a huge rock." Yana smiled remembering how she had felt when she first saw it.

"Then she became pregnant with Yousuf and the families became reconciled at the thought of a grandchild. Your father, with help from his father bought the house were you and your brother were born and all suddenly seemed so much better for them. I was so happy for them too. I had never seen Maria looking so beautiful, her, their happiness was a joy to see. However," she continued, "there was much jealousy. Maria had a number of young men in the town who had hoped to marry her. As far as they were concerned she had married a full-blown Muslim so that when the uprising happened it was all the excuse they needed." Daniella was silent, staring into the distance and re living the moment. "I warned Maria, several times, but she couldn't or wouldn't accept that people she had known, been friends with even; all her life, would turn…I can't say more. Not now, not now. One day I will tell you all I know."

Yana knew it was time to leave. She glanced at her watch, two hours had passed since Daniella had so warmly welcomed her. Standing, she bent and kissed the older woman on the cheek, noticed tears and the paleness of her face. Quietly she let herself out and walked, almost on autopilot back to the hotel. She had so much to think about.

There was light rain falling as she walked echoing her mood, and she knew the time had arrived to seek out Kurt. Casting her mind back to the time when she was seventeen she reflected on her several meetings with him including the walk up to the waterfall which at the time had seemed quite romantic. Then there had been the confusion she felt when he cut her dead in the street not knowing that he had just learned the truth of her mother's death at the hands of his father. Before she and Lucy had left the town he had written telling the history of his family living in the house from the perspective of a seven year old who believes what his parents tell him.

The day he cut her dead in the street was the day he had finally heard the truth from his father.

He had been so angry and appalled that he had left the town that day and had then written the long letter giving all the facts in a letter that eventually found her in England.

Daniella had told her he now lived in Belgrade and she decided after a late breakfast she would drive there. She realised she was extremely hungry having not eaten the previous evening and helped herself to the generous buffet of cheeses, cold cut of meats and orange juice, washed down with yet more coffee.

Having driven the route quite recently, she set off confidently arriving in the hour and forty-two minutes the sat navigation system, had, informed she would. She found a Park House and then wondered what next! She had no address for him and not even the name of the school he taught at. Cross with herself for being so stupid she checked that her I Pad was in her bag and set off to find an Internet Cafe where she could look for addresses of local senior schools.

There were, she discovered, only two major senior schools in the City and the helpful woman who ran the Internet Cafe kindly gave her a street map and put crosses on the locations of the schools.

It was not of course, the first one she found, after walking into the school trying to look as if she had every right to be there. She located an administrative office and quickly established that Kurt didn't teach there. "He used to," the pretty girl informed her. "But now he is Principal of the other one." She gave a merry laugh. "His school is much more important than this one." She laughed again somehow indicating she was perfectly happy to be where she was.

Holding the piece of paper with the complete directions she had just been given Yana walked fast for a good ten minutes. It was mid-afternoon and the children were streaming out whether going home early or for other reasons she had no way of knowing.

Waiting patiently by the gate as the young people streamed past she finally was able to make her way to what looked like the main entrance. As she approached the door she saw Kurt walking briskly along a corridor talking animatedly to a vivacious young woman with, Yana noticed very blonde hair worn in an elegant chignon.

She was quite petite and was looking up at him adoringly. For a moment Yana wanted to run back the way she had come; but during the moment of her indecision he turned his head and saw her. His face lit up, he said something to the young woman by his side; then leaving her he walked quickly towards Yana a smile on his face.

"How good, how very good to see you," he said holding out both hands. Yana answered his English in Bosnian, and took one of his outstretched hands which she shook. His grip was firm and his gaze was deep and direct. Yana felt a little shiver, not all unpleasant, shake her body.

"It's good to see you. Why don't we go and find somewhere to have a late lunch and catch up."

She had forgotten what deep blue eyes he had. What a lovely smile, showing perfectly white teeth against his lightly tanned skin. She was tall, but he was taller, about six feet three, she surmised as they walked side by side. She liked the way he inclined his head slightly in order to catch every word she said as they walked along the busy street.

They turned into a narrow alleyway and a short way down he indicated a door on their left. "My favourite eating place," he smiled. He was clearly well known and the two of them were shown into a courtyard garden that was a blaze of colour. Geraniums sprouted from pots in all sizes and their slightly peculiar scent hung in the air.

Yana enjoyed the food, but afterwards trying to recollect, when talking to Sue, she confessed she had no idea what she ate. They talked non-stop. Kurt wanting to know all about her career, and Yana congratulating him on being Principal of the school. The only silences were comfortable ones as they gazed at each other in a kind of wonderment.

"How did you find me?" Kurt wanted to know.

"Did you, have you done up the house?" She couldn't bring herself to say 'my' house or 'your' house. It certainly wasn't his but she didn't quite feel it was hers either. "The flowers, they were fresh?"

"I was telephoned when you arrived. What will you do with it?"

Yana was silent. She hadn't thought ahead – not recently anyway. She couldn't live there, her home was England and she was looking forward to going into a community medical practice after a six month placement at the hospital that she still had to complete.

A strange expression came over Kurt's face. "There is someone I would like you to meet Yana – he knew your mother too."

"I've met Daniella." Kurt looked pleased. "She has been brilliant arranging for the house to be kept aired and polished and the garden properly maintained," he looked at his watch. "I'm sorry Yana I have to get back. Can I see you tonight?" Yana nodded. They agreed to meet at the hotel where Yana was staying at eight thirty, and he was gone.

She sat for a while sipping her wine and enjoying the garden and the general buzz of conversation. It was good to be away from Bileljina where she felt somewhat under scrutiny at times.

Feeling pleasantly relaxed after the lunch, wine and Kurt's company, she left the restaurant and returned to the main thoroughfare. There she browsed around the shops feeling she should not drive for a while as the wine had gone to her head a little. Instead she bought little gifts for the family. A pretty plate for Sue, who would probably put it on the dresser with her collection and she choose several beautifully carved pieces including exquisite tiny horses for Lily's twins who seemed to have inherited her love of horses.

Finally, she bought an extremely pretty blouse for herself with coloured embroidery on the cuffs of the short sleeves and on either side of the buttons that fastened down the front.

Later that evening Yana dressed with care. Firstly, she tried on her new blouse but decided she did not want to look contrived ethnic. Instead, she wore a simple Artigiano dress that Sue had bought for her on her birthday. She loved the way the Italian clothes were made and they fitted her so perfectly. "She could be a model," one of the assistants had commented and Sue had agreed happily.

Yana had laughed, pleased and flattered, but modelling was not a career that either appealed or had even occurred to her.

Now, two years later the dress looked as good as the day she had first tried it on. It was as comfortable as a second skin and had an understated elegance about it. Tonight, she wore her hair loose; it hung like a silk smooth curtain just below her shoulders. She felt she looked good as she smiled happily at the girl in the mirror. Her heart was beating slightly faster than usual and the doctor in her recognised that her pulse was pounding. Over stimulated she thought taking a number of deep breaths as she walked slowly down the stairs to meet Kurt in the foyer.

Kurt was deep in conversation when a slight sound made him look up. The graceful figure with the shinning hair and an aura of calm she certainly didn't feel, walked closer. Kurt said a hasty goodbye to an old pupil of his and walked to meet her.

"You look stunning Yana." A smile lit up her face and he had a sudden longing to put his arms around her and kiss her with all the passion he felt. Instead they gravely shook hands, their eyes locked for a few seconds. Yana knew she had never felt like this before; the doctors she mostly dated were fun. Often a lots of laughs too, and occasionally a real attraction that sometimes led to bed, but never had her mouth felt so dry and her body so moist with longing.

Pulling herself together she made some inconsequential remark which gave both of them a much needed, breathing space.

"We are going to my favourite restaurant just outside the town, a mile or two so we'll take my car.

It's over there." Yana nodded and they crossed over the road while she wondered how they could maintain this casual conversation, unless of course he didn't feel as she did.

They drove the short distance and he heard her gasp slightly. "Are you all right?" he wanted to know. Yana nodded trying to keep her emotions intact. The village was Povia, the name she had only recently heard of. The place where her parents were secretly married. About to confide in Kurt, she was surprised to hear him saying they were to be joined for dinner by two of his friends. The moment for confidences was past.

She felt a slight sense of disappointment, followed immediately by a slight sense of relief that the evening would probably be less nerve wracking, for her at least! Nevertheless, still feeling a slight sense of disappointment, she followed the waiter as he led the way to their table.

There was Daniella wreathed in smiles looking so welcoming that Yana forgot any sense of disappointment. A tall, very thin man stood as they arrived at the table. His hair was thinning, but his face had a lean and interesting look. He held out his hand. "Milo Sezbrianni," he said, his smile warm and friendly, and Yana couldn't fail to notice that he and Daniella seemed very relaxed and comfortable together. Yana recollected that among the myriad of information she had received from her new friend Daniella had said she had been widowed some years ago. Milo must be a good friend or companion or whatever…

As if reading her thoughts Milo, who was now sitting opposite her told her that they, he and Daniella had been at school together – 'a long time ago' – he added cryptically, and he added, 'with your parents too of course'.

Yana couldn't speak, she felt a prickling of tears in her eyes that took a major effort to control. The last thing she wanted was tears falling down her cheeks. The waiter fussed over them filling their glasses with wine already ordered by Milo. It was another of the local Balkan wines that Yana was acquiring a taste for. Burgundy like, just a shade lighter. She sipped appreciatively letting conversation flow around her whilst she gathered her thoughts. She supposed it was nice having dinner in a foursome but she didn't really feel like light chit-chat with one complete stranger and Daniella who was now in full flow!

Kurt glanced at her noticing her tense expression with concern. Perhaps it hadn't been such a good idea after all.

Daniella had come up with 'a plan' she had said. It would get Yana back to where she belonged. Kurt had been intrigued. It was an interesting idea if, that is, Yana would even consider it.

The soup arrived and he noticed Yana was hardly eating. Her thoughts, had he but known were full of regret. The evening was not what she had hoped for, she had so wanted an opportunity to get to know Kurt a little more.

The conversation moved on she heard Milo mention retirement. "What are you retiring from?" she asked politely. "He is the doctor." Daniella announced importantly. "He is our doctor and what we shall do without him we just can't imagine." Milo smiled with a deprecating gesture.

"Oh Daniella, my dear. Another nice young man will arrive, you'll see." Daniella looked at Yana.

"Well," she demanded. "What do you think of that?" Yana was bemused, the conversation was so fast and quite idiomatic had meant she didn't feel she had grasped everything. He had acknowledged that he was retiring, that much she had understood and that he was a doctor, she thought she had grasped that too.

"When are you planning to retire?" again her question was polite etiquette more than anything.

"Well," he said slowly. "I am hoping to retire within the next twelve months. I just hope someone will step forward to take over my practice. It has to be someone acceptable to me and to the whole community," he added.

Yana felt rather than heard the emphasis. There must still be undercurrents here. Ethnic issues didn't just go away. She herself, had felt resentment from the lawyer when she collected the keys, and she had seen a headline only this morning about unrest in Pristina which was not all that far away.

Daniella said to no one in particular and everyone in general, in a voice that was meant to be casual – but to Kurt's ears at least sounded full of suppressed excitement. "You know Milo, Yana is a doctor. Fully qualified too." Milo nodded.

"I had heard," he said dryly. He turned to Yana. "Where did you study, where are you now, what…."

"Hey," Kurt interrupted with a laugh. "This is dinner, not an interview!" There was an awkward pause. Yana looked from one face to another. "This was a set up," she laughed but inwardly she had to assume that Kurt's interest in her was as a doctor to perhaps replace Milo.

Yana rose to her feet and placed her napkin on the table. "Thank you for the invitation Kurt, but I'm leaving."

"No," she held up her hand.

"Please don't move. I shall take a taxi back to the hotel." His face was stricken. *Good*, she thought, head held high she stalked out of the restaurant and walked down the road in search of a taxi. Her flat Ferragamo shoes were bliss to walk in and she almost contemplated walking the whole way thanking her lucky stars that she had not put on the strappy sandals she so nearly wore.

Passing a taxi rank she changed her mind and was soon speeding back to the hotel. Once in her room she pulled off her clothes and walked naked across the room to take a shower to wash the evening away. The cold water fell fiercely on her body cascading over her. She grabbed hold of her shampoo and started rubbing her hair vigorously turning the water to hot as she did so. As she did a favourite song of Michael and Sue's came into her head and she started humming. 'I'm gonna wash that man right out of my hair'.

She giggled. Here she was in Bijeljina humming a song she had heard and sung so many times when her English family played one of their favourite videos. Towelling herself dry she pulled on a silk nightgown Lily had given her at Christmas. It was cream silk and the usually pyjama-clad Yana had been instantly converted. Lily had generously given her two and her pyjamas seldom left her underwear drawer these days.

Chapter 22

Kurt stood up. "I'm going after her," he stated matter of factly feeling anything other. Daniella pulled at his arm. "Sit down Kurt. Give the girl some space."

"It was all your fault anyway," Milo commented glaring at Daniella. Kurt sat down.

"Oh stop it, you two. It was probably my fault for inviting you both along, I think she was expecting something different."

"Well thank you for that," Daniella said crossly. Kurt took her hand and kissed. "Don't you start please, I really don't need two women walking out on me in one evening!"

Dessert arrived and Milo offered to eat the spare one. "Most unfair." Daniella complained. "Eats for two and is skinny. I eat for half a person and look at me," she patted her ample bosom whilst Milo snorted unbelievingly.

"You two act like an old, married couple," Kurt spoke affectionately.

"Never," they answered together, and all three burst out laughing at the ludicrous thought. As Daniella wiped tears of laughter from her eyes she added.

"Why spoil a good friendship, eh Milo."

He nodded, still enjoying the second dessert.

Kurt looked from one to the other with real affection. They were old enough to be his parents and in a way they had been. When his mother died, Daniella had comforted him. Cooked him special treats and even sewed on lost or broken buttons and mended torn clothes. As for Milo, he had helped when his father was so ill. Afterwards, when Kurt spoke of his hatred for the things his father had done; things that had driven him to leave his own home and not speak to his father for a number of years. Milo provided wise counsel. Whilst not condoning Mikail's actions, he explained that history and circumstances sometimes changes people in ways that they would not even recognise themselves.

"He wiped it all from his mind." Milo had continued. "All he grieved over latterly was that he had driven you away." His words made a kind of sense but Kurt knew he could never forgive the man for the grief he caused Yana and her family.

As he sat drinking his coffee and while his old friends talked quietly, Kurt thought back to the day he had discovered the cot in the cellar. It had been taken apart and left there, now covered with cobwebs and very grimy. A number of screws were missing so he took it up to the old kitchen and scrubbed it. He had bought new screws and some non-leaded paint and had put it back together and re painted it before taking it upstairs to the attic. Returning to the cellar he had unearthed a little drum, dented and battered and finally a small brown Bear. He carefully removed the very dirty jacket and trousers and washed first the bear and then the clothes in warm soapy water. It took several goes but finally pleased with the results, the brown Bear with the little red jacket and blue trousers had been placed in the cot. He instinctively knew the cot and the bear belonged to Yana and he hoped one day she would find them…

Kurt felt he made one step forward and half a step backwards with Yana and still in a reverie he jerked back to the present when he heard Daniella repeating his name.

"We were talking about Milo's retirement again," Daniella said positively. "He wants to do no more than ten to twelve months. Yana must come back."

Milo raised his eyebrows to Kurt, who smiled back. "Daniella dear," Milo said, "We may all want her here, back in her home town, but we can't push her she must decide for herself."

"Ask her to tea then. Let her see for herself. The surgery – all the patients you treat and care for."

"If I do," Milo smiled as he spoke. "You, my dear Daniella, will not be invited," she gave a snort.

"I wouldn't come even if I was," she was satisfied though, Milo would invite the girl 'round.

Kurt insisted on paying the bill; it was, after all, he said his invitation. Milo drove Daniella home while Kurt drove back to his flat wishing the evening had turned out differently.

Yana slept soundly and only the early morning sunshine streaming through the open window woke her. She lay still for a moment running her hands lightly over her body enjoying the feel of the silk beneath her fingers.

With a sigh she threw back the summer weight duvet and stepped out of bed. She splashed water on her face, noting with surprise that the mirror over the washbasin showed she had developed a small scattering of freckles over her nose and that, despite using twenty factor.

Pulling on a pair of blue 'capris' and her navy and white spotted sleeveless silk blouse and headed down to the dining room.

The message from Milo was handed to her as she sipped her first coffee of the day.

Dear Yana, she read.

Please, will you make an old man happy and have tea with me today at four pm. If you are interested, I will show you my surgery and we can talk 'doctor talk'; if not, we won't!

You only need to let me know if you are unable to visit. It was signed simply. Milo.

After breakfast, and back in her room she wandered about thinking about the invitation. Her curiosity was roused. She knew she would go. To see his surgery would be interesting and to see what equipment he had if any, for minor surgery.

Having decided she would go she asked the hotel for a packed lunch and mid-morning found her walking again through the meadow and up the path towards the hill and the waterfall. She wanted to sit on the rock where the initials carved there she now knew for sure were those of her parents. The rock was part of her history. She sat there for quite a while thinking back over her life. It could all have been so different. A children's home could have been her childhood instead of the happy family life she had. Thoughts of Lucy, Lily and Bear crossed her mind. All so individual, all so special to her in their own way. Her face clouded as she thought of Michael's untimely death and the way Sue had tried so hard to hide her grief. The eventual move to the cottage where she seemed happy enough, particularly when surrounded by her grandchildren.

Yana ate some of her lunch and tucked the remainder under a large stone to pick up on her return. Walking onwards and upwards, she eventually reached the waterfall. It was as always spectacularly beautiful.

The sound of birdsong above the sound of cascading water seemed to surround her and she understood so well why her parents had loved this place – away from the ethnic stresses of their lives. Kurt liked it here too of course, and she grimaced wishing thoughts of him had not intruded.

With a sigh she turned and walked back to the rock her fingers, tracing, once again the carved Ms. She cleared some lichen that encroached and threatened to hide them if left alone then collecting the remains of her lunch she walked back down the hill to tidy herself up before going to tea with the doctor.

As he busied himself in the kitchen, Milo thought about the young woman he had met the previous evening. He remembered her a little from her visit as a teenager when so many people had commented on her likeness to Maria. Anna had been alive then and his life had been busy looking after her and the Practice. It made him remember Maria who had been several years younger than him. Bubbly personality, that red hair and all the boys fancying her. At that time, he only had eyes for Anna though, who became the love of his life. He always thought it a shame she had married Mustafa, life became complicated and most of the young men in their group, were jealous.

The ring of the doorbell alerted him to Yana's arrival. Drying his hands, he hurried up the hall and opened the door. He couldn't help himself, in this light she looked even more like Maria and he drew an involuntary breath. She held out her hand, he took it but instead of shaking it he kissed it lightly.

"You are a very lovely young woman my dear," he said warmly. Yana smiled in response enjoying his gallantry. He stepped aside and she walked into the cool recesses of the hall with its high ceiling and panelled walls. It was so unexpected and he noticed her surprise. "The panels were my wife's idea. The house was very shabby when we bought it and it was one of the many things we did in the way of renovating." Yana smiled, he almost sounded a bit nervous – and truth to be known, he actually felt a bit unnerved by her! She was as calm as she was beautiful and he for one, could never see her coming back to her home town. She had, he felt, an air about her. Life had been good to her far better than had she survived the traumas that followed the end of hostilities.

Yana followed Milo through the hall and kitchen into a lovely, if rather unkempt garden. "My wife was the gardener." Milo explained ruefully, waving his hand at the slight wilderness.

There were, Yana noticed lots of fruit trees. Apart from lemon and oranges, apricots and peaches hung on heavily laden branches. The smell of fruit seemed to fill the air along with the perfume of herbs. She recognised rosemary, and oregano among others, in one neatly controlled herb bed near the kitchen door.

Seeing her glance Milo waved his hand in the direction of the herbs. "My province," he smiled. "I love herbs to look at, smell and eat of course."

"Of course." Yana smiled as she spoke and sat at the white painted table that Milo had indicated. In moments he reappeared with a tray with tea and a cake cut into neat slices. She couldn't help but raise her eyebrows in slight surprise and Milo reacted by bursting out laughing. "My only culinary trick," he said. "Anna, my wife, taught me to make this cake."

"Then I must try a piece," Yana said simply, helping herself as she spoke. For a few moments there was a companionable silence as Milo poured the tea and Yana took an appreciative bite of cake. "Umm," she said – her mouth too full to say more.

"You like it?" Milo sounded anxious.

"It's delicious," Yana said happily before taking a second bite.

Milo relaxed. The first hurdle over. They sat for a while like old friends rather than two newly acquainted people. *Perhaps*, Milo thought, *it is because I knew her. I was there when she was born. I wonder if she knows that.*

I wonder how well he knew my parents. Yana was thinking. *Did he fall for Maria like so many of the young men in the town.* A sudden thought occurred to her – *was he perhaps there at her birth. How strange that would be, but equally how likely.*

It was as if he had read her thoughts. "I was there with Maria, your mother, when you were born. They, she and your father, were so happy. You were a little girl. They felt their family was complete."

129

Yana couldn't think of anything to say. Their minds had been travelling along the same path. It was somehow good to know someone who was there at her beginning. More and more she was feeling a sense of belonging in which Mishkin, her little bear played no small part.

Milo suddenly became brisk. He stood and suggested she might like to see his Surgery now. Yana was glad to move away from such a personal conversation and within minutes they were deeply engrossed in what Milo called 'doctor talk'.

The surgery was well equipped and modern. Milo had kept fully abreast of technology. It was neat and tidy with an interesting shelf of reference books organised alphabetically. There was an adjoining room with an electrocardiogram machine, a curtained cubicle for patients to remove their clothes as necessary and surprisingly two comfortable chairs for patients to sit down and feel more relaxed as medical problems were talked through.

Yana was impressed. Milo talked patient numbers, referrals and how local practices working in conjunction stood in for each other for holidays or illness. He explained he invariably had a trainee working with him as part of their course which was useful and also kept him on his toes.

"What about night calls?" Yana wanted to know.

"They happen," he answered cryptically. Yana was not surprised, she somehow couldn't see Milo sending locums instead of going himself.

"It's pretty lively at times," he added by way of understatement. He then insisted on showing her the house. It was slightly old fashioned and the colours were not particularly to her taste. Yana was not into minimalism but felt there was just too much everywhere.

The rooms though were beautifully proportioned and she lost count of the bedrooms. As if reading her mind Milo commented on the five bedrooms. "All this space," he said a shade wistfully. "And no children to fill it," Yana said nothing, if he wanted to say more, he would. As they walked side by side down the stairs he asked her the question she had been dreading.

"So Yana, what do you think. Would you be interested in taking over when I retire?" Yana bit her lip, she had to admit it was tempting – but there was so much to consider including her life outside this place. This was not home. England was home. Sue and her foster siblings and their children were her family.

"Milo, I'm sorry. I think it highly unlikely. There is so much to consider, but I am honoured that you asked me." If Milo was disappointed, he didn't show it. Instead he hugged the girl briefly to him. "You must do what you must do, but don't dismiss the idea completely. Think about it at least."

"I'll do that," she said giving him a brief kiss on either cheek. She liked him, he was easy to be with and she admired his obvious kindness towards patients and his absolute professionalism.

It was time to go home. Kurt had left several messages for her at the hotel, but she couldn't bear to speak to him. They always started out so well and something bad always seemed to happen.

Before she left she visited the house again. This time it felt less alien and despite herself she briefly imagined living there again. With an impatient sigh she closed the door behind her and slipped the key into her bag. Then she knocked on Daniella's door.

The older woman gave her a flashing smile. "I'm so very glad to see you – it was all my fault yesterday, it …"

"It was no one's fault," Yana interrupted, "It was just unexpected and I didn't deal with it very well," Daniella said nothing so Yana knew she had not dealt with the situation in very grown up way. Once again, she had let herself down in front of Kurt.

Daniella laid her arm on the girls. "Kurt really tries you know. He worked so hard to get the house right." Yana felt a pricking in her eyes blinking hard to stop the tears. She knew he had tried hard. She should have made more effort. On a sudden and unexpected impulse, she decided to stay a bit longer and furnish the house. She said a quick goodbye to Daniella and while walking back to the house telephoned Sue in England.

For once, she did not receive the support she expected. Had she but known once the phone call was over Sue hugged Dally to her while her mind raced ahead. Yana would go, she would leave England and she, Sue would feel lonelier and more useless than ever.

131

"Oh Dally, why did Michael get killed like that – we need him don't we." Dally looked at her with sympathetic eyes. He could always tell when his mistress was unhappy or worried. He fetched his ball and dropped it at her feet, when she didn't respond he nuzzled her and picked up the ball again dropping it in her lap. In spite of herself Sue laughed. "Wretched dog," she said in a tone that belied her words. She walked outside and obediently threw the ball. Dally collected it and brought it back carefully dropping it at her feet. After a while, she felt more cheerful, she stroked her faithful companion and together they walked into the woods.

Chapter 23

Yana telephoned Kurt. This time it was she who left a message saying she was going shopping for the house and would be gone for a day or two. Then she went around to Daniella's and told the surprised woman to pack an overnight bag – they were going shopping. As Daniella told her friends afterwards, she had never had so much fun.

They chose china and glassware. Cutlery and various accoutrements for the kitchen. Beds and rugs. Fabric for curtains. Yana having been assured there was the perfect person to make them for her back home. Comfortable chairs and a sofa for the sitting room. Duvets, pillows and bed linen.

To Yana the prices seemed reasonable and she spent nearly all her savings. Daniella though, with her eyes nearly popping out of her head, decided being a doctor must be a very good thing indeed.

They arrived back from their day and night away happy but exhausted and that evening Yana finally managed to speak with Kurt. To begin with it was a somewhat stilted conversation, but gradually the tone lightened and they agreed to meet for a picnic on the following Saturday only two days away as Yana was returning home on the Sunday.

Kurt had suggested they meet by the carved rock and insisted he would provide the picnic.

The next day all the newly acquired goods arrived and Yana with much help from Daniella and her curtain maker friend Anni – short for something Yana didn't quite grasp despite her now almost fluent grasp of the language.

When she returned to the hotel that evening happy but exhausted, she found a message from Sue to telephone urgently. She immediately checked her mobile which she had switched off in the early morning and found three messages. Lily had been in an accident, would Yana please come straight home. All thoughts of Kurt went out of her head. She requested her bill and within an hour she was on her way to the airport to get on the next available plane.

Saturday morning was bright with a pleasant breeze. Kurt packed the picnic with great care. It was a celebration; so beluga, salmon and freshly picked fruit to be washed down with a sparkling wine. He set off cheerfully arriving at the rock in plenty of time. He imagined their conversation. He imagined kissing her, and staying there by the waterfall under the stars.

After a while, he pulled himself together and looked at his watch. She was nearly an hour late. When the second hour had slowly ticked by he knew she wasn't coming. He was so furious he stamped around calling her all sorts of names. He shocked himself with his vehemence – but he found it hard to reconcile her sweet voice when talking on the telephone with her lack of appearance.

He started to worry. Perhaps she was ill. Perhaps she had gone to the house, fallen down the stairs and was lying helpless, unable to move. Almost forgetting the picnic neatly laid out on a rug, he threw everything at great speed into the basket and set off rapidly down the hill only pausing when he stood in front of his old home.

He could hear movement inside and rang the bell impatiently, but to his surprise the door was opened by grey haired lady of indeterminate age, with a tape measure hanging around her neck like a necklace. They looked at each other for a moment then Kurt pushed past her. "Yana," he called. "Yana are you all right?"

"She is not here," The woman who had opened the door appeared at his side. "She has gone home to England. I'm just here measuring curtains," she added by way of explanation.

Kurt couldn't bring himself to speak. She had tricked him. Was this her revenge for the other evening – or revenge for the past. He was confused as well as angry. He turned on his heel and left the house vowing never to go inside again.

Yana couldn't drive quickly enough to the hospital. The conversation she had with Sue made it clear Lily was in real trouble. It was of course a riding accident and Yana knew as did everyone how bad they can be. By the time she arrived she was shattered but seeing Sue, so white faced and worried pulled her together. The doctor within her, taking charge of the emotions she was dealing with herself.

They talked quickly for a few moments, Sue bringing Yana up to date with the situation. "Lucy has been here, so has Bear. They will both be back soon." She squeezed Yana's hand tightly. "We needed you here too. Paul is with her of course, but she is still unconscious." Sue gave a sob and Yana put her arms around her and held her close.

They walked in together to see Lily. She was moaning softly but still seemed to be unconscious.

Paul looked ashen-faced. "Why is she moaning? Is she in pain?"

"I'm sure not," Yana answered firmly. "It is good that she is making noises, it means that she is not in a deeply unconscious state."

Yana went off to find the duty doctor. Nurses were with Lily all the time as she was in intensive care, but Yana wanted to see the scans for herself. She found the doctor and together they looked at the scans. It was not good. Lily's spine was cracked in two places. She might never walk again. Yana felt physically sick. Lily, always the active one, always impatient with people who sat around.

How would she cope with this? How would Sue cope too. All her excitement about furnishing the house, the medical practice and Kurt seemed so unimportant now. She had entirely forgotten her arrangement to meet Kurt and it was several days before she remembered.

Lily gained consciousness. No fool, the first thing she asked was, "Can I walk?" Diplomatically, the doctors encouraged her to think positively whilst at the same time warning her of the struggles ahead. "Cut the crap," she said to Yana and Lucy. "I want the truth." They both knew there was a faint possibility that Lily might walk again. If determination and effort were the criteria, there would be no problem; but there was the unknown factor. How much damage had been done that could not be evaluated at present because of the bruising and swelling.

Lily was looking from one to another. "Tell me the truth. I don't want platitudes. Tell me."

Lucy looked at her twin and the three girls held hands as if giving strength to the other. First Lucy, then Yana told her that

135

her fitness and strength would help her. Her youth would also be an important factor in her recovery, as was her determination.

"I might never walk. I'm right, aren't I?" Her sisters nodded and the three girls had tears pouring down their faces. They knew Lily. She had to deal with it head on, that way she might stand a chance.

It was as if a lamp had gone out. Lily gave up. She lay staring at the ceiling ignoring all who came to visit her not saying a word to anyone.

They were all worried. Paul even blamed Lucy and Yana for being so honest with her. Sue tried to mediate explaining that the girls believed it was right to tell her the truth so that she could put up a fight. It had never occurred to them that the previously feisty Lily was no more.

Paul was so angry that he decided that only Amy and Andy could visit their mother. They had wanted to come before, and Sue had suggested it might be good all round. Now, finally he allowed them to visit and excluded everyone else except Sue.

Lucy and Yana had gone through all the notes and scans again and before they both left to go back to their work the girls explained everything carefully to their mother.

Sue was more confident now. When bleeps went off, she didn't panic and although Lily hardly spoke to her she was there every day despite Paul's curfew. She was there when the children were finally allowed to visit.

"What the hell are you doing here?" she snapped. Sue beamed, the silence was broken. The twins had been told she wouldn't speak so for a moment they were taken aback. "Mummy, I jumped the big fence today," Amy said.

"I told her she shouldn't," Andy said quickly expecting his twin would get one of their mother's lambasting, instead Lily smiled. "That was brave Amy."

"I did it for you Mummy. I made a pact. If I could do it, you would get better – and I did, I did."

The child's voice rose with excitement. Sue, and Lucy who had just arrived, held their breaths. Lily smiled. "That was brave, and that was clever Amy – but you are not to do it again until I come home – you too Andy." The twins nodded happy that for once they seemed to have pleased their mother.

Paul who came in as Lily was speaking put an arm around each of them. "That's enough excitement for now you two. Say goodbye to your mother and go and get some orange juice from the machine. You can come again soon."

Sue went with them. "You are so clever Amy that was just what your mother needed to hear – but please promise me you won't do it again. We don't want another accident," Amy started to protest. Of course, she would do it again – but not, as she had confided to Andy until Mummy came home.

It was the beginning of better days for Lily. It was as if she wanted to see Amy do the jump, it was all she talked about. How clever and talented Amy was. What courage to tackle something that could have been so dangerous. Now X-rays showed her back was healing. She sat in a wheel chair. The lack lustre attitude had gone replaced by a strong will make a complete recovery.

She had a purpose again and all she thought and talked about was a future for Amy. Olympic medals were, as far as she was concerned, in the bag. Amy would achieve what she had been unable to.

If Sue felt it was, as ever with Lily, a rather over the top attitude and to the detriment of Andy she held her counsel. Lily had something to fight for and she was getting stronger every day. It was time for her to go home.

Dally was duly collected from a kind neighbour who had looked after him for the last four months. Her cottage had a neglected air and her garden was overgrown. With a sigh, Sue settled back into her old routines with one quite major exception she starting writing down all the stories she had made up over the years for her children and grandchildren.

She wrote by hand rather than on the computer, though she knew at some point she would have to computerise them. The Land of Blue Grass, such a favourite with all the children started to come alive on the pages with the interesting Catellymonk and the Giradonk taking the stories into the realms of fantasy.

Walking Dally now had to be fitted in as with visits from Bear and Chantelle with their little boy now chattering in a delightful mix of French and English. Yana coming towards the end of her final placement in Accident and Emergency came down when she could telling of the pressures they were all under and the problems of drunk and frequently violent patients.

Yana and Sue discussed the chances of drunk patients ever being sent to a separate unit with medical care but also the option of a locked room for them to sleep off their stupor once they had been medically assessed thus leaving the Department to look after really needy patients. A pipe dream, they both reluctantly agreed.

They talked about the locum job Yana was so looking forward to in a small Sussex town. It was a six-month placement and Yana was looking forward to working in a Practice and getting to know her patients.

Christmas this year was going to be very different. The local social life of dinners and drinks parties would be the same, but Meg and Adrian, Lily's in-laws had invited all her family to join them. It would be a big crowd and Sue wistfully thought of other bustling Christmas in the old days at the Rectory when the aroma of her home cooked turkey had filled the air. However, to have all the family under one roof would be amazing, something no longer possible in the cottage.

On Christmas Eve Yana came to collect her and they drove to Wycliffe Hall, delighted the threatened snow had not yet put in an appearance.

They arrived at around four pm. In time for tea as Meg had suggested. It was dark, of course, and lights seemed to shine from every window.

Meg greeted them warmly, a huge fire burned in the fireplace of the large hall and the Christmas tree sparkled in the centre. The non-Father Christmas presents were placed around the base of the tree looking very inviting in their festive paper and ribbons. The children would have stockings on their beds left for them personally by the man himself of course!

Once unpacked, Sue and Yana who were sharing a room, added their gifts to the pile. The housekeeper brought tea into the drawing room helped by a young girl, who it transpired was her niece. She had inveigled her way in to spend Christmas there as an extra pair of much needed hands, to the delight of her aunt.

Lily and her family were already there and Lily, still in a wheel chair looked happier than she had for years. She was deep in conversation with Adrian. Her eyes sparkled, her hair shone and she chattered as she had as a child.

Lucy observing her twin felt she was almost high with excitement about something but before she could get involved, more family arrived and excitement among the children was palpable.

The large family rocking horse had been brought down from the old nursery and put in the hall and the younger children were in and out of the drawing room vying for their turn under the careful eyes of the chauffeur / houseman.

Amy and Andy stayed protectively close to their mother, whilst Leila and Louisa enjoyed playing with Bear and Chantelle's little boy Michel.

"When are you going to have a baby Aunt Yana?" Louisa asked politely. Everyone laughed but Sue saw a slight shadow cross Yana's face. She had sent a Christmas card to Kurt with a warm message. She had felt mortified when she had finally realised she had not turned up for their planned picnic and had written apologising and explaining the circumstances – but she had heard nothing.

"When I find a nice man like your daddy," she replied winking at Peter who grinned back quite unable to fathom why she was still single

It was a happy Christmas. Adrian and Meg were generous and delightful hosts. Everyone ate too much. The adults drank rather freely of the excellent wines from Adrian's cellar and Sue seemed to have been given enough bathing products to last her until the next Christmas!

Her children had bought her a new laptop which she had craved; her writing was going really well. Dally had enjoyed Christmas too but on the drive home slept tiredly. Yana stopped at the cottage but decided not to go in as she had her last week in A & E then off to her first Practice placement in Pulborough, West Sussex. Having hugged each other Yana waited to see Sue and Dally go into the cottage and then she drove off.

Sue looked at Dally. "Just the two of us again Dal," she said as she turned off the downstairs lights and they both somewhat tiredly went up the stairs to their bed. Dally's bed was in the corner of Sue's bedroom and with one bound she was in it and curled up tightly. Sue laughed to herself thinking not for the first time that there is no bed like your own.

Chapter 24

Kurt had a rotten Christmas. Several of the staff had invited him to join them but he never believed it was a good idea to socialise too much with them. Business and pleasure could at times make for complications. Daniella and Milo, who were spending Christmas together, also asked him to join them. He made some excuses about being elsewhere which fooled neither of them and in the end he spent Christmas alone surrounded he felt, by numerous, meaningless cards and a few gifts from staff, friends and pupils. The card from Yana, made him mad, the message of just 'best wishes', and of course making no mention of Lily and the accident which after all she had clearly spelt out in her abject letter of apology; which unbeknown to her, he had never received. As far as he was concerned no apologies, and no explanations as to her non-appearance at the picnic.

Sue's Christmas card and long letter arrived after Christmas. She wrote copiously apologising for not corresponding much lately and explaining Lily's slow but steady progress although still wheel chair bound, but bright and positive, which after such a terrible accident was amazing. She explained how she had stayed there for quite a while and how the family doctors Lucy and Yana had been such a support. She also enclosed her first published children's book, signed of course!

He read and re-read the bit about Lily. Kurt realised she had no idea he wasn't fully informed about the accident. He felt a pang of guilt – was it perhaps the reason for her precipitous departure.

But he still couldn't understand why she had not been in touch, either at the time or at any time. He decided to write to Sue and find out exactly what happened.

The school term started badly with a Muslim boy being beaten up. Despite a whole school assembly, no one owned up to it, and the boy still seriously hurt in hospital, was in no condition to be cross questioned. The police seemed to be dragging their heels and on a visit to the boy's parents Kurt found himself defending the police although his every instinct told him something was amiss.

He decided to go back to his hometown where he knew the Chief of Police. When the previous man had retired he had been replaced by a Muslim which, of course, was not viewed very positively by some in the Town. Kurt thought there was a chance he might be helpful.

The new man was friendly and receptive and heard him out. He was non-committal in his response and could offer no firm answer to Kurt's concerns. However, he did say he would make enquiries and it made Kurt feel slightly better in that he had at least aired his concerns to someone he knew quite well and trusted.

The winter days dragged on. Kurt couldn't wait for the spring. He felt he needed the colour and smell of flowers and hoped the new spring would give his own self a spring too.

******

Yana was having a ball – her own words to Sue. She loved the Practice in Pulborough. The doctors were caring towards their patients. Even telephoning one or two of them to check how things had been whilst the doctor had been on holiday. She worked hard, but thrived on it, having more sleep than she had for years was an added bonus. She enjoyed home visits although they were discouraged by her 'boss'. She, however, felt some of the particularly frail elderly and a few of the young mums with no transport and several small children were deserved of a visit.

Night calls were fairly rare and the four of them did a week each in rotation. Because Pulborough was a little remote, on call doctors might have to travel quite a distance and Dr Griffiths, the head medic, felt the calls, when they happened were better dealt with 'in house'.

It was all Yana had dreamed about, particularly as the six months drew to a close and they asked her if she would like to become a junior partner. Her mind though, was tending towards other directions. She decided she needed a few days with Sue. She had a week's leave due and Sue, having received Yana's call bustled about happy as a sand boy. Yana was going to be home for a week. Her head was filled with plans – so much so that she hardly noticed Dally was particularly quiet.

Half an hour before Yana was due she decided to take her much loved dog for a quick walk in the woods. She had been slower of late, no longer chasing rabbits but quietly pottering, and enjoying the scents. She called and when Dally didn't come trotting to her she went into the kitchen,

Dally lay very still. She looked at Sue her eyes full of love. "Oh Dally, darling Dally, don't die." Dally put her unusually dry nose against her mistress's hand. She gave what sounded like a little sigh and she was gone.

Yana found them. Sue with Dally in her arms sobbing as she held the still warm body against her. Gently Yana eased Sue's hands from around the dog. "She's gone Sue darling." Sue nodded, sobbing and unable to speak. Quietly and firmly Yana led Sue to the sitting room. Once there she fetched a small glass of brandy and gave it to Sue. "I have no one Yana, no one." It was not the time to argue – to tell her she had a loving family and grandchildren. Yana just held her and after a while they talked and a calmer Sue asked Yana to call the vet.

With Dally on the way to the pet crematorium with a promise that the ashes would be returned for burial in a day or two; Yana collected Dally's bed and put it at the far end of the garage. That night she slept with Sue in the large bed where they talked at intervals during a long night for both of them.

By morning Sue had herself under control. She started to apologise and Yana stopped her immediately. Over breakfast Sue was chatting about her plans for the week ahead and perhaps they could visit some rescue centre like Dog's Trust, and find a dog that needed a good home.

Yana seemed a little distracted, and after a while Sue realised that although the girl was paying polite attention to what she was saying, her mind was obviously elsewhere.

Sue stopped mid-sentence and Yana barely seemed to notice. "Come on darling – spill the beans.

What is going on in that head of yours?" Yana looked relieved, she needed to talk and Lucy was so busy these days with family, and almost full-time work at the hospital. A sudden idea struck her.

"Sue come with me to Bosnia. I am going there for all sorts of reasons." Sue looked amazed,

"You want me to come?"

"Definitely!" She then explained to Sue what she had been thinking for the last few months. Milo's idea was not as mad as it might seem. The house was ready. Daniella had written to say the curtains looked lovely. The gardener had been encouraged to plant lots of spring bulbs. Yana told Sue all about the house, even talking about the crib and the little bear Mishkin that she always kept with her. She talked of Milo and his retirement plans and his proposal that she take over his Practice.

Sue was flabbergasted. The thought of Yana being so far away was horrible. "I suppose I could always keep house for you," she laughed.

"You know that's not such a bad idea!" Yana laughed too, glad that Sue was perking up again.

That evening the diaries were bought out and plans were made. Sue felt more excited than she had for ages. This sounded like a real adventure. Diaries agreed, Yana returned to West Sussex to say she needed time to think the junior partnership through, and also to arrange to be away prior to making a decision. Fortunately, Dr Griffiths was relaxed about her taking her time and with his blessing she and Sue left for Bileljina.

It was Daniella who told Kurt Yana was arriving in a few days. Milo had received an email to that effect and although Daniella did not know the contents of the letter she knew that Milo was pleased. The major news for Kurt though, was that Yana was bringing her English mother. He felt this was very positive and although on tender hooks re his relationship, or lack of it with Yana he really looked forward to meeting the lady who had written him so many charming and informative letters over the last years. He had developed a fondness for her over time, it would he thought, be so great to meet her at last.

He had no idea where he stood with Yana and how he really felt. There were times when he felt she was the only woman for him – and times when he almost hated her.

There was so much history between them and between the two families.

143

Chapter 25

Yana felt so proud of her country. This time she had bought a car, a silver Volkswagen. Perhaps she thought on reflection, she should have hired again but as she proposed to visit her homeland regularly it seemed good sense to her to have her own car. If Sue was surprised, she kept it to herself.

Spring was breaking through, wild flowers growing in hedgerows were abundant. A small Inn where they paused for lunch, was welcoming and friendly. They stopped at the bridge where Yana had stood so pensively on her first visit. Together, mother and daughter watched the glistening water gently flowing by before returning to the car for the last part of the drive.

There were lights on in the house, and when they went in warmth emanated from the old stove. Spring nights could turn cold and the welcome warmth was enjoyed by both women.

A fresh bowl of flowers was beautifully arranged on the round dining table, the one that Kurt had 'rescued' from the cellar. The newly made curtains hung, generously full, at the windows. The soft lighting Kurt had installed when the house was re-wired, made for a cosy atmosphere and Sue was enchanted.

Yana, sensing this, and wanting to see for herself how the new furniture and curtains looked suggested they do a tour. Everything was better than Yana expected. A lamp shone in each bedroom. The beds were all made up with the new duvets and linen. "Daniella has been busy," she exclaimed happily.

Finally, they climbed to the former attic. A bedside lamp was a light on either side of the large double bed. Full red and gold curtains hung at the windows and matching cushions made the comfortable chair placed by a window, which looked down on the garden particularly inviting.

Curiously, Sue opened the door into the new bathroom. Soft white towels hung on the rails near the washbasin. A thick white bathmat was on the floor by the glazed enclosed shower. "It's gorgeous, isn't it Yana?" Yana nodded. She loved her new bedroom. It was hard to imagine it had once been a dark and gloomy unused storage place. Kurt had been so clever, she thought, to have the extra window and the bathroom. It had transformed the space completely.

The two women returned to the floor below. "You have a choice Sue, the front double room or the back single!" Without hesitation, Sue choose the back bedroom. Although it was dark and she was unable to see the garden, she knew from what Yana had said that this room not only overlooked the garden but with a view up to the hills too.

Yana left Sue 'ooing' and 'aahing' and fetched their bags upstairs. "Coffee?" she asked. "Or something stronger?"

To Sue the bed looked so inviting. "Just bed I think darling. If you don't mind." They kissed goodnight and Yana returned downstairs. Walking over to the stove, she touched it gingerly. It was warm, not hot but she felt a serenity standing there. It was as if her mother and father were welcoming her homecoming.

They breakfasted quite late. Yana had been out to buy fresh bread and milk and had of course bumped into Daniella at the bakery. She had hard work getting away from her as she wanted to be sure everything at the house met expectations. She admitted to being the person responsible for the flowers, lighting and heating. "It was a perfect welcome Daniella dear. It really was."

Daniella looked delighted. "That's all I wanted," she bubbled happily.

Sue was downstairs wearing a light cotton dressing gown fussing over cups in the kitchen. The smell of the hot bread hurried the coffee making along and soon they were sitting in the garden enjoying the warm bread spread thickly spread with some home-made jam Sue had secreted in her case. They talked as they relaxed enjoying each other's company and planned the day ahead.

Yana had a meeting arranged with Milo at two pm but until then she wanted to show Sue around the neighbourhood probably unavoidably introducing her to Daniella en route. Then a light salad lunch in the garden before going to her meeting.

After her shower, Sue had a closer look around 'her' floor. The double room next to hers had obviously been the original main bedroom. She noticed the entwined Ms and wondered why Yana had not chosen to use this room; but of course, the attic room was so charming too.

They had a happy morning wandering around bumping into a number of people who greeted Yana warmly. Daniella had been spreading the word that she might be coming home. That she was a doctor too. Yana couldn't but remember her first visit with Lucy, how different her reception had been then – almost bordering on hostility at times. With hindsight she realised that some of the attitudes had been caused by embarrassment and even in some cases fear.

The town had gone through hell in living memory as well as those with guilty consciences. Now, on this lovely spring day it almost seemed like a different town. The market stalls were out in the main square and Sue was enchanted with the place, but extremely frustrated that she was unable to communicate.

After lunch whilst Sue sat sipping a second coffee in the garden Yana walked slowly to Milo's. Her mind was in a kind of turmoil. The warmth of her welcome back had unsettled her. Her home here. The offer of the partnership in Pulborough nagged her. It would be so easy to live there – she had even looked at some properties, and her current landlord was encouraging her to continue renting the cottage she had taken on a six month lease.

She stood outside Milo's house looking at the adjacent surgery linked by a corridor from the house. The house was not on offer. Milo hadn't decided yet whether to stay in it or move somewhere smaller. The Surgery was easy walking distance from her 'home'. It could actually work. Her language was now totally fluent and her medical qualifications only needed ratification.

It was a major decision but she would be so far away from the family, her English family who were the most important people in her life.

Milo opened the door. "Do you plan to stand there much longer?" he enquired genially. "Or are you planning to ring the bell." He spoke with a smile on his face and she had a feeling he understood her turmoil.

She followed him into the house and through the door that led to the Surgery. "Best talk business in here," he nodded in the direction of one of the comfortable leather chairs. Yana sat, feeling incredibly nervous – almost as if she were a student again...

They sat in silence, each waiting for the other to begin, then they both spoke at once, which released the tension and made them both laugh.

It was easier after that; Milo of course wanted to know her decision. Yana wanted to know so many things. Would she be acceptable to the local people? Could she work alongside him for a while. When exactly did he propose to fully retire. "My sixty-fifth birthday is next week, the eighth. I would like to retire as soon as possible and yes I would be prepared to work together for a short period, say three months for you to adjust, acclimatise etc."

Was that some kind of portent or what, Yana was thinking. Sue's birthday was the same day and she would be sixty five too. Yana was not a fatalist – but it seemed like a good omen to her.

They talked for two hours, discussing advances in medicine. Yana's ideas and Milo's regrets. There were always regrets in family medicine – babies who die at birth or earlier, babies handicapped. Elderly folk becoming so dependent on their families or friends. Advances in treating dementia and the longevity of the population in general. They both agreed longevity was great but more must be done to support families caring for the elderly.

By the end of two hours they had formed a comfortable relationship, though Yana had yet to make a final decision, there was so much to think about. She told Milo she would let him know within a few days.

Milo saw her off with some regret, he had enjoyed his afternoon and he felt confident she would slip right back into life there as if she had never left. He hoped she would make the right choice both for her and for him...

Yana was quiet and a little withdrawn over dinner that evening. Sue had cooked chicken with her special garlic sauce which she knew Yana enjoyed. Tonight, though Yana picked at her food and finally Sue could contain herself no longer. "Come on Yana, spill the beans." As if to belie her slightly jokey tone she laid a hand over Yana's and gave a gentle squeeze. Yana's eyes filled with tears.

"Oh, Sue I am so torn – you have no idea." Sue waited patiently, smiling encouragingly at her 'daughter' and squeezing her hand gently again.

"Tell me," she said.

Yana told her about the conversation with Milo, even smiling as she mentioned that he shared his birthday with her, Sue. She explained that she felt drawn here despite herself. Yet everyone she loved, especially you Sue would be so far away. "There is no one here," she concluded.

"I could always visit for several months at a time," Sue countered. "Providing I am at home for Easter and Christmas, and you could come back for those and other family occasions. My life in England can sometimes be rather lonely. I have never said this out loud before, perhaps never even let myself admit it – but it is true."

Yana looked aghast. Why had it not occurred to her – to any of them. Sue was always so lively, so happy to see them, yet unbeknownst she had been lonely. "Sue if you would come for several months a year, in fact all the time as far as I am concerned it would make me so happy and make my decision so much easier."

They talked then, the two of them until the early hours of the morning. Yana would take over when Milo retired but would expect him to be around, at least part of the time for the first six months. Finally, with warm hugs and as the early morning birdsong started they said their good nights.

Sue lay in bed trying to imagine life divided between home and here. How strange that she would be living in a town where the little Yana had arrived from. Her mind drifted back over years to Michael's telephone call. She remembered strapping the unhappy, tear stained little girl into Bear's car seat. Talking softly knowing that not one word was understood. Only soft tones reassured the child who looked with such bewilderment at all the new faces at The Old Rectory.

They were happy days though and Yana had learned quickly. 'please and thank you' and the names of the family. She was terrified at first of Abby, the little black cocker spaniel, but Abby seemed to sense this and would lie quietly on the floor waiting for this new little person to become braver and make the first move. Sue smiled remembering the first time she found Yana on the floor with her arms 'round the patient dog. She couldn't tell who was the happiest. Abby who was enjoying the affection she always craved or Yana, who missing her little bear had found a small black dog to cuddle instead.

Yana, Sue remembered had never cried, but if she didn't like the food she was given she would just close her mouth very firmly. They soon found she liked spicy things and roast peppers and garlic were an early favourite that Lily, Lucy and Rupert as he was called then turned their noses up at.

From the beginning Yana and Lucy seemed to form a special bond and there were many mornings when she had found Lucy in Yana's bed, her arms wrapped protectively around the little girl as they slept.

They were such happy days, but they were over. Michael would want her to try a new kind of life, she was sure. Still thinking of Michael, she drifted off to sleep with a smile on her lips.

Chapter 26

Daniella invited Yana and Sue for dinner. It happened to be Sue's birthday and, at first, she was reluctant to accept thinking Sue might prefer to do something else. However, Sue was thrilled as she had by now met Daniella several times and although her English was very rusty and Sue's Bosnian was non-existent, they seemed to have formed a friendship.

Saying nothing to her other guest, Daniella invited Milo and Kurt. It was, she knew, Milo's birthday too and it would make a real occasion of it if it was more of a party. Kurt was not told about the other guests and as he had the occasional dinner with Daniella he accepted happily.

It was going to be a great evening Daniella promised herself buying her meat and fish carefully. Fish soup then her special boiled beef. For dessert she decided on a chocolate cake which she ordered from the local bakery.

Once she had it home, she wrote 'Milo' and then 'Sue' in white icing and put two candles on it; one for each of them. It was all rather childish, she knew that, but birthdays were special, weren't they she rationalised.

Sue's birthday started early with phone calls from Lucy, Lily, Bear and the grandchildren. Yana had been entrusted with the presents and Sue opened them in surprised delight. A new pashmina from Lucy and Peter, plus a home-made card from the children. Lily and Paul had sent a small brooch with small seed pearls around the edge. Amy had made a tray cloth and Andy a small carved boat. Bear and Chantelle had sent a card with a token for the local garden centre.

Finally, Yana handed over her gift, a small jewellery box containing a pair of earrings that Sue had admired on one of their several visits to Povia.

"What a lovely morning," Sue exclaimed happily. "Not just the gifts. They are special too, of course, but talking to the whole family and," she added, "you making it so special too Yana dear."

Later that morning, Yana took Sue for a walk. She wanted to show Sue the beautiful waterfall and more especially 'her' rock, as she always thought of it. She stopped at the rock and as ever let her fingers feel the carved M's. She sat down suddenly putting her face in her hands. Sue sat down too, and put her arm around Yana. "Whatever is it," she asked.

"Oh, my God," Yana repeated, remembering the picnic she had missed. Remembering the brief note she had scrawled and sent by way of apology several days after the event, not even bothering to check whether she had the address properly. "He must have been up here, waiting for me."

At this point Sue decided that silence was golden, later when Yana had things back in perspective she would explain that Kurt knew about the accident. He had been very bitter until he found out the facts from Sue in their letter exchange, and even now couldn't quite believe she had never written. Her letter sent in such haste having never found him due to the incorrect details on the envelope.

Sue dressed carefully for the dinner party at Daniella's. She wore her pale, coffee-coloured silk palazzo trousers with a cream blouse and narrow belt showing off her still trim waist. Wearing a rose silk scarf draped over her shoulders and her new brooch and earrings she felt quite acceptable!

Yana told her she looked lovely and she returned the compliment. Yana's hair shone and her Armani suit looked what it was, simple and quality. "You look wonderfully elegant as ever." Sue said giving her a gentle kiss on the cheek. "Three women spending an evening together and look at the trouble we've taken," They laughed happily.

They walked arm in arm chatting easily as they walked to Daniella's home. Yana knocked on the door and within seconds a beaming Daniella welcomed them in.

Milo stood up as they walked in, and if Yana and Sue were surprised to see him, he was bowled over by the two contrasting, but equally beautiful women. "Milo, how nice," Yana said introducing Sue to the doctor. "My English Mother, Milo. A very special person."

"I can tell," he responded taking the outstretched hand and shaking it firmly. Sue felt a little shiver. His look seemed to see more than felt comfortable, and feeling herself unusually reserved with him, she started an animated conversation about nothing in particular with Daniella.

Sue spoke more quickly than usual and Daniella understood about one word in three, but she sensed a need in Sue to be with her so she invited her into the kitchen thankful she had hidden the cake well away!

Another knock at the door surprised Yana and when she went to open it, her hostess having disappeared with Sue; Kurt stood there carrying a large bouquet of flowers. They were equally surprised to see each other. "The flowers are not for you."

"I didn't suppose they were," she replied turning away from him and heading back to Milo.

It was a strange evening. Daniella sat herself at the top of the table with Milo on her right and Kurt on her left. Sue sat next to Kurt and Yana next to Milo. One side of the table behaved as if the other side barely existed. Sue and Kurt in deep and animated conversation. Yana and Milo talking to each other and Daniella.

The dinner was delicious – although asked the following day what they had eaten, probably only Daniella, who had prepared it could say. Milo kept glancing at Sue and Sue caught his eye from time to time and immediately became even more engrossed with Kurt whom she found utterly charming.

Finally, it was dessert. Daniella bustled out to her kitchen and Yana carried out the remainder of the used plates out in time to see Daniella lighting two candles. "How lovely, Daniella. A birthday cake for Sue."

"For Sue and Milo. They are both sixty-five today." For some reason it seemed hilariously funny and they collapsed against each other trying to laugh quietly. Finally, getting themselves under control, they walked in stately file. Daniella first, carrying the cake, followed by Yana with the plates. As they walked they sang 'Happy birthday to you. Happy birthday to you. Happy birthday, Sue and Milo, happy birthday to you'.

Everyone clapped and cheered – Milo and Sue meeting each other's eyes for the first time since their introduction. Daniella put the cake in the middle of the table and turned the lights lower.

The two candles burned brightly. "Both of you blow," she said in English. "Blow and wish."

Milo and Sue inclined their heads towards the cake, the candles fluttered and went out. More cheers and Daniella raised the lights again and cut her guests a piece of cake. It broke the ice at last and the rest of the evening was jolly and convivial. Neither Sue nor Milo could get over sharing not only the same birthday, but the same year too.

In all their conversations in the earlier part of the evening, Sue explained more clearly why Yana had missed the picnic. He had heard about the accident of course, in one of Sue's letters but he had not connected the two events. Now he could kick himself for being so pig-headed.

Kurt caught Yana's eye and smiled. Slightly uncertainly she smiled back. The exchange did not go unnoticed by Sue who felt quietly pleased with herself – a special birthday after all. The family telephone calls this morning, all the thoughtful gifts including the brooch and earrings she was wearing tonight, a lovely dinner party, that wasn't over yet.

They moved into the sitting room for coffee and brandy. "What are your thoughts?" Milo enquired in his formal English. "You look happy!"

"I was thinking how fortunate I am to have such a loving family," she answered.

A slight shadow seemed to cross Milo's face. "You are indeed fortunate."

Once again, linking arms Yana and Sue returned to number twenty-five. Yana never said the word 'home' always referring to the 'the house' or the number. Sue thought she understood. It would take time for it to become home.

The next morning when they got up for breakfast, an envelope lay on the floor. Yana somehow expected it would be for her but very clearly written on the envelope was the name 'Sue'.

When Sue came downstairs for breakfast, the envelope was propped up against her coffee cup. She looked surprised and sat down to open it, looking first at the signature. Milo! *Excuse me addressing you so informally*, it began; *but I do not know you married name.*

Last evening, he wrote, *it was a pleasure meeting you and to share a birthday. Daniella informs me that you like gardens and I would like to share my love of gardens with you. Will you please visit me at four o' clock today and perhaps afterwards you would allow me to take you to a favourite place of mine to enjoy a light dinner.*

Silently she handed the short letter to Yana. Yana read it and handed it back. "You'll go?" Sue shrugged imperceptibly. "Should I?"

"Why not."

"Why not indeed," Sue smiled.

She spent the entire day wondering what to wear. It wasn't as if she had brought much with her. Never one for thinking too much about clothes, she knew what she liked. At one time she had dressed to please Michael, not that he probably ever realised. These days she dressed to please herself. Jeans and shirts in the summer and jeans and sweaters in the winter, saving proper clothes for rare outings, or smart family events, particularly when with Lily, who although still living in riding gear, though not riding now, expected her mother to 'dress up', her phraseology, when Meg and Adrian were involved at family occasions. Sue even wore jeans when she met with her Agent re her children's stories.

Finally, she decided to wear part of what she had worn the previous evening. The palazzo pants but this time with a tank top and light loose jacket that she had bought at the same time and worked as an alternative. Over one shoulder she hung her new pashmina and she wore the double string of pearls given to her by Michael many years ago.

Exactly five minutes before she was due there, she kissed Yana goodbye and feeling somewhat nervous, quickly completed the walk to Milo's home. The house a lovely square building, pointed out to her by Yana earlier that day looked welcoming with its pathway to the front door. The flower beds on either side of the path were a riot of colour.

Sue noticed the double front doors painted green though faded by the sun and shutters at all the windows the paint work equally faded but so attractive giving the house quite a French feel.

Before she could raise her hand to the large brass knocker, one of the doors opened and Milo stood there greeting her in a friendly manner. They shook hands and talking as they went he led her into his garden. Sue couldn't help but gasp. It was such a wonderful profusion of flowers and colour. Heady smelling lilies grew in large drifts. Agapanthus in blues and whites intermingling with alliums with their purple heads and in various varieties. Daffodils almost over, but their leaves providing swathes of green among the other colours. Everywhere she looked there was form and colour. "Would you like to…?" Milo indicated she might like to walk down the garden. Sue was in her element. She walked through honey suckled archways enjoying spotting an early clematis that was one of her favourites.

"It's enchanting," she breathed, her nervousness forgotten.

"I heard you liked gardens," Milo smiled happily. "Perhaps you can help me with one corner I've never been able to organise. Following a path, they arrived at a shady sloping bank. Tall trees also making it an impossible place to plant up.

"Water," Sue said spontaneously.

"Water?" Milo was intrigued.

"It's a good slope – place rocks strategically and have a small waterfall tumbling down into a little pond at the bottom. You could have water lilies and marsh buttercups, it could look lovely I believe…" she finished a bit lamely afraid she had been over enthusiastic.

Milo clapped his hands in delight. "My dear Sue, that is splendid – we shall drink to your splendid idea."

They walked back the way they had come and sat at a wrought iron table where a bottle of wine was keeping cool in a wine cooler. "Daniella gave me this for my birthday; I thought I should try it out with my birthday partner!"

Sue sank into the comfortable looking wicker chair and took a glass from her host. At least, she thought, if nothing else, they could talk about gardens all evening. They didn't need to, somehow the evening turned out to be easy and enjoyable. Indeed, as she confided the next morning to Yana.

One of the most pleasant evenings she had spent in a long time. She hadn't been out for dinner alone, with a man since Michael and later, much later when she lay in bed thinking over the evening she felt Michael would have approved.

155

After the glass of wine, they had driven to a small village about eight miles away. A modest restaurant, looking from the outside like a private house turned out to be a delightful venue. Only open three evenings a week – serving a limited but excellent menu. Clearly, a favourite haunt of Milo's and they were both warmly welcomed.

For a while they sat in the garden, then when their starter was ready they moved indoors. Sue was not sorry, for the air was already turning a little chill and indoors the inevitable stove threw out a welcome warmth.

Dinner was perfect. A cold soup followed by grilled fish accompanied by small steamed potatoes and a delicious salad. She declined dessert and instead enjoyed a strong coffee and a small brandy.

Now lying in bed looking out of the window at the star strewn sky, she found herself smiling in the darkness. He, Milo, had been gallant and charming and surprisingly easy to be with. He had been surprised when she had told him Michael had been a doctor. "That was how we found Yana," she told him. He told her about Anna and how she had developed pre-senile dementia. It was hard for him to work and look after her properly so he had employed a full time nurse / housekeeper who was with them until Anna died.

"She didn't know me for years," Milo had explained to Sue, "Until just before she died she looked straight at me and said 'Milo'. She hadn't spoken for several years and I could hardly take it in. It was as if she wanted to say a proper goodbye." They were both quiet for a few minutes then Sue told him about the accident. The suddenness of Michael's death had been so hard to accept," she explained. "She had kept expecting him to walk through the door and hug her like he always had."

It was good to talk, Sue decided, they probably both needed to, and afterwards, when talk about Michael and Anna was over they talked books and films and travel, coming back to gardens at intervals as they discussed the pleasures as well as the vicissitudes.

"Michael, I love you," she whispered to the darkened room. She felt a warmth as if he was near her, then, as suddenly as it had been there, that feeling, it was gone. It was as if he was saying a final, loving goodbye.

******

Kurt telephoned twice, each time asking Yana to meet him. Sue was her excuse on both occasions and Kurt read correctly between the lines, and didn't call again.

After a few days with no call Yana felt aggrieved, he really shouldn't be put off quite so easily. The few weeks sped by and it was time to pack their things and reload the car. Sue had been out twice more with Milo and they were now kissing hello and goodbye on the cheek. She told him she wasn't sure when she was coming back as it was rather up to Yana's plans, but she did plan to spend about two months a year with Yana when she moved.

Milo had to be content with that although he felt time was not 'on their side', he was also aware that Sue was not going to be rushed into anything. He had lived as a bachelor for a number of years now he knew he could be patient, though he had felt a stirring in his loins unknown for a long time.

On the journey home they talked of everything except Kurt and Milo. Yana was due back in Pulborough to explain that she would not be taking up their offer of a junior partnership. The cottage she rented would have to be packed up and cleaned and before she left the country she planned to spend time with each of her foster siblings and their families.

Sue's cottage seemed orderly, quiet and lonely. After Yana drove off, she automatically unpacked and put a load of washing in the machine. There were welcome home messages on the answerphone, but no dog to collect or take for walks.

It was midday so she decided to go for a walk in the woods anyway, but realised after a few minutes that she had made a mistake. With no Dally to call – or come bounding delightedly up to her, it was simply not the same.

Her thoughts turned to Bosnia, of Danielle, Kurt and Milo too of course. She was aware she had kept him slightly at a distance and now rather regretted it. She had sensed he wanted to move forwards and in hindsight she realised, to her surprise, that she would have liked to have felt his arms around her. She missed the tenderness of lovemaking and the closeness lovers share. There would never be anyone to take Michael's place but

157

she realised there was a place in her life for the right man and perhaps, just perhaps, Milo was he.

When she arrived back from her very short walk, the telephone was ringing. For a moment she thought it was 'him', but instead it was Kurt, full of apologies for not saying goodbye and insisting she must return soon. "We are all missing you Sue."

"Who is all?" she enquired innocently.

"Why myself, Daniella and of course Milo." They talked for a few minutes then said their goodbyes. Sue was smiling again. It was nice to be missed.

Chapter 27

Lucy couldn't believe what she was hearing from Yana. Not only was she going back to Bosnia but she was giving up her chance of a partnership in Pulborough. "Why?" she demanded.

"It's what I've always wanted," Yana smiled. "Luce, you know it's what I've always wanted and to have the opportunity to be a community doctor, where better than where I was born," Lucy exploded.

"Where your mother was raped and murdered. Where your father and brother were killed. I just don't understand you; and how dare you encourage Mum to come with you."

Yana was sobered. Lucy hadn't even listened. Sue was only coming for a month or two each year.

For the first time there was a gulf between the two girls and Yana was glad she hadn't mentioned her plans earlier, she had at least had five lovely days with Lucy, Peter, Leila and Louisa.

Lucy and Yana parted with the strain still between them, and the moment Yana had driven away, Lucy telephoned her mother.

Sue found the conversation both bewildering and hurtful. Yana had made it so clear how much she would love her foster mother to spend a month or two a year with her. She, after all, saw so little of Lily and Lucy these days – their lives were so busy. Lucy with her work at the hospital and all the clinics she had plus her family.

Lily with her new coaching classes on top of the other programmes; and, she still walked with a stick. So apart from the Easter Holidays when she had all the grandchildren and Christmas when they all got together there were long gaps when she hardly saw them.

Bear and Chantelle came for a long weekend every half term, but their main holidays were spent in France where Chantelle's parents had a holiday home in Royan.

By the time Yana arrived at Lily and Paul's, Lily had already been acquainted with her mother's plan. She couldn't understand why Lucy was so upset and told Yana it was a 'bloody good idea'.

"I know Mum is lonely these days," she told Lucy. "She either needs to move into town and make a new circle of friends or spend time with Yana in Bosnia. Since she moved to the cottage she is too remote from most of her old friends – that's partly the trouble – and missing Dad of course."

It silenced Lucy, perhaps she had been unreasonable, perhaps even a bit of a guilty conscience. She knew, she didn't see as much of her mother as she should. Lucy didn't bother to telephone Bear. She would leave it to her mother to tell him her plans.

Yana had a great time with Lily. She was impressed with her will and determination which was all that had got her where she was physically. Andy and Amy had developed into super kids Yana thought, and despite Lily's total lack of interest in them as babies now as 'people' they seemed to have a great time together.

Amy was besotted with her ponies and Andy, whose hero was still Uncle Bear, was determined to follow his uncle into County then, National cricket.

Yana said her goodbyes feeling closer to Lily than she had ever felt and only sad that there was still tension between her and Lucy.

Next stop she thought, driving through a light summer shower towards Marlborough, to see Bear and Chantelle. Their house was just outside the College grounds and provided a home for junior boys. She drove up the drive and parked near a garage. Taking her overnight case with her she walked towards the front entrance.

Chantelle had heard the car on the gravel and was already waiting with the door open. "Come in quickly Yana, out of the rain." Yana loved the way she talked with the lightest of French accents it seemed a charming part of her personality. The two young women hugged. "Rupert will be here soon. He take the preparation now with the little boys." Yana loved the way she said Rupert sounding like Rupaire, and was the only member of the family who did not call him Bear, but somehow that seemed right for the two of them.

Yana followed Chantelle into the pretty little kitchen and when Bear arrived they were deep in conversation either side of the kitchen table.

"Yana, so great to see you." Bear gave her a warm hug. "You two look as if you have put the world to rights. You were talking so much I could hear the non-stop rattle as I walked down the hall."

Yana thumped him good-naturedly then sat down again with Bear now sitting beside her. The children came in with the au pair. They had been to the park, and suddenly the kitchen was full of noise. Yana looked from face to face, this 'family life' was what she had loved as a child, and now as the years passed, she wondered if she would ever find this sort of happiness.

The au pair stayed in the kitchen to start getting the children's tea while Bear, Chantelle and Yana moved into the sitting room. They wanted all her news. Yana told them of her future plans in Bosnia. She also explained Sue's wishes and Lucy's reservations.

Bear listened gravely, nodding from time to time. Finally, he told her that if this is what she wanted to do – perhaps even felt called to do – then of course she had his and Chantelle's blessing; providing of course, they could come and visit her there. "Lucy will come round," he added with a smile. "You two have always been so close, and she will realise it's a marvellous opportunity for our mother." Yana felt an enormous sense of relief. Bear was right, Lucy would come round.

******

Sue heard the post drop through the letter box. As she picked up several items, fashion and gardening magazines and a couple of letters she couldn't help but think of Dally who used to rush to the door at the sound of post and bark at the postman. Putting on the kettle for coffee she started going the post. Noticing the letter with the foreign stamp she presumed it was from Kurt. It was not his writing, perhaps Daniella she thought slitting the envelope open.

My dear Sue, the letter began. She turned the sheet over to look at the signature. Milo! The exclamation was hers. How strange, but nice she thought, continuing to read. *My dear Sue,* she read again.

By now you will be home in the delightful English cottage you described with its low beamed ceilings and special fireplace that has a 'nook'. I think you called it that. (he means inglenook, she smiled to herself). Where will you be when you read this? Sitting in your bedroom overlooking your very English cottage garden. Or perhaps by your English style stove I believe called an Aga.

You will be wondering why I am writing to you, and so soon after you have left here. I feel nervous, like a young man and yet it is because I am not a young man any more, that I write to you in this way. (Sue smiled again. His English was correct and yet slightly different and rather charmingly old fashioned. She continued reading).

When we met Sue, I believed, felt, there was a certain frisson between us. We talked easily together did we not? We laughed together and found a love of gardening and music. Sue if I was forty-five not sixty-five, and you were also forty-five then I would perhaps not have the courage to write this way.

I can never be your Michael. You can never be my Anna, but we can start a new life together; a life of Sue and Milo. I am asking you Sue, to marry me.

I can imagine you gasping (she did) *– but you see every day NOW is more precious than it was twenty years ago when we took the continuation of our lives as our right and due.*

It is, I know a big step – for you particularly – but I know you plan to be near Yana for several months every year. This way you will be near her always and the rest of your family can fill this big old house as often as they would like. Also of course you would go to see them, perhaps taking me with you to see your so English cottage.

I want to put my arms around you. I want to feel your arms around me. Can you find it in your heart to consider, most carefully, what I have written, every word is written with my whole heart.

With love, sincerely yours,
Milo.

Sue put the letter on the table, coffee forgotten. What a surprise. Though was it really. There had been a frisson – but was that enough. She didn't feel like she did about Michael – but then he had pointed that out. He didn't feel about her as he had felt about Anna.

She read the letter through again. Her mind was racing. He was so right, they were both lonely.

True, they didn't have time to waste. Loneliness was not the reason for a relationship, but it was a consideration if the relationship was right for all the other reasons.

On a sudden whim she decided to drive the thirty miles or so to The Old Rectory. For some reason, she felt the answer might come to her, seeing the place again. She hadn't been back before, and now, as she parked in the lane that passed by the lower paddock she could look through the gate and up to the house.

Children darted about on the lawn. Putting her window down, she could hear shrieks of childish laughter. She heard a steady ping, ping, and realised the tennis court was in use. Out of sight from where she was parked, her mind though had a lovely image of times past. She sighed a deep sigh, not an unhappy one more a reflection. The time for The Old Rectory was in her past now a new family was living their lives there, happy ones too by the sound of things. She smiled as she heard a good-natured curse coming from the direction of the tennis court.

Time to move on in every way. "Goodbye house. Goodbye my dearest Michael," she whispered to herself as she put on one of her favourite Mozart CDs and drove off feeling a contentment she hadn't felt for a while. Her mind was made up, she would not exactly rush, but she would not drag her heels either, Milo's words running through her mind as she drove.

The next day found her at her computer. She had decided to send an identical email to all three of her children. To tell Lucy of her plans would not be easy as there was still a tension between them.

Lily would just say 'great idea' and get on with her own hectic life. Bear – now Bear would be different. He would want to know if she was sure. If she really believed she could be happy living with a man she had met so recently and in a country where the language was fairly incomprehensible!

Thinking of Bear thinking that, brought Sue up with a jolt. Language! She would have to learn the language and learn enough before she married Milo.

The letter was not an easy one to write, and a number of go's later she thought perhaps she had found the words she needed. It was addressed to all of her children, including Yana of course.

My dear children, she wrote.

This is probably the most difficult even the most awkward letter I have ever written. I ask that you think about what I am writing very carefully, and also the reason for my writing to you rather than speaking to you individually.

You are all such wonderful and caring children no mother could have been more blessed – and no children could have had a more wonderful and loved father than yours.

You all know how happy your father and I were and how, looking back, his awful death, I felt at the time almost killed me too. I missed him so much. I will always miss him – but life moves on.

That's what kind people said to me at the time and I couldn't really believe them. But now I've realised how true it is.

Children dearest, I have received a proposal of marriage – at my age… and, after careful, very careful, consideration of the very many implications; I have decided to say yes.

At this point Sue paused. She gazed thoughtfully ahead realising she could hardly send this email without letting Milo know her answer! She carefully saved the email and looked at the telephone number on Milo's letter.

Picking up her mobile and taking a deep breath to steady herself she keyed his number. With the two-hour difference she realised it would be lunchtime there, a perfect time to get hold of him.

The phone rang several times before he answered it. It almost threw her at first as his voice speaking his mother tongue sounded different. "Milo, it's Sue," she said quickly. There was a pause.

"Sue, you have my letter?"

"Milo, thank you. I will marry you." There was another pause. Sue's heart beat faster. Had he regretted his letter. *Was he wondering how to get out of it.*

"I'm sorry, Sue. I am so happy you have taken my breath away." Sue laughed with relief. Immediately they talked easily again, Sue suggesting he come over to meet her family and to make plans.

"I have to learn your language too – there is so much to think about."

Milo smiled, he loved her enthusiasm; he equally had no doubt she would learn to speak Bosnian. Life would be more enjoyable for her if she could communicate locally. He assured he could arrange locum cover and they arranged a date, two weeks ahead for him to come over for a long weekend. After they had finished their conversation she returned to the email.

Milo – she continued, *will be in England from the fifth to the tenth of July. It will probably be too much of a squeeze here so why don't we have drinks and canapés here followed by lunch at The Golden Hen.* They would enjoy that she knew, as the G H as it was known locally, was renowned for its Sunday carvery and amazing puddings.

Without more ado she moved to the 'send' icon and the die was cast. She had signed off 'your very loving Mother'. She had never signed mother before, but somehow a modicum of formality seemed appropriate for such a missive.

How she wished she could be a fly on the wall when her family went into their emails. Lily would leave it to Paul. He always checked her emails as a matter of course. They were usually business and he dealt with that side of their life. Lucy would check her emails when the children were in bed. Bear and Chantelle, she had no idea and it didn't matter anyway, they would read it in due course.

Yana was the first to call. She was bubbling with excitement and enthusiasm. "I almost can't believe it," she said, "and yet it seems so right and so perfect. It will be amazing having you live so close. I can hardly believe it," she repeated. She finished by saying she would supply the canapés.

"Some of my choux stuffed with cheese, and some other bits too." Sue demurred, but was actually delighted. One thing less to think about…

Chantelle was next. Bear was taking some pupils on an outing, he had not seen Sue's email but Chantelle assured her, he would call her on his return home that evening. His mobile was off though Chantelle said she had tried to reach him. "It is so exciting Sue, we will get cover for the weekend and we will be there to meet your new man." She talked in quick excited sentences and her enthusiasm matched Yana's.

Paul telephoned. Lily was in the riding ring. He had been instructed to ring! He said he also told his parents Meg and Adrian who offered straight away to have a wedding reception at their home, and if Sue wanted the wedding could be in the family chapel in the grounds.

Sue felt bemused, everything was sort of happening to fast. "Please thank your parents, but we are way off plans yet," she laughed. "What does Lily think?"

"That it's a cracking idea. She doesn't envy you learning the language though. What a challenge," he laughed.

"I am going to do it, however challenging," was Sue's instant response.

Lucy didn't call that day or evening. The longer the time went on, the more Sue worried. She really did want unanimous approval. Why hadn't Lucy telephoned. That night she hardly slept and when the telephone rang at six am she nearly jumped out of her skin. "Lucy?"

"Mum, what an earth were you up to in Yana's town." To Sue's immense relief, Lucy didn't sound cross. "I'm sorry I didn't call before Mum, but I was standing in for a sick colleague and have been up all night, so only checked my emails five minutes ago before going to bed."

"You don't mind?"

"Mum darling it's your life. If you are sure and you are happy, then I am happy for you. We perhaps haven't understood how much you missed Pa. I'm sorry," she said. For being unreasonable the other day, I was overtired and crotchety when I spoke to you and Yana before. Am I forgiven?"

"It goes without saying darling."

There was so much to do. Sue rang several language schools to find out how she could do an intensive course in Serbian-Croatian which she found were quite similar languages, also she learned that Bosnian was also a language spoken there but it seemed they had strong almost interchangeable formats.

She booked herself in for a five-day intensive course in the hope that when Milo arrived she would at least have made a start. She would then restart once he had returned to Bosnia.

Going by train to London two days later, she reflected on how her life had changed. The language school had recommended a small bread and breakfast style hotel in the same street as the school. Sue wondered what it would be like. Fairly basic she presumed.

In the event it turned out to be pleasant. Clean, smallish room, nice en suite and sparkling white linen on the bed – always a good sign. Monday morning, dead on nine am found her waiting to be shown her classroom.

By lunchtime she was totally exhausted. Tutors changed every hour on the hour as she faded they appeared fresher. She began to feel more and more confused, frustrated and dim!

She seemed unable to grasp anything at some moments and repeating and repeating became ever more difficult. By five pm, with just a short break at lunchtime she almost crawled back to her hotel, and once in the bedroom telephoned Yana. "What a language," she greeted Yana with. Yana smiled remembering her early difficulties on her first visit back to Bosnia with Lucy, and at least she had some knowledge in the deep recesses of her brain. The fundamentals of basic, albeit childish memories of Serbian.

"I'll never do it." Sue wailed. "I can't possibly marry him if I can't speak the language."

"You can and you will, Sue. You have learned other languages, this will get easier and what motivation you have! Sue darling, I must go, I'm meeting someone." Then for the first time she spoke to Sue in her mother tongue, "Bogom mala majka. It means goodbye little mother."

Sue heard the click of the phone. What had Yana said? 'Bogom' was the only thing she remembered.

It meant 'goodbye'. Sue turned off her mobile, her determination grew strong again. "Bogom," she repeated, "bogom." It was the only word she remembered from a whole day of learning.

She thought back. Yana as a nearly three-year-old had been faced with English. A completely foreign sound to her. She had coped – and learned surprisingly quickly. She too would cope, and learn. Too tired to go out for dinner she resolved to have an early night and an exceedingly good breakfast before starting DAY TWO. The capital letters were written in her brain. Learn she would…

Day two started well with her extremely hearty breakfast. Knowing what to expect helped the day flow more easily. She had remembered a few things from the previous day that she hadn't realised she had taken in. Tutors came and went and Sue greeted them formally with her newly learned.

"Dobro jutro kako si?" (Good morning, how are you?)

By the end of the day she was tired, but sensibly ate on the way back to the hotel. Yana phoned. "Jutro kako si?"

"Well, thank you," Yana replied in Bosnian, then repeating what she had said in English.

Sue was thrilled. It was such a small beginning, but she had to begin somewhere. Days three, four and five sped by she now had a few days at home to prepare for the influx and Milo's arrival. She booked him a room at the hotel thinking it the most appropriate thing to do. For her, for the family and for him, too.

It was one of those idyllic July days. The garden was heaven with the roses in full bloom, the scent of sweet peas wafting in the air, and a profusion of colour where ever she looked. She was delighted that Milo would see her garden at its best.

At seven am she cut the grass, still slightly wet with dew. She trimmed the edges. Then she showered and afterwards put all the flowers she had picked for the house earlier into large and small containers as appropriate. The perfume of the philodendron filling the air throughout the cottage with their heavenly scent.

She had decided what to wear the evening before, so having done some basic chores, she pulled on her white linen skirt and red and white spotted short sleeved silk shirt; then she set off to meet Milo at Gatwick airport.

Sue didn't have to wait long after the flight landed. Milo only had hand luggage so he was quickly out through customs. He seemed to tower over everyone. *He must be six feet three or four to my five foot six,* she mused, thinking what a distinguished air he had about him as he walked towards the barrier his eyes searching for her.

Their eyes met and his face lit up with pleasure. "You are more beautiful that I remember," he said kissing her lightly on the lips for the first time. Sue felt a tingle of excitement. He took hold of her hand. "Lead the way please." So, Sue led and holding her hand lightly, he followed closely.

Down one ramp and to the car park. He put his case on the back seat and as they drove out of the airport, he looked favourably at the neat green fields and well-kept roads.

The sun was still shining and Sue was pleased that his first glimpse of England was at its best.

They stopped once for coffee and the toilet, then, talking easily as they had done when they had been together in Bosnia, they finally arrived home.

He found the cottage totally perfect. "You are prepared to leave this for me?" he asked incredulously. She showed him the downstairs and the garden which he marvelled over. "You will keep the cottage?"

"Yes," she answered thinking it would be a sanctuary, if she ever needed one. It would be a holiday home, and it would also be a solid financial investment in her name. She had thought very carefully about money. Michael's insurance had left her a comparatively wealthy widow. Her children's stories were selling well too. All those monies belonged to her and Michael's children, including Yana of course. From what she understood, Milo had no immediate family, but he could have distant cousins and perhaps other far flung relatives and she was determined her will, re done after Michael's death would remain as it was. Milo didn't need any money anyway and their two monies, she decided, should be kept separately.

Now was not the time though, to discuss it in detail. "And where do I sleep?" she detected a slightly impish tone, and looked at him sharply. "In the hotel. I thought it was better, the family and all that," she finished lamely. If Milo was disappointed, he didn't say anything and for that she was grateful.

Busying herself making some tea, putting out a lemon drizzle cake she had made earlier. She suddenly remembered she had planned to greet him in his own tongue – bother – she would surprise him later.

They had tea in the garden where bird song filled the air as they worked at collecting the last food of the day. "A perfect English evening," Milo said. "Even more perfect because we are together. Tomorrow may we go shopping?" Sue was surprised. So, unlike a man, wanting to shop.

"Of course," she replied. "There are some really good shops in Guildford."

"I only need one sort of shop, for jewels." Sue looked puzzled. "Would you not like a ring to signify we are to be married?" Sue laughed happily.

"Oh, an engagement ring. I hadn't even thought about that!"

Later they walked to the hotel, Milo pulling his small case. He checked into his room and then they had dinner in the oak-panelled dining room. He insisted on walking her home afterwards, and this time kissed her properly.

His arms were 'round her and she could feel the beat of his heart. She felt herself weakening. Perhaps she should let him stay after all. "Good night Sue," he turned and left quite suddenly, and Sue suddenly feeling bereft nearly called him back.

As arranged, he called for her at ten am and they drove into Guildford. Milo had very definite ideas. It had to be a special ring he told the jeweller in the second shop they visited. As she had no idea what he proposed to spend Sue stayed quiet until she saw a ring that made her gasp. It had a central ruby surrounded by smaller ones then edged in diamonds that formed a flower like scallop.

"You like this one?" Milo asked. Sue nodded feeling slightly embarrassed, not having any idea of the cost. When the jeweller quoted the price, she nearly fainted. So much for a ring, surely Milo wouldn't buy it. He handed over his American Express card without turning a hair. "We have to check the limit I'm afraid, sir."

"Of course you do," Milo replied equably. "Try it on for size Sue my dear and then I will find a more appropriate time to give it to you properly." Picking up the ring he handed it to her and she slid it on her finger. It fitted perfectly and looked astonishingly beautiful.

The jewellers' assistant returned with a smile from her telephone call. The jeweller nodded to her, she nodded back. *It was,* thought Sue, *all a bit theatrical!*

"Oh Madam it really does suit you," the jeweller wreathed in smiles reached for a ring box. Sue slid the ring off her finger, glad that she had put her original engagement ring on her right hand before they went shopping. That was the past. This was the future. Sue feeling somewhat still bemused they walked out into the bright sunshine. "Shall we go back to the cottage for lunch?"

"That would be delightful," Milo said, waiting while she climbed into the car before walking around and getting into the passenger seat.

Encouraged to sit in the garden while Sue quickly prepared the cold chicken and salad she had planned. Milo put his hand on the small box in his pocket thinking about how and when he would give it to Sue.

They ate in companionable silence, broken only by short sentences about the morning, the food, the cottage and the garden. Milo also commented on the staff at the hotel whom he found amazingly polite. Sue didn't argue, she had found some of the places she and Yana had stayed immaculate but sometimes not particularly friendly.

Sunday dawned. Sue was up at six thirty. Showered and hair washed, she pulled on a pair of lightweight jeans and a cool shirt. Flowers were re watered and tidied. Glasses put out, wine in the fridge to cool. She consulted her list. Canapés! Thin brown bread and butter with smoked salmon cut into small triangles. Stuffed bacon rolls with her secret ingredients of thyme, finely chopped and precooked onions, fine brown bread crumbs and some spices. Curried eggs spread on small rounds of flaky pastry which she had made before going to bed the previous evening. Now chilled it rolled perfectly.

The family were due to arrive by eleven. Ten thirty already! Sue almost flew upstairs to change into the pretty chiffony dress worn with a pair of her favourite heeled-sandals.

Lucy arrived first with Peter and the girls. Leila and Louisa greeted their grandmother with hugs and at the same time saying in unison, "And Gran, can we be bridesmaids…please…?" Sue burst out laughing.

"It's not that sort of wedding." The disappointment was painful to see. "I know darlings we'll buy you matching dresses and your cousins and you can be 'sort of' bridesmaids."

The girls were satisfied, to be sort of bridesmaids was perfectly acceptable. "Mum, what a beautiful ring!" Lucy couldn't fail but to notice the new sparkle on her mother's finger, and in her eyes. Sue smiled at her daughter remembering, as she did, the proposal in the garden as they had enjoyed their after lunch coffee. It had been so romantic. The things he had said, how he felt about her, how he longed to take her in his arms and make love to her and how he would hold her close afterwards. He had kissed her tenderly, then with mounting passion and they both felt a longing to consummate their relationship.

Lily and her family arrived at the same time as Yana. The noise level rose a number of decibels. Everyone talking at once, glad to be altogether which didn't happen as much as they would like. Amy and Andy went outside with their cousins and it was there that Sue first spotted Milo. She had been glancing anxiously out of the window at regular intervals and there he was!

He was sitting on the swing, all the children were with him. "There's Milo," Sue said to the room in general. Yana went straight out to greet the doctor while the others had a sneaky look at their mother's fiancé.

He looked good, Sue thought pleased. His dark hair streaked with white, his lean build and his obvious delight with the children. He stood as Yana approached and noticed his warm smile as he greeted her. If he was overwhelmed by her family, he didn't show it, gravely shaking hands with them one by one, and amazingly, identifying them as he did.

"Mum must have given him very accurate descriptions of us." Lucy laughed, the last one in line.

"My very dear Sue," he said turning to her with a smile, and taking her in his arms and kissing her.

For a moment she was worried but at that moment Andy noticed. "Oh gross," he intoned – and the entire group laughed. It really broke the ice.

The children came in from the garden for their home-made lemonade and things to eat. In no time it seemed to Sue the food was almost gone. Paul and Peter tucking in as if they had had no breakfast.

The rest of the day passed happily, with games in the garden and strolls in the woods. Finally, it was time to go for dinner.

Milo walked with Lily on one side, still walking with the aid of a stick. Lucy on the other. Sue walked with Leila, Louisa and Amy who wanted to talk bridesmaid's dresses!

Chantelle, Yana and the little ones with Paul, Peter and Bear, walked in an ambling group at the rear and finally they all arrived at the hotel.

They had been given a room off the main dining room – but were able of course, to help themselves to the Carvery. It was a happy, if at times noisy, lunch and once the adults were enjoying their after-lunch coffee, Andy led his cousins to the play area in the grounds.

Milo stood. He smiled at Sue and her slightly worried expression changed as he said how much he had enjoyed meeting the family. He went on to make them a promise. "Your mother has become most dear to me – at a speed which has surprised us both. I promise you, each of you that I will treasure her and take care of her as long as there is a breath in my body. Thank you."

He sat down abruptly. Sue swallowed hard. She had practised with her tutor, practised on the telephone with Yana and now she stood. In perfect Bosnian she said. "Milo. Welcome to my family. You have already changed my life and I know we shall find happiness together." Milo and Yana beamed. "Translation," yelled the family with one voice. Sue repeated her words in English and everyone clapped.

Peter stood. "As a once outsider Milo. I can say that this is a great family to belong to. I'm sure Lily's husband, Paul, would agree." Paul nodded emphatically. "So," Peter continued. "I would like you to raise your glasses to what I am sure will be one of many proposals. Sue and Milo."

Everyone stood – apart from the couple concerned who sat holdings hands like young lovers, and smiled at each other and the family.

By six pm, the cottage was empty. The girls had cleared up the plates and glasses and put the few items of food leftover into the fridge.

Sue and Milo were alone. "Let's have a G and T. Milo looked mystified. "Very English I'm afraid."

"Then I'll try it! Umm I approve of this," he smiled a few moments later taking his first sip of Sue's favourite evening tipple. "A pleasant way to end an eventful day. Did I do all right?" he grinned.

"You know you did, they loved you." The telephone interrupted their peace. It was Meg. "Paul's mother," she mouthed to Milo.

"I didn't want to ring earlier as I knew you had the family." Meg began. "Adrian and I really hope you and your fiancé would join us for lunch tomorrow. I know it is short notice but we gather he is not here for long."

"He leaves on Tuesday." Sue's was remembering what Lily and Paul had said about her parents offer to host the wedding reception at their home. . Just in case this might possibly happen they should meet Milo and vice versa. "Just one moment please Meg," she said, covering the mouthpiece while she repeated the conversation to Milo. "Of course, let's go. I shall be able to see more of your lovely countryside on the drive." Meg was delighted and told Sue how much they were looking forward to seeing her again and meeting Milo. They agreed to arrive around twelve thirty which being an almost three-hour drive from door to door, would give them all the time they needed.

Chapter 28

Sue and Milo had their first talk about the wedding. It had all happened so quickly that they had no opportunity to make any plans at all as to when and where.

Sue explained the situation , We could even use their own family Chapel which Lily had mentioned they could have the use of. Last time Sue was there was for the baptism of the twins when the local vicar agreed to perform the ceremony. "He was so nice," Sue explained. "Perhaps he could do our wedding."

Milo had gone a little quiet and Sue suddenly realised she was proposing all sorts of ideas without him having even a say!

"Daniella and Kurt," he mused. "Oh, Kurt could be your best man," she bit her lip in frustration and her own enthusiasm. "Milo, I am so sorry, all these ideas and you may feel so differently. I am sorry," she repeated.

"Sue, my dear wife-to-be, I love your enthusiasm. Never change please! All the things you have talked about and even the idea of Kurt being Best Man, whatever that is! Let's do everything possible, this is going to be a special beginning to the rest of our lives. There is just one thing. Would you consider having a Catholic blessing when we get back to our future home."

Sue nodded, and kissed him warmly. "I love you Milo," she said smiling as she spoke.

After a while of quiet conversation about their future, Sue whipped up a cheese and ham omelette for their supper. They were both still replete from lunch and the omelette plus some salad suited them both fine.

They sat at the kitchen table Milo commenting on each member of the family, saying how well she had described them, and adding that he was really looking forward to playing the role of grandfather at last, having missed out on being a parent. As if reading her thoughts, he explained that Anna had been unable to have children having suffered from severe anorexia it had left her with problems that made it difficult for her to conceive.

It was eleven pm. Milo stood to leave. They walked to the front door where he put his arms around her. "Milo," Sue heard her voice as if coming from someone else. "Would you like to stay for the night?" There was a silence that seemed interminable to Sue. Then Milo smiled warmly down at her, his eyes seemed to be twinkling. "You mean you don't banish me to my cell tonight?"

"You'll stay?"

"I have longed for you to ask me!" Wordlessly they walked up the stairs, Milo ducking his head, at Sue's behest so that he didn't knock himself out on one of the lower beams.

It had been a long time for Sue – she felt surprisingly nervous. It had been an even longer time for Milo and his only concern was that he would make her happy and that the hydraulics were still in good working order.

In the event, neither of them need have worried. The love-making was gentle and complete. They both felt an aliveness they had not felt for years. Not once did Sue think of Michael, not until afterwards anyway, and then it was with a sense of gratitude that because he had been such a caring and at times exciting lover she was able to help Milo, who she felt had perhaps never had the happy sex life she had known.

"Never before," he breathed heavily afterwards.

"Never before what?" she asked.

"Never before so perfect." She cuddled closer, not speaking, words were unnecessary. He knew he had made her happy as he waited for her body to indicate the beginning of an orgasm and although it was their first time together, they came joyfully, gorgeously together.

He left before breakfast to get a change of clothes and check out from the hotel. They had showered together, but had become distracted by each other's bodies. Now they would both re shower and dress separately before leaving at nine thirty to drive for the MacDonald home..

Milo enjoyed the drive and halfway there she offered him the keys after they had had a speedy coffee break. The car was insured for any driver and he had an EU driving licence and he was obviously quite keen to try driving the car.

He drove steadily and carefully, asking questions if he was unsure of signs or directions. When they turned in the gates of the estate he made suitably impressed noises. Sue told him was right to be impressed as it was one of the finest houses in the country. "It is a palace, not a house he commented. "I know what you mean," she laughed.

As they pulled up outside the flight of stone steps leading to the front entrance, Milo commented on the magnificence of the big doors. They had no further time to talk as Meg and Adrian walked down the steps to greet them. They were ushered in and proper introductions and greetings were exchanged in the spacious hall that last time Sue had visited, had been full of Christmas decorations for the festive season. The fire in the hearth had blazed along with the lights on the magnificent Christmas tree.

Milo shook hand gravely. "Lady MacDonald, Lord MacDonald."

"No, no, please." Meg responded. "We are such friends of Sue's – you are family now too." Milo looked pleased. "I have so much of a family now, thanks to Sue," he flashed his fiancée a warm smile.

Meg led the way into the magnificent yellow and gold drawing room. As Milo said afterwards, he felt it impolite to comment on everything but he couldn't resist commenting on the two Canelettos which he assumed correctly were originals. He noticed the Rembrandt and a beautiful Reynolds portrait. The four of them enjoyed a leisurely glass of Champagne and after a short while the housekeeper informed Meg quietly, that luncheon was served.

The starter was a cold avocado soup followed by a filet of beef served with new potatoes, which along with the green kidney beans and baby carrots came from their kitchen garden. Dessert was a crème brulee and it was all washed down with firstly, a crisp white Chablis followed by a red Bordeaux.

Over lunch, Meg raised the subject of the wedding and suggested after coffee they might like to look at the Chapel. It was, she explained not a big enough venue for Paul and Lily's wedding – but it is perfect for a small family affair.

"Amy and Andy were baptised there. It was charming, wasn't it Sue?" Sue nodded, Meg didn't need to sell the idea to her – the thought of all the family being together there was a delight. They talked dates. "A few months at most," Milo quipped with a glance at Sue, that to her immense embarrassment made her blush. Meg clapped her hands as a sudden thought hit her.

"Christmas," she said. "Everyone here for Christmas – the wedding on Boxing Day!"

Milo looked thoroughly mystified. "Boxing Day. What is this?" Sue quickly explained about it being the day after Christmas day and so called because, in bygone days, it was when servants in and outside of the great houses would receive a Christmas gift from their employers. A Christmas 'box', so the day became known as Boxing Day for that reason.

"What an interesting insight I am having. I am learning so much about your country in such a few days."

At four pm they had afternoon tea in the Conservatory. Neatly cut cucumber sandwiches and a ginger cake which the two men tucked into with equal pleasure. An hour later Sue indicated that it was time to head home. She and Meg agreed to talk regularly to make sure of all the arrangements.

"How many guests will you have Milo?" Meg asked conversationally.

"Just two," he answered after a slight pause then looking at Sue he said, with a smile. "I don't think I dare not invite Daniella, and of course Kurt," he went on to explain to Meg and Adrian that Kurt was like a surrogate son to him and that Daniella was not only his oldest friend, but additionally had been a close friend of Yana's mother.

There were laughs and kisses all round as goodbyes were said and Sue, driving again, felt it had been a wonderful introduction for Milo to meet a couple who were not only becoming amongst her closest friends as well as extended family by marriage.

The following day, it was goodbyes at the airport. Sue feeling somewhat sad and totally exhausted drove back home to the cottage knowing she would face an unmade bed and breakfast dishes still on the table.

Once again, she missed Dally and wondered how Milo would feel about having a dog. They had talked briefly about Dally, but Milo had, unusually, been somewhat unresponsive.

The bedroom brought back memories of the previous night where their lovemaking was becoming ever more relaxed and adventurous, and had, Milo confessed, achieved heights he had seldom, if ever achieved before.

It was strange, Sue couldn't help thinking. Perhaps it was the newness of the relationship or was it the fact that she had been on her own now for some time, but her whole body seemed to be super sensitive and she had seldom felt more alive. Slowly she stripped the bed, making it up again with the crisp white sheets she liked. Her mind wandered back over some of the conversations she had shared with Milo. Admiring her Aga, he suggested she have one installed when she refitted the kitchen to her taste. He also encouraged her to think about what else she would like to do to make it totally their home rather than the one he had shared with Anna. Nothing had been done for a number of years and Sue felt a tinge of excitement. What fun it would be…

They had talked about the family visiting them, and Milo had suggested putting in a swimming pool in what was currently a plum orchard. They had talked of their wedding and of the generosity of Meg and Adrian wanting to host the wedding . They had talked of a winter honeymoon, but Milo had suddenly gone coy and Sue was left suitably mystified. They had also talked about Yana, her future, and the hope perhaps she and Kurt might find a way through the maze of complications that seemed to colour their relationship.

Putting the laundry in the machine she glanced at her watch. Milo would be almost home by now. Kurt was meeting him at the airport in Belgrade and driving him home.

She sat down suddenly. Everything buzzing in her head. Milo home, her here. A wedding to plan for. What on earth would she wear???

Meg telephoned early the next morning. They had taken to Milo, and, did Sue have any idea what she was going to wear for the wedding because, nearer the time the flowers both in the chapel and the house could complement her choice.

Sue thought rapidly. Meg always dressed so elegantly perhaps she would like to go wedding / honeymoon clothes shopping.

Before she could formulate the question, Meg mentioned Lily's continued progress, Paul's flair with the rescue horses and Amy's astonishing riding prowess. Suddenly, Sue made a decision. "Meg dear, will you meet me in London to shop for the wedding?" Had she but known, Meg had mentioned over breakfast only that morning, how much she would like to accompany Sue on her outfit shopping. "Well tell her then!" had been Adrian's swift and cheerful response.

Meg came clean and said she had been wondering how to angle for that particular invitation. Both women were delighted and put a date in the diary towards the end of September.

"The autumn fashions will be well established and we don't want to be rushed why don't we make it the inside of a week." Meg continued. "We can do a show or two if we feel inclined ..Leave the accommodation to me Sue. We can use the suite Adrian keeps at the Dorchester for all his Business trips."

Sue who had never stayed at the Dorchester was so pleased with herself for having asked Meg's help. An equally happy Meg was delighted she was going to have a fun few days in London with someone she had become increasingly fond of.

Chapter 29

As good as his word, Kurt was waiting for Milo. They greeted each other warmly and walked out to the car. As they drove through the darkness Milo sensed his younger friend was low-spirited, so he talked far more than he felt like doing. He talked about Sue's cottage – her family – the grandchildren, and last, but by no means least. Yana.

Kurt was not to be drawn though and when they finally arrived at Milo's home, he wouldn't even come in. Milo let himself into the house, a few lights were on and the hall stove lent a welcoming warmth to what had tuned into a chilly late evening.

Already past eleven, he poured himself a small brandy before picking up his case and going upstairs to his bedroom. Anna and he had not shared a room for years. The big front bedroom had been unused since she became so ill and he had felt she would be happier in a smaller one. He had moved all her things into a smaller bedroom overlooking the garden, with the bed placed by the window so she had something to look at. There was a small balcony too, but she could seldom be encouraged to use it. At least she had fresh air tinged with the perfume of flowers from the garden below, though her interest in the garden had become minimal he had felt it a more relaxed space for her.

Now, he pushed open the door of the big bedroom. It looked shabby and uncared for and he resolved to get rid of everything in it, and ask Sue what colour she would like the room to be and how she wanted it decorated in total. They could shop together for furnishings after they were married and until it arrived they could use the smaller bedroom he had used for some years. No doubt she would refurbish that too!

He chuckled with the thought of Sue with her excellent sense of style let loose on this rambling shabby house of his.

******

Yana was saying her goodbyes at the practice. She had loved being in Pulborough and although knew she was right to leave, she had not quite realised what a niche she had carved for herself.

The three doctors, pharmacist, receptionists and secretary threw a big party for her along with their spouses. The event was held in an upmarket hotel in West Chiltington, an adjoining village.

They presented her with a framed photograph of them all. "So you won't forget us," Doctor Griffiths said as he also handed her a small box holding a lovely gold watch. "We know you lost yours," added one of the other doctors. "We can't let you go off to Bosnia with that horrid cheap watch you have worn lately. Whatever would they think!"

Yana took the watch carefully out of the box. "Turn it over," one of the receptionists called out.

Engraved on the back was her name, the year, and Pulborough.

Yana was both touched and surprised, she knew she would miss the camaraderie they had given her and she knew she would miss them all and the support and learning she had achieved there.

It made her realise that one day she would like to expand her practice in Bosnia, she could see the sense in having colleagues to 'bounce things off'. She was also aware Milo sometimes worked twelve hours a day and knew it was not a good plan for her.

Although not due to begin until January, she was planning to stay in her house for the month of November working alongside Milo and getting to know some of his patients. Meanwhile, she planned to spend some time with Sue and they could both talk and plan their new lives.

They also had a secret plan that Yana would continue where the three weeks' intensive language course that Sue had now completed, finished. She had learned an enormous amount, but lacked the confidence to build on it, and also lacked the opportunity to use it. Yana coming to stay for a month, unbeknownst to everyone in the family, and certainly not Milo was a real bonus. The plan was Bosnian all day every day, stopping only when Sue could take no more, couldn't make herself understood or they both became hysterical with laughter at some mispronunciation or a grammatical error that totally changed the meaning.

Evenings were English Sue decreed, for her sanity and Yana's time off. They grew even closer, the two of them, if that was possible, and Sue marvelled sometimes, at the quirk of fate that had brought Yana to them in the first place; and now it was the beginning of a whole new chapter in both their lives.

November arrived and Sue and Meg met as arranged at The Dorchester. They shared the luxurious twin bedded room Meg had mentioned with a view over the park. Somehow in conversation at one time or another they had discovered neither of them had seen The Mousetrap. Sue had bought tickets for their first evening in London as a small thank you to Meg for organising the hotel, among many other things.

They enjoyed their evening at the theatre, at least up to a point, they confessed to each other, deciding that another time a good musical might be more fun.

Meg was ruthless. After a nine am breakfast she verbally presented the itinerary for the next two days. "But what if I find something at the first shop we go to?"

"You won't," Meg assured her. "But if by any remote chance we do, we can go back and buy it later. Don't forget you have a trousseau to buy as well."

"Oh yes, I do, don't I. What fun!" To hell with the expense, she thought. When she and Michael were first married they didn't have much money. A home was the most important thing. Her parents had paid for the wedding, the dress and the bridesmaids three dresses and of course the reception.

But she had bought the trousseau, which as far as she could remember consisted of two pretty nightgowns, good old Marks and Spencers undies and a couple of summer dresses.

Times and circumstances had changed. Meg took her to Janet Reger where they both enthused over delicate silk knickers and matching bras. She bought five sets and some slips and camisoles.

"That's a good start," Meg commented, sounding very satisfied.

They stopped for coffee in Peter Jones then looked at some clothes. "There is too much choice," wailed Sue.

Meg put on a serious face. "We shall have lunch and make some colour decisions. It's a winter wedding. Matching coat, or what?"

"I wish I knew. All I know is that I shall know immediately." It was shortly after this conversation that Meg had her 'idea'.

"Sue, what would you wear for a Christmas wedding if you were going as a guest?" Sue brightened. "Oh, that is so much easier," she thought for a moment or two. "I think I would look for a red wool dress, with a red coat. Perhaps with black velvet collar and cuffs and a hat with a wide-ish brim turned up at the front. Also, perhaps a flower on the brim. If the hat was red, a black flower and vice versa."

"That's your answer." Meg looked smug.

"But I can't wear red for my wedding, can I?" she finished uncertainly.

"You can do as you choose." The two women were silent for a few moments. Sue trying to visualise herself in red. Meg wondering what she would wear as red had been a possible plan for herself.

Renewed after lunch, they decided to take a taxi to Harrods. Sue had said earlier that she found the vast areas full of clothes was confusing and a little overwhelming. With these comments in mind Meg took Sue straight to the personal shopper services. There they explained their thoughts to a helpful and charming lady, who had welcomed Meg warmly. In no time they were ensconced awaiting the arrival of the outfits deemed desirable by the expert. By the end of the day they were both exhausted. Sue had forgotten more than she remembered; but ultimately THE dress and coat arrived and as soon as she saw them, Sue knew.

They both fitted perfectly. Her five foot six figure looked tall and slender and she looked a good ten years younger than her sixty-five years. When a series of hats made their appearance she immediately pounced on one. It was exactly what she had been looking for.

Meg and the personal shopper guide stood back and admired their handiwork. "Shoes," they breathed as one. Soon a simple pair of black court shoes, with a higher heel than Sue would normally choose, completed the ensemble. Sue was ready to be the bride!

On the way back to The Dorchester, they discussed the bridesmaids. Sue still felt she shouldn't or didn't actually want bridesmaids, but she knew her littlest granddaughter had set her heart on it and the others two were quite happy to go along with her.

"They could wear navy velvet and carry red rose petals scattering them before you. Like they do in American weddings!"

"I like the idea of them walking before me. But no scattering of petals!" Meg said she had a really good dressmaker who would make the dresses, and after conferring they agreed Meg would take charge of organising the bridesmaid's outfits completely. It was a wonderful relief for Sue.

The following morning, they visited The White House to choose new bed linen, duvets, towels, pillows and pillow cases. She arranged to have them sent directly to Milo. It would have been perfectly possible, of course, to buy them there, but she wanted to start off with everything new and theirs, not his and Anna's. Also, Milo had casually dropped out that he didn't have much in the way of linen, which gave Sue the excuse, if one was needed, to go ahead. There would be so much other shopping to do in the way of refurbishment when she got there. It was good to get this out of the way... Milo had mentioned replacing some furniture as well. It really would be setting up home together. A new start for them both.

"What are you thinking about?" Meg interrupted her thought process which had drifted from furniture to beds and from beds to lovemaking. "Oh, this and that," she answered vaguely. Meg wanted to know where they were going for their honeymoon. For a moment, Sue looked startled. They hadn't even discussed a honeymoon – she must mention it to Milo when they spoke next, which would be this evening. "Milo is planning something," she half lied.

The two friends finally said their goodbyes and both agreed the whole expedition had been great fun. To Sue's horror Meg informed her that Adrian had arranged for the account to be charged to him. Sue was not pleased, but after making a protest and saying it must not happen again she could do no other than accept the gesture graciously.

As she told Yana later. "It was so kind, but I don't want to be beholden to them. We could so easily have split the cost." Yana agreed, but poured oil on slightly troubled water by saying it would probably not even occur to them to do anything differently.

They were back to speaking Bosnian again. Having a day or two off seemed to have benefited Sue. Words seemed firmer in her mind and her conversation was beginning to flow more easily.

******

Milo was in his study when Sue rang. It was nine pm his time and he had just finished a particularly hard day. To his surprise and delight, Sue greeted him in his own tongue and for a moment he didn't realise it was her and he automatically replied in Bosnian; and it was only when she next spoke he realised who it was!

They talked for about half an hour. Sometimes, Sue spoke her new language and Milo at the other end of the telephone smiled at her sterling efforts.

She told him to expect a big package from The White House, which was she explained not the one in the USA. But the shop in England. Sue asked him about the honeymoon. Milo proved evasive, but after a while, at her insistence disclosed that she would need summer clothes and perhaps a few smart things for the evening. "Long or short," she demanded. He of course had no idea. Sue persisted. "Will you be wearing a dinner jacket?" he agreed he would. "Black or White?"

"White I think," said Milo, thinking he must get his act together. He had no dinner jacket at present his life style in the past fifteen years had hardly been social.

They finally said their goodbyes with Milo adding it was good that he could now picture her in her cosy bedroom, and he only wished he was there too.

Sue put the telephone down thoughtfully. Smart summer clothes – where was he taking her. She hoped it was not a cruise, she and Michael had read with horror of some of the big cruise ships with up to four thousand people on board and decided that would be three thousand nine hundred and ninety-eight to many for them! Perhaps the Caribbean, Barbados, Antigua or St. Lucia. It had been a dream of theirs – hers and Michael's to head that way, but there had always seemed hurdles to prevent them Doctor business or family or financial commitments that made it impossible.

Later that night, she dreamed of Michael again, the first time in a while. They were dancing, very much in the style of the old Fred Astaire and Ginger Rogers films. She felt the music and felt the movement of the dance with neither of them putting a foot wrong. Suddenly it was Milo, not Michael. He was smiling down at her and she realised the other had been a dream and this was real. They danced through soft clouds, floating, their feet hardly touching anything.

She woke suddenly. It was dark. She looked at the digital clock on her side table, two, forty-three. She tried to recapture the mood – the music was still in her head. It had, she decided been nice dancing with Milo.

******

Daniella was extremely excited. All her friends knew by now that she was to spend Christmas in the home of an English Lord and Lady. She had no idea of the connection to Sue, but assured her friends that Sue came from a 'grand' family. Looking at her clothes, she decided she needed four new dresses for the occasion, to cover the four days she would be there. She had heard somewhere that old English houses were very cold. No stoves in England, she gathered. She would choose warm fabric and possibly line them too, even the thought of being cold made her shiver.

Daniella had already decided to travel in her old but good fur coat with a warm black sweater and skirt for when they arrived. For the day before Christmas she made a dirndl style rather Bavarian looking dress copied from a fashion magazine, to wear with a new cream blouse and a Loden wool jacket. She would she decided wear it with a yellow and scarlet silk scarf, which she felt would look very elegant. The three other dresses were more cosmopolitan in design and she felt a sense of relief that she would always have her fur coat to fall back on for warmth.

******

It seemed to be a frenzy of fittings for the girls. Leila, Louisa, Amy and Bear's little daughter Chloe. There many have been no official bridesmaids, but the cousins had made up their minds to be 'proper' bridesmaids. Their deep blue velvet dresses had little puff sleeves, trimmed with narrow white lace which was also used to make a narrow belt of twisted velvet and lace to provide 'interest' at the waist.

The dresses reached to mid-calf length, and because of the potential cold they each had a fully lined cape to wear on arrival and departure from, the chapel.

It had also been agreed by Sue that they would carry little posies of red rose buds and 'Alice bands' to hold their hair off their faces.

Meg was in her element, driving Mrs Bennett firstly to Marlborough to measure little Chloe. Then to Lucy's for Leila and Louisa fittings and finally Amy, who lived near them at the extreme end of their land with her parents Lily and Paul.

Meg felt all four children would look enchanting, properly finishing off the ceremonial side of the wedding. Amy, along with support from Andy and her mother Lily, had originally decided she was too big for all that sort of stuff. With reluctance at first, Amy agreed that her other grandmother's happiness was important to her, and Milo seemed 'okay'. So, to Meg's delight, she finally agreed to become a bridesmaid. Meg breathed a sigh of relief. It was all coming together.

Time marched inexorably onwards. Yana had left England for her month working alongside Milo.

The two of them really hit it off and Milo enjoyed having the extra help as much as he enjoyed her company. They talked of Sue, and Yana told him about her early years with the James family. How from the start she had become their extra daughter.

The one subject they never discussed was her on/off relationship with Kurt who kept well out of their way. Yana met the locum who would stay over during the Christmas period when she would be back in England for the wedding. He was a mild mannered bachelor who was awestruck by Yana. They had the occasional meal together, but Yana felt nothing except friendship, though Jan would have liked more.

Yana told Milo about the dogs she had grown up with. How Abby had been her first 'friend'; and how Sue had grieved at losing Dally. Together, they hatched a plot to buy a Dalmatian puppy for Sue, which Yana would organise whilst they were on their honeymoon. The puppy – Milo's extra wedding present to her would be there to greet her when she arrived in her new home.

Chapter 30

It was Christmas. Presents had been chosen and wrapped. Sue's car was weighed down with them, in the largest case she had. Also hanging very carefully in a protective cover, her dress and coat. And in the large hat box on the back seat sat 'the' hat. The second case was more modest in size, and it was packed with what she needed for her wedding day, and the rest was trousseau for the honeymoon.

She had left her cottage keys with Jayne, the lady from the village who had cleaned for her, and would now pop in weekly to collect and forward any mail and keep a general eye on the place. It was, thought Sue comforting to know that the cottage would not be alone and she was sure that although she had arranged for her mail to be redirected occasional things would slip through that Jayne could deal with. The house would be kept fresh and aired and during the winter months the heating would be kept on very low to stop the house getting a damp feeling.

Before she had driven off she had taken a lingering look at her little cottage that had provided such a good home. "I'll be back in the spring," she whispered to the air, closing the gate firmly she climbed into her car and set off for the drive to the MacDonald's

It was about three fifteen when she arrived and it was already dusk. Lights seemed to shine from all the windows and as she parked she noticed Lucy and Peter's car already there.

Once again, before she could even mount the steps the doors were thrown open and Adrian big and beaming as ever, strode down the steps to meet her. "Well, and how is the bride to be?"

"Incredibly nervous," she laughed lightly to belie the words – but truth to be, she was. Adrian collected the largest case from the boot of the car. "This weighs a ton."

"Presents, all presents. I had quite a struggle to get it into the car myself!"

Leaving her honeymoon case for now, she collected her large handbag and the carefully shrouded wedding outfit.

Meg appeared in the hall and greeted Sue warmly. "Your granddaughters, well two of them insisted on trying on their dresses. I had hard work persuading them they could not wear them for family dinner tonight!"

Adrian put the large case by the Christmas tree. "That's fine Adrian, I'll unpack it when the little ones are in bed. Father Christmas was still believed in, especially by Bear and Chantelle's children. Sue had her suspicions that Leila and Louisa played along with the idea, in the hope of getting more presents…

Soon Bear, Chantelle and the little ones arrived and lastly Lily, Peter and the twins who living within the grounds were not staying overnight.

For Sue it was wonderful catching up on every one's news. The only ones missing now were Yana and Milo, Daniella and Kurt. Peter left for Gatwick to meet their plane and the rest of them sat down for tea. The nursery had been re decorated and the smaller children with their au pair in charge disappeared for tea in the nursery leaving the adults and older children sitting comfortably around the fire in the drawing room. They wanted to know all about the wedding arrangements for the day after Christmas. "Please," said Sue earnestly. "Let's get tomorrow over first. Enjoy Christmas Day, then we'll talk about the wedding." Everyone laughed, Paul saying there wouldn't be much opportunity to talk on THE Day.

At seven thirty, Peter returned with his car load, who all arrived in high spirits. Lucy and Yana went into an immediate huddle, any coolness between them long since forgotten. Sue took Milo to his bedroom saying very pointedly that they must observe the proprieties and not share a room.

"Can't I even sneak along in the middle of the night?" Sue shook her head regretfully.

"No way!"

Soon they were all seated around the long dining room table. It had been decided as the smaller children were tiring, and over excited, they should have their supper in the breakfast room with the au pairs. Meg had engaged a cook for over the Christmas period, leaving the housekeeper time to run the household, and deal with the multitudinous situations that would undoubtedly arise with such a large number of guests.

The Christmas cook – Christine, proved a great success and they all enjoyed dainty salmon cakes followed by beef Stifado; that was basically a Greek stew cooked in reduced red wine with lots of delicious herbs making it a most tasty dinner. It was served with roasted peppers in balsamic, and baby roast potatoes.

Afterwards they had homemade mango ice cream – one of Meg's specialities, served with miniature meringues. "And tomorrow we have Christmas Lunch!" Peter said with a wry expression on his face. "No wonder I put on weight every time we come here."

"You put on weight, Peter dear, because you eat too much." Lucy quipped.

They continued sitting for a while when they had finished eating, enjoying an excellent port produced from Adrian's cellar. The children were excused, and the adults continued chatting on a range of topics, from world politics, the European union and the future of the monarchy.

Eventually, they returned to the drawing room for coffee before saying their goodnights. Sue and Milo lingered by the fire and had a quick cuddle before walking up the stairs together. Milo heading for the room he was sharing with Kurt and Sue to her solitary state.

They had unanimously agreed not to attend the midnight service but were all happy to go the ten-thirty Christmas Day service the following morning. The children had received their Father Christmas stockings left mysteriously on their beds during the night and the big presents around the tree would be opened when they returned from church.

Sue had discretely put a small package for Milo under the tree adding to the large number of gaily wrapped gifts already in situ. Unbeknownst to him was that the gifts she bought would be from them both.

It was, of course, an early start with so many children of varying ages in the house. After a good breakfast of scrambled egg and bacon they set off in a fleet of cars for the church.

The local vicar, a friend of the MacDonald's, welcomed Sue who was then introduced to his wife and teenage son who had also been invited to the Reception.

Amy was secretly pleased, as she had a crush on Robert, a spotty faced youth who Lily felt was gauche beyond belief. She indulged her daughter's fantasies, feeling confident no harm would come from a pubescent crush.

"It hadn't been the easiest of flights," Milo confided to Sue on one of their rare moments together on Christmas Day. It had been a long service that morning, because so many people attended, being the day it was, and with most of them going to the altar for a blessing or to take Communion it had taken one and a half hours.

After wonderful Christmas Lunch, with all the trimmings including the Brandy flamed Christmas pudding. Adrian appeared dressed as Father Christmas with many a merry ho, ho, ho, and weighed down by a heavy sack!

After much excitement, with happy and delighted children of all sizes exclaiming over their gifts. Milo thanked Sue for the gold cufflinks engraved with his initials and Sue was thrilled with her choker pearl necklace. Dear Michael, she thought. He had always asked her what she would like, then because he was so busy she invariably went out at the last minute to buy it on his behalf!

Presents and lunch over and together in Sue's bedroom Milo told her about the constraint between Yana and Kurt. "They sat in adjoining seats on the flight," Milo explained, "and barely exchanged a word." He had then consulted Daniella who told him they were both equally stubborn. As the third seat in their row was unoccupied Milo explained to Sue he had decided to sit by them

"I don't know what the problem is," he had said. "But we are flying to England for my wedding. Your foster mother's wedding, Yana. Whatever your difficulties, I am telling you now it must not show to the rest of the family. Put on an act if you must. Sort out your problems if you can, but don't spoil our wedding, being difficult with each other. Understood?"

"What happened then Milo?" Sue couldn't wait to hear. Milo smiled.

"It seemed to help a little. They both looked at each other guiltily and Yana had spoken first. I will repeat what they said verbatim."

"Of course, Milo, how right you are."

Kurt apparently had nodded in agreement and his response was. "Quite right Milo, of course."

With a sense of relief, Milo had returned to his seat where the ever curious Daniella had asked how things had gone. "What did you say,"

"They'll behave. They'd better," he had muttered.

Sue listened to the saga with sympathy. Sympathy for Milo having to deal with it and concern for Yana wondering at the same time what else that thoughtless young man had done.

She told Milo about the picnic Yana didn't attend. "But more than that," she added. "It's all the 'history'."

"I know," Milo said, squeezing her hand.

"Let's go for a walk," Sue said springing to her feet. She always felt better walking anxiety off.

Milo fetched his coat, hat and gloves and Sue put on the old Barbour she had brought with her for such eventualities. Hand in hand they walked out of a side door like guilty teenagers.

It was a cold winter day with the palest of sun. "I hope it's like this tomorrow." Milo looked at her fondly. "My dear Sue – it doesn't matter, does it?" She looked up at him and knew it didn't, but in her heart of hearts she still hoped the sun might shine.

They talked of renovations to the house. How large a pool to put in the old orchard; and how nice it was being alone like this. Sue tried to wheedle the honeymoon details out of him, but he was unmoved by her pleas, enjoying the secret surprise he had planned so carefully.

To Sue's amazement, she slept soundly that night. No dreams, no tossing and turning – in fact she was still half asleep when there was a light knock on the door. Not Milo, surely she thought – hastily arranging her nightdress to make her decent, rather than one generous bosom so obviously exposed.

Before she could even say 'come in', the three girls Lily, Lucy and Yana appeared, all wearing cosy fleece dressing gowns. They looked so happy that Sue's heart soared with pleasure. "What are you up to," she began. Then as the girls carried a drop leaf table into the middle of the room and Lucy rapidly placed a pretty embroidered cloth on it the Housekeeper appeared, as if on cue.

"Bride's privilege," she announced with a smile, putting down a large silver tray laden with delicate looking china, and with a delicious aroma of bacon and eggs drifting from under a lidded chaffing dish.

The girls collected chairs together and Sue climbed willingly out of bed to join the merry trio.

"Who is Mum today?" she asked eyeing the coffee jug longingly.

"You are!" They chorused in unison.

Breakfast tasted as delicious as it had smelt. Hot croissants, accompanied by crispy bacon and scrambled eggs. Freshly squeezed orange juice and, surprisingly, Sue's favourite brand of Brazilian coffee washed it down.

"There is a clue here," Yana said looking conspiratorially at her sisters with a wink.

"A hot country," Sue began, thinking of oranges. "Or France, the croissants?"

"You'd never guess, Mum," Lucy said.

"So don't try," Lily added. They giggled just as they had when little girls, and Sue felt an overwhelming love for them all.

"You will come and visit, won't you? Milo is even putting a pool for the grandchildren."

"And us," they chorused indignantly!

It was a happy breakfast. Sue couldn't help wondering what Milo was doing. The wedding was at eleven, and at nine thirty she shooed them out of her room. They left armed with the breakfast tray, putting the table back where it belonged and leaving their Mother in peace.

Sue breathed a sigh of relief. It had been simply wonderful – but now she needed some space. Hair wash, dry, and shower. Suddenly she felt there wasn't enough time. Just as she began to panic there was another light tap on the door. "Bother," Sue muttered to herself, almost simultaneously saying. "Come in." It was Meg, full of apologies for disturbing the bride – but just checking to see if there was anything at all Sue needed or wanted.

Assuring Meg she was fine and thanking her for organising the lovely bedroom breakfast, Sue closed the door, grateful, but determined that should another knock occur she would not answer it.

She decided to have a bath, not shower, and poured in her favourite bath oil, the aroma filling her senses with pleasure.

Her hair was still wet from the hand shower, and lying back, she relaxed in the warmth of the water.

In her new underwear, she stood and dried her hair with the dryer, pleased that the good cut she had recently meant it would just fall into place. Her dress, uncovered now, hung on a hook on the bedroom door. The special coat hanger ensuring it hung perfectly. The grand hatbox was on the bed. She pulled on her ultrafine lacy-topped hold up stockings and surveyed herself in the mirror.

Her face glowed from the bath. Her figure was neat and slim. Not bad for sixty-five she thought gratefully. Everyone told her she looked ten years younger and she used to laugh and say a polite 'thank you', and it must be in the genes! Thinking back, both her parents had looked way younger than the years belied.

She made up her face quite lightly, putting on a little blusher and her usual eyeliner and mascara.

Finally, she stepped into her dress, and after a little struggle managed to do up the long zip. The dress did look lovely. It flattered her figure with its excellent cut, and the round neck was perfect for her new pearl choker. The sleeves, though short, were not too short, reaching to just above her elbow. She fixed her pearl earrings, the ones Michael had given her years before and decided it was totally appropriate to wear them today. Twisting the wedding ring, now on her right hand, the one he had given her on their wedding day, she decided to keep it on. Her new wedding ring would be on her left hand and somehow it seemed acceptable to keep Michael's as a memory.

Glancing at her watch, she was surprised to find it was already ten thirty. She slid her feet into her sleek new court shoes which she had 'worn in' around the cottage for several weeks; the last thing she needed today was painful feet!

Next, the hat. Lifting it gingerly out of the box she carried it to the dressing table. Once seated on the padded stool she placed it carefully on her head. It, the hat, was magnificent. Sue felt relieved and excited. The tilted up front meant she could be seen, and Milo could kiss her more easily after the ceremony. The crown slightly raised above her head gave her some additional height which she felt all added to the overall look. Finally, the coat. It was deceptively simple, slightly fitted with a single self-coloured button at waist level.

She had decided to carry nothing at all and a small lace handkerchief, for emergencies, was discreetly tucked into the neat little pocket on the right seam of the coat.

As she surveyed herself from all angles there was a gentle knock on the bedroom door. For the third time that morning she called. "Come in." And her handsome son Bear stood smiling broadly.

"Wow Mum, you look a million dollars. What a fabulous colour!" She kissed him lightly.

"Is it time?" he nodded.

"We are the last to leave." Slightly solemnly they walked side by side down the wide staircase.

The housekeeper and holiday cook stood at the foot of the stairs looking in admiration and Sue was greeted with a small round of applause. "Thank you, how kind," she murmured.

The sun – a pale wintry one – just what she had ordered, was shining as they walked the few hundred yards to the chapel. She could hear organ music and as they drew closer she saw her three granddaughters in their deep blue velvet dresses with their capes still on to keep them cosy.

Lucy was there with them and as Sue arrived she collected the capes, ushered the girls forward and managed to whisper. "Gorgeous Mum, gorgeous." Sue gave her a flashing smile and then she and Bear, arm in arm followed the trio of girls down the short aisle. As arranged each of them went into a pew by their respective parents and Sue saw Milo for the first time that day.

He looked so handsome in his morning suit. She had been surprised, in a way, to see Bear wearing one it was, after all meant to be a small family wedding. She had then rationalised that as he was accompanying her down the aisle he had rationalised it would be the correct 'look'.

Milo took her hand and raised it to his lips. Her heart raced as the familiar words of the service began. It seemed to be over in a flash, then signing the register and out again to the smiling faces of the family.

Meg had organised everything from the beautiful flowers in the Chapel to a photographer. Eventually they meandered back to the house for champagne followed by a magnificent wedding breakfast. Milo disappeared and returned after a short while in smart/casual trousers and an equally smart jacket.

Meg whispered that a car was due in half an hour. Surprised, Sue dashed back to her room, put her make up bag into her new black leather handbag. Took off her hat and brushed her hair, picked up her gloves and returned downstairs.

Their two cases were already in the hall and the goodbyes started in real earnest. It was hard saying so many goodbyes, as particularly, apart from Yana she knew she probably wouldn't see the rest of the family until Easter.

Meg and Adrian hugged her warmly, and when she tried to thank them, they assured her they had loved every moment of the whole occasion. A large white limousine stood on the drive and a chauffeur driver ushered them into the magnificent vehicle as, though they were royalty.

Sue had a strong desire to giggle and didn't dare meet Milo's eyes. "Where are we going?"

"Gatwick."

"Then?"

"Wait and see."

"Oh, you are impossible," she said with mock severity.

"Ah, you have found me out already," he grinned at her. They held hands all the way, talking quietly about the day. How smoothly it had gone. How handsome he looked. "Thank you," he said modestly. "You looked, look totally stunning. I've never seen you in a hat before – wonderful. Will you wear it again?"

"Every morning for breakfast!" He leaned over and kissed her.

"And little or nothing else I trust." She tried to appear shocked and giggled again instead.

They arrived at Gatwick. The chauffeur lifted their cases out of the car and hailed a porter.

"Goodbye sir, madam. Have a wonderful honeymoon." They thanked him graciously and headed indoors.

"I need to know what I am looking for." She was annoyed that she had not heard what Milo had said to the porter. He took them straight to the first class check in at British Airways. Milo handed over the passports and within moments they were handed their boarding passes and directed to the First Class lounge.

Once through passport control, Sue had sneaked a quick look at the tickets, but hadn't quite managed to read the small print. It was only when they were informed they could board that she finally found they were heading for Rio de Janeiro. "How fabulous," she said, and he smiled slightly mysteriously.

It was a smooth flight travelling First Class and also a first for Sue. She and Michael had never managed to travel beyond Business, and then only very occasionally.

They landed in the dark and bright lights everywhere woke Sue up as she tried to take in the scene. They drew up at a white marble looking hotel and as the car drew to a halt a smartly attired doorman opened the car door and welcomed them to Rio.

Milo had taken a suite. They had a large double bedroom with a balcony. A sitting room, two bathrooms and a tiny kitchenette. Out of curiosity she looked in the tiny fridge and found it stocked with orange juice, wines and a bottle of champagne.

She was so tired she could hardly move and Milo seemed to feel the same. They disappeared into their separate bathrooms and reappeared refreshed after showers. Even so, the first night of their married life they lay chastely in each other's arms, content just to be together.

Sue woke first and for a moment wondered where she was. She thought about the last twenty-four hours. The grandchildren had looked so sweet. Milo looked handsome and she was so proud of Bear and the way he had escorted her down the aisle, and the girls. What fun breakfast had been. Milo stirred, she rolled over to look at him. He smiled and held out his arms and they made love, and whilst the world around them continued on, they were on a plateau of their own.

Chapter 31

Kurt and Daniella were taken back to Gatwick the following morning. Meg and she had struck up an instant friendship and Daniella had made Meg promise to come for a visit in the spring. Meg assured her that she was visiting Sue then so she would be able to combine seeing her two friends.

Kurt, slightly more formal, but nevertheless made it clear how much he had enjoyed the whole visit. Staying in their beautiful home, being 'best man' and being part of an English country wedding. "I shall see you in Bosnia," Meg said gaily.

"We both will." Adrian added, shaking the younger man warmly by the hand. Meg, spontaneous as ever, hugged him, sensing unhappiness behind the smile, and having heard some of Yana's story from Sue, realised what a burden he carried.

Yana had already left to spend a few days with Bear, Chantelle and the children. Marlborough's broad High Street, with the school set at the far end, seemed, even on a cold winters day, far more civilised than her town in Bosnia.

It was quiet. School was closed for the holiday and Bear, Chantelle and the children had the house to themselves. For Yana it was a peaceful three days before she returned to Bosnia to re take up her role as doctor, relieve Jan, the locum who had been standing in for her during her during her absence, would stay for a few more days to de brief her.

Finally, and somewhat reluctantly she said her goodbyes. Bear was such a darling. Definitely Bear was the right name for him rather than his baptismal name of Rupert, which no one used these days, except Chantelle and on official documents.

The flight home was uneventful. Yana collected her car and drove carefully on the snow packed roads, glad that the chains were already in situ. Not totally to her surprise, lights shone through her shutters. She smiled inwardly. Daniella had been in. A warm glow hit her as she went in, the smell of burning logs entwined with beeswax which no doubt dear Daniella had polished her table with. Yana smiled, Daniella had a 'thing' about polish. She always said when you walked into a house you should be greeted by the smell of beeswax and the perfume of flowers. No flowers this time of year, though the smell of the beeswax and wood smoke made Yana smile.

Putting her case down she went into the kitchen and prepared some coffee. Soon, the smell of the freshly ground brewing coffee added to the other aromas. Quite suddenly, and with a big sigh she felt at home. For the first time, here in this house she felt at home. Cup in hand she climbed the stairs to the front room. The room her parents had shared. The room where she had been conceived.

Tonight, the shadows that hung over it seemed to have lifted. Once more she traced the double Ms on the headboard. She lay back on the bed savouring this new feeling of peace, and in moments, coffee cooling on the side table she was asleep.

She woke to the sound of birdsong and the early morning light peeping through the slats in the shutters. A slow smile defused her face. She was home. This room had become her parents haven again, the ghosts of the last years were driven away.

Stretching, she sat up noting with a grimace the cold coffee. Leaving it on the landing she went up to her bedroom to take a shower and change her clothes. Any tiredness she had felt had completely dissipated, and after the shower she felt ready for work.

Her hair still wet she went down to the kitchen collecting the cold coffee en route. Daniella had, as promised, put fresh eggs, bread and milk in her fridge and very soon she was sitting down, music playing quietly in the background as she hungrily ate scrambled eggs and toast.

By eight am, she was in the surgery wading through a pile of messages left for her by Jan, who preferred hand written notes to emails. Having carefully read everything through and made notes to herself on various follow ups that were necessary she turned on her computer to collect her emails.

Lots of family emails, but nothing from Sue. Yana smiled. By now she would be on the cruise! When Milo had first mentioned a cruise, Yana remembered Sue saying she would hate to be on a ship with thousands of people. "Trust me Yana," Milo had smiled. "The ship I have in mind has two hundred guests for a cruise around South America." Yana was relieved. Sue would, she was sure, enjoy that immensely. She looked forward to hearing all about it before too long, she felt sure the month would speed by for them as well as for her.

Jan had done a good job over the Christmas holiday which was generally quite a quiet period, but she knew that historically she was heading for the busy season of colds, sore throats and 'flu, and the hypothermia problems, all of which would be most likely to hit the elderly in the community harder than anyone else.

Yana worked long hours over the next few weeks. At her desk by eight am, she would receive calls for visits which she then slotted into her day. By nine, the waiting room was full. The record system was not as she wanted it. A lot of records were computerised, but not all, and the cross check she wanted to establish was not yet in place.

The young woman Milo employed as a Receptionist, was not particularly friendly, and at times Yana found her attitude actually unhelpful. One evening, at the end of another long day, she sat the girl down to find a solution to the problem, and realised in moments that there were unresolved issues connected with her taking over the practice.

Her brother, it transpired, had also recently qualified as a doctor and had approached Milo with a view to taking over the practice when Milo retired. Yana, not knowing Milo's reasons for selecting her over a genuine local could only make polite, conciliatory noises. At least, knowing part of the problem might help ease the situation a little. But, in the event it seemed not to improve relations at all, and Yana knew she would have to employ someone else as soon as possible.

The house buzzed with activity. Yana, with help from Daniella had unpacked some of the 'goodies' from The White House Linen Company in England. Now Milo's king size bed had been made up with new sheets, pillows and duvets. The walls in the bedroom had been painted in 'magnolia' – Milo's choice for the neutral Sue had requested. Soft white towels hung in the rather antiquated bathroom. Daniella had found some inexpensive but bright fabric and had run up a pair of curtains, as a temporary measure to brighten the room, and had covered a few cushions in the same fabric which Yana threw, casually, but with a certain precision on the bed. They could do nothing about the shabbiness of the rugs, and both women chattered about what changes would soon occur.

They had been surprised to find the big front bedroom empty. Again painted 'magnolia'. "At least," Yana said with a smile. "A blank canvas in here for Sue to weave her magic!" A few days later, the honeymooners returned home, both looking lightly tanned and very relaxed and happy. For a moment Yana even felt a pang of jealously, they were so obviously happy and she seemed to be unlucky in love.

The local carpenter was already building a bed for the master bedroom. Sue had been shopping in Belgrade and had chosen everything from new kitchen and bathrooms and also ordered fitted furniture to turn one of the smaller bedrooms adjacent to their bedroom, into a dressing room for Milo. The room on the other side of theirs was being converted into an en suite bathroom for them.

Sue ordered new rugs, curtain fabric, new pots, pans and china. "Milo's," she confided to Yana, "were beyond redemption!" She had, however, found in a cupboard in the drawing room a dinner service of the most exquisite porcelain. "Apart from dust," she confided to Yana. "It was in perfect condition, not a crack or a mark. In fact, I don't think it has ever been used." Later Sue found it had belonged to Milo's parents and Anna had refused to use it. Sue made a mental note that at their first dinner party, she would surprise Milo by using it. When she knew he was out for a while, she carefully collected a few pieces at a time and carefully washed them, longing for her new kitchen to be fitted so the whole twelve-piece service would take pride of place.

The dining room with its heavy wood panelled walls, lent itself to becoming a room full of depth and colour. The furniture was excellent. A long mahogany table, several glass fronted cupboards and a marble topped serving table. Sue chose a rich fabric for the curtains of deep red with stripes of cream running lengthways, the room took on a look of elegance and warmth. The rugs were cream, and lay on the newly refurbished and polished floorboards adding a certain charm.

It was the second room Sue re did, the first being of course, their bedroom and the new bathroom. The new bed, now finished had a firm but comfortable mattress. If Sue had been somewhat surprised to have a built in bed, she was delighted with the finished article. It was a large bed, six feet by seven feet, giving the tall Milo plenty of leg-room.

Creamy yellow curtains now hung at the two windows, and a matching spread covered the bed. Extra pillows were in abundance and two comfortable chairs sat companionably either side of a small round table on which fresh flowers sent out their perfume. It was an oasis of peace. Milo loved its style and femininity. The bathroom had a generous bath and an attractive and spacious shower. Big enough for two, Milo had insisted. Power jets sprayed from all sides, and the overhead spray fell gently onto the body below. The wood floor had been tiled over with non-slip tiles, and fluffy thick bath and shower mats provided the soft finish they both liked.

Sue was in her element, and as winter gave way to spring, room after room came alive under her spell. Gone was the gloomy, though lovely, house. Now, it seemed light and welcoming and before long, with work now starting on the outside they would be ready for their first visitors.

Chapter 32

Yana was glad Milo was home. Apart from some questions she had about one or two of the patients she wanted his views about the Reception situation. Despite their conversation the Receptionist's attitude seemed, if anything to have hardened and Yana was discovering a certain amount of disinformation involving her in the occasional wild goose chases.

Equally some requests or concerns mentioned by patients was not being passed on to her, or if they were it was often in a hit or miss manner. Yana's mind was resolved, but she felt Milo should know her reasons before she advertised the position. She wanted to avoid the possibility of more misinformation being put about.

The problem of when she could do this was solved by Sue's call inviting themselves around, as apart from wanting to see her they had one or two gifts for her as well. They arrived promptly at seven carrying several interesting packages. "It's like another Christmas," she told the happy pair as she opened package after package.

A richly embroidered full-length shawl. A bracelet and matching necklace based on Inca designs and finally a book about South America, with lots of stunning photographs. "To whet your appetite," Milo explained. It was a real 'coffee table' type of book and Yana knew that curled up on a winters evening it would excite her imagination.

She poured wine. Red for Milo, white for Sue and herself. Giving Milo a long look she decided that social occasion or not she had to unburden herself. She explained fully all that had taken place, including her talk with the young woman. "Let her go," Milo said. "She was never the best, and she has taken advantage and more."

Yana felt a great sense of relief and Sue saw her relax. Tension that had etched her face as she spoke, was lifted. "Thank you Milo."

"For what? You already knew," he smiled. Conversation turned to the house garden. Sadly some trees had to be removed from the orchard to make way for the building of the new pool. But while the pool was being dug out a small feature pool with a miniature waterfall was going in to what Milo described as 'Sue's corner'.

"I shall have rocks and wild flowers," Sue added, going into rapturous descriptions of her plans.

Yana looked from one to another of them. They were so obviously happy in each other's company, each indulging the other. "Lucy, Peter and the girls arrive in the spring and I want it all finished by then and we shall have a pool warming party. Inviting everyone," she concluded, looked steadily at Yana for a reaction. Yana deliberately misunderstood the look. Of Kurt, she had seen nothing since the wedding. After Milo's banishments on the flight to England, she and Kurt had been polite and civil to each other and yet Yana had thought sadly there was nothing, and at the same time wanting there to be.

******

Kurt had been seeing quite a lot of the member of staff Yana had seen him with what seemed a long time ago. He had denied then, that she was no other than just a member of staff, but that had changed and they were involved in what turned into quite a long affair.

For Kurt it was just that – almost meaningless sex with someone who was nice – but so bland – so willing to be his everything. In truth, he was bored by her, resulting in him trying to make her leave. It seemed the meaner he became, the more she 'gave'. *I am becoming my father*, he thought feeling melancholic again. His moods didn't affect his teaching, In the classroom in front of his pupils, he could banish all personal thoughts and every year grateful pupils thanked him for what he taught.

When he touched 'her', he thought of Yana. He hated himself for his mental disloyalty. He hated Yana – she had caused all the problems. It was she who had opened the can of worms that made him turn away from his father. He rationalised that Yana's mother had probably 'asked for it', the rape – women did. Then he hated himself more for he knew this was not the case.

Finally, he had enough. He told the girl she must leave. When she refused he packed her things, changed the locks and when she still waylaid him, telling of her devotion, he broke her heart telling her that when they had made love he thought of someone else, someone he really loved. Even in her abject distress she loved him. She loved him so much that she decided she must track down this female and tell her some home truths.

Daniella was her conduit, she had heard Kurt talk to her about 'her'. She knew from the wedding Kurt had attended at Christmas that Daniella had gone too. She would know who this woman was.

The following weekend, with the pale spring sunshine encouraging her to roll back the canvas roof of her small Fiat, she drove to the town where Kurt had, if not been born there had certainly lived at some stage. She went to a small hotel looking for a lady called Daniella. Finally, after a number of false starts she arrived at the hotel where Janus son was now the proprietor. Slightly suspicious at first, he was soon charmed by the vivacious little blonde and soon provided her with the address she sought, after, and only after, making her promise to come back and at least have a drink with him. She gladly agreed, thinking it was a small price to pay.

Leaving her car where it was, she set off following the directions she had been given turning off the High Street into the quieter road that she was seeking. Had she but known it, Yana coming out of the surgery in a rush to deliver a baby, noticed her and wondered why she looked familiar. Then with thoughts of what lay ahead for the next few hours turned her mind to the mother to be.

Daniella was quite surprised to see the petite pretty blonde on her doorstep, but, when the girl started to speak and was clearly in distress, Daniella almost dragged her indoors. Soon the whole sorry story was told. Unwittingly, she had betrayed Kurt's behaviour towards her and Daniella found herself getting angrier than she had been for a very long time, since the war years in fact.

What to do, that was the problem. How could she give Yana's name and address and be sure all this sorry creature wanted was to face her and tell her the truth. 'When in doubt, make coffee' was her motto. So, taking the girl by the hand she led her into the kitchen and pushed her into a chair while she busied herself.

"Stay the night," she said suddenly. The girl looked startled. "If you do, I will arrange for you to meet – if not, I won't." The girl nodded miserably.

"I will go to the hotel."

"You will stay here." Daniella responded sharply. The girl looked up, the face looking down at her was implacable.

"I will stay, but I have nothing." Daniella shrugged her shoulders.

"What I have, you are welcome to." She saw the girl's shoulders sag – then surprisingly she sat bolt upright. "I promised to have a drink at the hotel. It was the only way I found you," she added, feeling that it sounded as if she was already 'over' Kurt.

Daniella picked up her mobile. "The young lady you propositioned is staying overnight with me. You can see her in the morning. Yes, yes," she said somewhat impatiently, in answer to his response wondering if everything was all right.

"She seemed upset."

"She's fine," Daniella said abruptly, turning her mobile off as she spoke.

A light supper of omelette and salad and Daniella excused herself from her guest having first shown her where she could sleep. Lent her a nightgown and provided a new toothbrush and directed her towards the bathroom. Then quietly letting herself out of the house she walked past a few houses to Yana's.

It was ten pm. Yana had just returned home after an unusually speedy delivery. There had been a slight haemorrhage and blood had been hastily supplied from the local hospital. All prospective Mums had their blood pre-matched as a precaution, so all went smoothly and mother and baby were cuddled up in bed, with the new father proudly watching his new family.

If Yana was surprised to see her friend so late in the evening, she didn't show it. Daniella stepped inside without even waiting to be invited in. Unusually, she declined coffee or anything else.

"Sit down Yana please. There is something you should know." She explained how the girl had arrived and her story about Kurt packing her things and changing the locks. "Aah," said Yana.

"What's that supposed to mean?" Daniella demanded, somewhat crossly.

"I saw her arrive and I couldn't place her. I'd seen her you see, a long time ago when Kurt assured me he thought business and pleasure shouldn't mix."

"I'm sure he meant it at the time." Daniella commented somewhat dryly. Yana was silent.

"So, what am I supposed to do?"

"Hear what she has to say. That's all. Then decide." Yana tried to look bored with the whole saga, but Daniella was not deceived. Yana still had feelings for Kurt, of that she was sure.

It was Sunday morning. Yana had no idea what time to expect her visitor. She had her breakfast in the garden. It was a bit chilly, but she enjoyed watching and hearing the birds and was well wrapped up. The birds were in and out of the nesting boxes she had put up in every suitable place. Lulled by the soft spring air and the sound of birdsong her mind was wandering. A myriad of thoughts passing through her mind like a series of quick photographs.

The bell rang. The girl, not tear stained today. Her short blonde hair freshly washed with Daniella's shampoo and with her red trousers and white tee shirt and carrying a light jacket, looked remarkably fetching. *Why on earth*, Yana wondered, *did Kurt want to dump such a pretty thing.*

Yana held the door open and the girl stepped inside looking about her curiously. Yana indicated the garden feeling their meeting might be more relaxed in a garden setting. They sat, the two of them. Yana with her creamy skin and auburn hair, tall and slim with an air of worldliness about her. The girl five foot nothing. Curly blonde hair, curvaceous but not heavy. *Eyes as bright as buttons and lips*, thought Yana, *naturally ruby red*.

"You have something to tell me I believe," She said feeling one of them had to break the ice. The girl nodded, her bottom lip trembled. "He loves you," she blurted out. It was not what Yana expected to hear. She had expected a tirade, listing Kurt's faults and blaming her. She sat bolt upright.

"What did you say?" she almost thought she must have misheard.

"He loves you. He thinks only of you when he makes love to me." Yana was silenced.

"How do you know that?" she finally asked as gently as she could.

"Because he told me, more than once." Yana had seldom felt so angry.

"How dare he. How bloody dare he," she muttered in English. The girl looked blank.

"I've left my job. How can I be his secretary?"

"Why don't you work for me instead?" The girl laughed. At first it was bitter, then slightly hysterical and finally a short dry laugh and… "You can't mean it!"

"But I do," Yana insisted thinking this girl is loyal and she must be efficient or Kurt wouldn't have employed her. "Work for me. Secretary, receptionist, confidant." She named a salary that was half as much again as she was getting at the school. She suddenly smiled. Her whole face lit up. *She really was incredibly pretty,* Yana thought. "Is it too far to come." The girl shook her head and held out her hand.

"I didn't expect this," she said smiling.

"Neither did I." Yana shook the proffered hand which was dry and firm. A good handshake, a good indication she thought momentarily. It was to be the beginning of a lifelong friendship.

Later feeling as if the weight of the world had been lifted from her shoulders the girl, Ramiza, returned first to Daniella's and then to the hotel. Daniella was given a shortened version of what had happened and felt a quiet sense of satisfaction that she had done the right thing. Janus's son Muris, brought her a drink and she explained she would soon be working in the town. The pressure off, he did not pursue his original action plan. Time was now on his side! He felt good about her and said goodbye with no regrets and full of hope and expectation of a new and perhaps special friendship.

Yana was not quite sure what to do. She felt like telephoning Kurt, then writing. He had used his supposed feelings for her to rid himself of Ramiza. She was convinced she had been an excuse, no more. If he loved her, why didn't he do something about it.

One week later, Ramiza came to work for Yana. She literally transformed Yana's life. She updated the computer programme. She was pleasant and helpful to patients, and had such patience with them to even the most querulous. They hit it off from the start. Yana only had to mention something as a passing thought and it seemed to be implemented overnight. Her desk was tidied into neat, organised order with pressing matters unmissably, centre front. There were no more wild goose chases after non-existent patients. Or calls on patients that had not called her! As a consequence, her own image started to improve and as a bonus Ramiza said she had never enjoyed a job more.

Someone else in town was happy too. Muris was ever at the surgery on one pretext or another, Ramiza pretended not to notice, but Yana could tell she was secretly pleased, and it was not too long before they started dating properly.

Daniella talked with Sue and Milo, and it was not too long before a dinner party was planned. Jan would 'cover' for Yana. Coincidently it happened, to be very near the date of Daniella's birthday, so Sue and Milo decided to turn it into a birthday party for her. Unbeknownst to her, of course.

The party started at eight pm. Yana arrived at 8.15 to find about twenty people already there. She wore her new Inca style jewellery, her hair washed and brushed to a gleaming auburn copper. Her entrance caused several gasps. Kurt had his back to her when she walked in and he was not altogether surprised when he turned around and saw her looking lovelier than ever. They had wasted so much time, the two of them. Surely the time was ripe for a reconciliation after all these years.

He took a step towards her and she turned as someone called her name. For once, Kurt felt he was responsible. He had been resentful and stupid and he determined that tonight, this evening would be the last ever, chance he would have. It was tonight, or put her out of his mind and life forever.

It was a happy evening. Daniella enjoyed her 'surprise' party, though of course she had suspected Sue and Milo would 'do something'. She noticed as the evening went on that Yana and Kurt were talking together in a corner of the room. She was perhaps the only one who noticed them discreetly leave the party and she hoped that at last there would be a proper reconciliation.

It was dark by the time they left, but by mutual consent they decided to head to the rock. They returned briefly to Yana's to collect a large torch and set off up the hill. They didn't talk. When Yana nearly tripped, he grabbed her arm – she thanked him politely, and they continued upwards.

By the time they reached the rock, they had both reached certain conclusions. Yana's were: *Well this is it. I love him, I have for years, perhaps since I was seventeen. I've made mistakes, but then so has he. Tonight is the beginning or the end.*

Kurt walked steadily up. *Well this is it*. He thought. *I love her, I have for years. I've made mistakes, but then so has she. Tonight, is our real beginning or the end.*

They reached the rock and sat down. Yana as ever reaching and touching the nearest 'M', "Kurt."

"Yana." They both spoke at once. It made them laugh, perhaps a shade cautiously. "I love you Yana – we have wasted too many years."

"I love you Kurt, and yes we have."

There were no more words as the torch was turned off and they held each other closely, wondering why they had not taken such a simple step before.

They made their way down the hill as the morning light started to fill the sky. They walked hand in hand knowing that, at last, their lives would be together in the town where they were born. A place that had been so full of heartache in the past, but now would give them a future. A future that they would share.